POPPYLAND

RAFFAELLA BARKER, daughter of the poet George Barker, was born and brought up in the Norfolk countryside. She is the author of seven other novels, *Come and Tell Me Some Lies*, *The Hook*, *Hens Dancing*, *Summertime*, *Green Grass*, *A Perfect Life* and *From a Distance*. She has also written a novel for young adults, *Phosphorescence*. She is a regular contributor to the *Sunday Times* and the *Sunday Telegraph*, and teaches on the Literature and Creative Writing BA at the University of East Anglia and the *Guardian* UEA Novel Writing Masterclass. Raffaella Barker lives by the sea in north Norfolk.

Also by Raffaella Barker

RAFFAELLA BARKER

POPPYLAND

B L O O M S B U R Y

LONDON · NEW DELHI · NEW YORK · SYDNEY

First published in Great Britain in 2008 by Headline Review
This paperback edition published 2014

Extract from 'The Hollow Men' from Collected
Poems 1909-1962 by T.S. Eliot.
Copyright © 2002 T.S. Eliot Estate. Reprinted by
permission of Faber and Faber Ltd

Extract from 'The Invitation' by Oriah Mountain Dreamer. Copyright
© 1999 by Oriah Mountain Dreamer. Reprinted by permission of
HarperCollins Publishers Ltd (UK) and HarperCollins Publishers (USA)

Bloomsbury Publishing Plc
50 Bedford Square
London
WC1B 3DP

www.bloomsbury.com

Bloomsbury is a trademark of Bloomsbury Publishing Plc

Bloomsbury Publishing, London, New Delhi, New York and Sydney

A CIP catalogue record for this book is available from the British Library

ISBN 978 1 4088 5063 3

10 9 8 7 6 5 4 3 2 1

Typeset by Hewer Text UK Ltd, Edinburgh

Printed and bound in Great Britain by
CPI Group (UK) Ltd, Croydon CR0 4YY

For the man I met at the station

All my life I have been running away so that someone will come and find me, and it wasn't until I stopped and turned round that I saw you walking towards me.

PART 1

PART I

PROLOGUE

Between the black sea breakers, like hurdles on a racetrack, the sections of beach are private spaces. On the cliffs above, a man leans on a higgledy-piggledy run of white railings, a sketch pad balanced on the gloss-coated metal of the top rail, looking first out at the summer sea then down at his drawing. The beach curves into the distance, disappearing into the sea in a haze of spray and sand along to the east. Each of the long rectangular spaces between the groynes is the same at first glance then different, never the same again. In the section directly beneath the drawing man, pebbles are scattered like freckles on the smooth shoulder of sand leading to a shadowy pool like a hollowed collarbone beneath the breathing mouth of the sea.

At the tide line, handfuls of mussels, flung by the waves into the cracks between the high, wet sleeper fences, hang in festoons on ropes of slippery neon-green weed, heavy with the life within each shell, which

I

is laced shut and sealed tight by clamps of white barnacles across its blue-black surface. A breeze swings a necklace of shellfish and they clatter against the black wood, and shells jut from cracks in the breakers like hungry beaks. The breeze plays on the beach, flipping a wave up to slap the groyne, catching an empty paper bag off the sand to dip it in and out of the meandering tide line. The mood is idle and nonchalant.

Without warning, the breeze changes gear, the wind breathes in then blasts out in a crashing rush of waves. Frilling like torn lace they gain momentum and loom, walls of water pounding, hurling stones up the softly scooped sand, more freckles emerging on the skin of the beach.

Over the breakers in the next compartment of the shore, the wind leaps upon a child digging with her pink spade, bent back, squatting, intent. The little girl sings a nursery rhyme while she pats a heap of sand and turns to the hole she has started. In a rush her hat falls backwards off her head, her curls whip into her eyes and sand stings her bare arms and legs. She straightens up, mouth open, her green swimsuit sharp edged and bright like a new leaf, and scuttles sideways a few steps, seeking safety behind a woman who is bending over a basket pulling out a towel. There is no one else on the whole long shore, just this small group, a woman and her two children, laughing and content in their own world, safe on a beach which at high tide will be consumed by the sea. To the backdrop of the whisper and crash of the sea she hums, and a snatch of her voice flies up and over the cliff. The man smiles; he recognises the tune well enough to know it is out of key and he finds it delightful that she is oblivious of him and singing really quite loudly and tunelessly.

The wind curls around her and throws her skirt up, showing a flash of black underwear and a slice of stomach, creamy like the new moon. The upside-down skirt swallows her up to her shoulders; and as she is unaware of being watched, her movements are unhurried. The skirt is still rucked up, and she reaches for the child, arms extending as if from a flower.

'Let's bury someone,' she suggests to the child, and the child proffers a doll.

'Her,' she says firmly.

'OK.' A sudden strafe of wind picks up a yellow beach towel, a stripy doll's chair and a spray of sand and throws them high into the air. An open newspaper bowls towards the woman. She is in the middle of chaos, none of it her own, and for a moment she seems in danger of being engulfed by it. On the cliff the man is watching intently, alert and ready to rush to the rescue, even though it is only paper. It may be foolish, but the impulse is real: she is alone, there is no one to help her, and she looks way too fragile to withstand the mad intensity of the elements. The bundle of newspaper is solid enough to knock her off her feet, as if it is wrapped around a cannon ball. He expects her to turn round, her face white with panic, but she laughs and shrieks in mock alarm and the little girl laughs too and they are turning, dancing on the sand, and the woman tries to untangle her clothes and pull down her skirt again.

'We almost got bowled over, are you OK, sweet-heart?' she asks the child, who nods and begins scampering in and out, zigzagging towards the water, past the baby who sits on the sand and smiles. 'Wait!' calls the woman, 'I'm coming too.' She runs towards the waves, her skirt tucked in somewhere and the tops of her thighs flash pale as she moves.

From the cliffs, the man watches. He is possessed by a sense that this small scene he is witnessing is exactly what is meant to be happening today. None of it was planned by him, nor by the woman on the beach. It is all part of a greater universal order. In other words, they were both meant to be here today. Why? It's a good question. Maybe she has the answer. Is she asking the same question as she stands with the foaming tide around her ankles, playing with the baby? It's impossible to know what she is thinking except that she looks content, not yearning, not tragic, but fragile. Who is she, and how can he know her?

A seagull floats dreamily on an air current. The small girl in the green swimsuit starts to cry, pulling at the newspaper wrapped around her doll's chair. The woman doesn't hear her as the sound floats up the cliffs and away. The baby smiles and pats the sea. She is scooped into the woman's arms, and the woman nuzzles her to make her laugh. The wind has moved on, throwing chaos further down the beach.

A small starfish hand reaches up as the older child looks to the woman for reassurance. With the baby on her other hip the woman stands in the stillness, glanc-ing about as if she is looking for the whirlwind, hoping to actually see the invisible force at the heart of the erratic movement of all the chairs and clothes and paper on the beach.

The little girl laughs again. Pointing as a ball whips up on a curl of air and bounces to the sea where waves rise and fall, as if the water itself is panting. It is loud now, like a shell pressed to the ear, shingle dragging back the weight of it, pulling it away from the shore, tugged by the moon. Spitting and sighing, the wind mutters off, slapping a knot of netting on to the breakers.

Another gull drifts over, too big, like a cuddly toy on a wire as it floats awkwardly on an air current. It is almost drawn into the spin then swoops out again sounding raucous laughter. Pointing, the baby laughs too, crawling along the beach as the gull soars up over the pitted cliff, where chalk crumbles like cheese and small lumps tumble in the still air.

The man sits down at a table outside the café and turns the pages of his notebook. Distracted, he half stands again, looking over to see where the group on the beach are. They are self contained, absorbed, and have no idea he is there; suddenly he wishes they would see him. Sound fills the tranquil space around him now the wind has moved away, and voices carry up from the beach.

'She's like a crab,' pipes the child. 'They have to go back to the sea or else they might die.'

The woman's answer is slightly breathless, 'Yes, but at least crabs come from the sea in the first place. She's a human and she will just get capsized.'

'I was a stone before I was born,' says the child.

There is a pause before the woman, her voice buoyant and full of smiles replies, 'Maybe you were.'

The words resonate, amplified by the cliff, fluting over a tangle of lobster pots drying at the top. The man writes 'I was a stone before I was born' on a blank page, and he shuts his notebook. Across the beach comes the sounds of the family approaching. He looks around, squinting in the fall of sunlight hitting the pavement. There is no one else on the street. No one on the grass between the cliff edge and the café. No one trudging up the switchback tarmac path from the beach. No one anywhere in this dozing seaside village. Even the parked cars have settled anthropomorphically into sleeping creatures in the lazy afternoon, mirroring the black-and-white cat coiled on the seat of an old tractor nearby. No one is here save the man and the family on the beach. He lights a cigarette. A peal of laughter and a squeal fly up from below, and it takes just a step and he is by the railings looking down. They are right below the café now, and the woman is bent over the child, helping her put her shoes on, while the baby sits solidly beside them on the sand. He gasps on his cigarette then chucks it over the railings. It's a reflex reaction, he recoils, swears under his breath and watches helpless as the salmon-pink head of the lighted cigarette flares, dropping down the cliff like a stealth missile towards the baby.

'Oh shit!' The cigarette lands near the three of them but touches none of them. The woman is kneeling, one child on her lap, her hair falling over her shoulders, the baby clambering on to her too. Three faces lift like flowers to see whose voice they have heard, and the skirt is like petals around them.

1

Grace
Copenhagen
Five years earlier

How do I do this? Hurtling from the airport in a cab, adrenaline pounds through me, shaking me up and out of the trance of my flight. Copenhagen. I have never been to this city before, I am not sure where I am going or what will be there when I arrive, but at least the sense of panic is familiar. Jumbling along rather than travelling is what I do. Less glamorous than I would like, but isn't everyone a bit less dazzling than their wildest dreams? I have been to so many cities and arrived like this, alone, disorganised and sometimes with my case tied together with string, which is less a bohemian touch and more of a zip-locking problem. It's always such a rush. Something weird happens to my brain when I am planning a trip and the planning gets suspended until some time after the last minute. So here I am, zooming along on a familiar rush of anxiety, a bit like, I imagine, the Cresta Run, with a taste in the back of my mouth which reminds me of green wine gums mixed with gin.

It's very unrelaxing, and I try to regain a trance state in the back of the taxi so that I can summon a nice plump guardian angel to coo at me that all will be well. It isn't really happening right now, but usually that is what gets me through. And the best thing is it's true, despite endless squalls of drama; I have never stepped blindly off the edge of what I know and hit the ground, something has always broken my fall.

All this is metaphorical, of course. For in real life, I am clumsy and I bump into bits of furniture all the time and miss my footing on steps. Even just now, on the escalator at the airport, I got a strap from my handbag caught in the moving banister and my bag whooshed away, gliding like an unreachable prize down the escalator next to the hordes of unheeding people who also looked like prizes or trophies waiting to be scooped off rather than human beings making their own way somewhere. I watched in the suspended state that I am so familiar with for a moment, but then action seized me and I ran up the down escalator. A teenage boy, clean, blond and smartly dressed like everyone else I have seen so far in Copenhagen, noticed me dashing in the face of everyone else, and he grabbed the handle of the bag before it was crushed into the floor by the inexorable motion of the escalator. My guardian angel was clearly still on duty then.

Generally, I have a lot to be thankful for, and, as I live near to a gospel church on the Lower East Side in Manhattan, I have every opportunity to remember it and even to sing harmonies about it if I want to. The choir leader is a huge cushion-shaped lady called Jezebel who wears orange wafting dresses and has flowing sensibilities. Maybe she joined the choir to override her scandalous name. I don't know, but I was once there when her husband Ezra arrived to pick her up, and the moment of their meeting was operatic. Jezebel burst into a chirruping riff of song and rushed to hug him, her hugeness engulfing his slight form like a blazing fire as their bodies met and began to sway together. Thinking of them now, dancing in the dusty church room in Manhattan, makes me smile and I feel less nervous with them in my head.

I am a bit worried about seeing my work, a lot is riding on it – not least me getting all the way here from New York, and I always have a pre-show terror that I have been painting the wrong thing all this time. Anyway, I am going to focus right now on the cheerful and solid image of Jezebel and Ezra dancing, and it is appropriate, as they are the inspiration for one of the pictures in the show. When I do this, I know all of it is going to be fine.

I am by the sea now, on the quay by the harbour. Somewhere nearby is the famous mermaid. I can't see her, it is too dark beyond the street lights and although I am sure she is lit up, I don't know where to look, but

I can picture her supplicant pose, her head bowed, her naked grace. The only thing I know about her is that Eric Gill made her and he also designed the script that is used for the London Underground. Oh, and she is the Little Mermaid who lost her voice to the King of the Underworld. That's quite a lot to know about a statue, in fact. Especially one I haven't seen. The cab swoops out from among tall, coloured warehouse buildings and along the harbour. The street is wet with pewter skimming all surfaces, a dull grey gleam, too cold to evaporate and dry out, and not yet crystallising into frost. Beyond the fizzing street lighting, night begins to swallow roof tops and awnings, and needle-pointed church spires. Further along the harbour the opera house glows like a space-age pagoda out of the dark. In the cab the indicator ticks, otherwise all sound seems swallowed by the dark. Outside, above the invisible horizon, the moon is like a flower, purple shadow staining petal imprints on the solid silver disc, hanging as if nailed on to the flat, black sky. Looking at it, I can't help feeling it's hung a bit too low. My forehead is pressed against the cool window of the taxi, and I am so hot that my skin sticks to the smooth glass; my eyes flicker with a need to sleep and it is refreshing to look at something so clean and restful.

My brain chatters with rushing thoughts. What if my show is hung too low? What if my pictures are all drooping below the plimsoll line I carry in my head when I am painting them? What can I do? Nothing, is the sensible answer. There is an hour before the doors of the gallery open to the public and the press, so I suppose I could get them all to help me and call it an installation. I'm about to arrive and at last I'll meet Hans Stettjens the gallery owner. When I realised I wouldn't be here to put up the show, he called me for an hour to talk about the hanging and said he would do it for me. He said to delay the show would have a drastic domino effect on me and the gallery.

'But I can't come until after the funeral.' I was on the phone in London, sitting on the floor in my sister's bedroom overlooking the canal.

'The funeral?' There was a long silence in which I heard him swallowing, then he said, 'My dear, I am so sorry.'

'It was my mum,' I said, and my throat swelled with the loss.

'You poor child,' he said, and his sympathy was like a warm blanket around me.

'It's really hard to believe,' I said. 'I didn't used to see her very much, but I can't grasp that I will never see her again.'

'You need time for your grief. Let me take care of your work. The paintings are beautiful and we will show them well for you.'

'Thank you.' Once I began crying about my mother, it was hard to stop; all the regret I felt for not having seen her, and not having liked her much got muddled with the relief that she was not alive to drink herself to death now. Hans Stettjen's kindness and his interest and his capability all reminded me of what was impossible between me and my mother. It's funny how much easier it is to express a whole range of emotions on a canvas than it is to sit face to face in a family and talk. Somewhere along the way I got scared of saying anything to my mother because I knew she was fragile and it might be too much for her. The small phrases people use can echo in a child's head and I didn't dare ask her what she meant when she shook me, aged five, after I had spilled ink across the whole of the sitting-room sofa, and said fiercely, 'The trouble with you is that you can't keep still. You even got out of your cot on the wrong side and everything since then has been a struggle.' She had then stalked off and the door of her room had closed with a crisp click. I had told Lucy, my older sister, and she had looked very frightened. 'Which is the wrong side?' she whispered.

'I don't know,' I wept in reply. 'Mummy didn't say.'

The next telephone conversation I had with Hans Stettjens was more businesslike: 'Let's talk about how you would like them hung,' he said. 'The nudes are very arresting; I see them as a triptych, no?'

'No,' I almost yelled. 'They don't go together at all. Well, not close together. They need space. Everyone needs space, Hans.'

For me, hanging an exhibition with my pictures in it is an act as intimate as the removal of my clothes. I had never imagined that I wouldn't do it myself, or even be there for the final adjusting and changing of light and space between the work. And I hardly have the vocabulary for talking about them and how they should be. I can be articulate on paper or canvas, but not in conversation. I don't actually even know my right and left, which baffled Hans when he was hanging my pictures with me on the phone guiding him.

'Yes, do it there! Do you see? I mean up a bit from the green one on the same side as her hair and the tree.'

'The left, you mean?'

'Do I?' I was waving my arms in front of me with the phone under my chin, mouthing at my sister Lucy to tell me which was left and which was right.

Hans Stettjens was unfailingly polite. 'Yes, very good indeed, left it is,' he said as though I had performed a rabbit-from-hat miracle. I must say, it felt a bit of a miracle. I have never shown my work before without seeing the gallery space and the pictures hanging in it. And now I am about to arrive and they will all be there, ready and waiting for me. I was trying to explain to Lucy why it was weird, and the only comparison I could find was a bit random.

'Well, Lucy, imagine if you had a baby and it wasn't with you one day and you went to a party and the baby was there all dressed and ready with someone else.'

I knew exactly what I meant and how I would feel; I could imagine a baby all dressed in a red satin outfit looking all wrong, but Lucy raised her eyebrows and nodded in a special 'You are bonkers' way and said,

'Mmm. Maybe, but I haven't got a baby, so it's hard to imagine any of it, Grace, and it's a lot of fuss to make when we've got to deal with all this business of Mum, you know.'

I groaned, then bit my lip. She wasn't going to understand and it didn't matter that she couldn't. Lucy has always been very down to earth, and she couldn't understand the battles I had with Mum.

'Oh well, just believe me when I tell you that I need to hang my own show, it's very personal, I always do it myself.'

Lucy hugged me, 'Oh, I'm sorry,' she said, and tears were swimming in her eyes.

'And I'm sorry, too; the timing of everything is making this all so hard.'

So in the end, doing this show differently is only one of the myriad things that has changed in our lives, and it is nothing to do with Lucy, and it is no one's fault. Mum died. That's the thing that makes life different for ever more. And now is not the time to try to come to terms with it. I have to get through this evening in Denmark and then there will be time. I shiver, afraid of just how much time there will be from tomorrow.

I would have been in Denmark for a week by now if things had been different. I pull my knees up to my chest and hug my shins, making myself tightly small on the back seat of the cab. I wish I had someone who could have come with me, someone to talk to. Leaning back against the plumped seat back, I flirt with a wild notion of escape, of opening the door at the next traffic lights and stepping out into nowhere.

Three weeks ago in New York, when the paintings left, I wanted to call them back, to look at them again, to give myself another final chance with them. Shock and grief are playing havoc with my mind and I am scared to admit even to myself that I have no proper memory of Mum's face when I think of her now in the aftermath of her death, and in the same way, my pictures dissolve in bewildering chimera in my mind when I am trying to visualise them. I couldn't command any sense of them once they had gone, and I couldn't remember what I was trying to do with them. I kept expecting another chance, and it's the same with Mum. I did not expect never to see her again.

A year ago I won the award to be shown here in Denmark in a new amazing contemporary art gallery. I worked towards the show as a date, a deadline, an end in itself, without thinking much about Copenhagen or what it meant to be coming here all the way from the States on my own. To have a one-man show so far away from my life was a bigger deal than I could imagine, so I just didn't let myself think about it. I didn't really have time to think about anything else either; the show took a while to take shape and I was so wrapped up in the work that I didn't notice time slipping by until all the jumbled events that make up everyday life had loomed and cleared in methodical disorder, and when it was almost time for me to leave, my work was already shipped.

Mum was the last big thing in the way. Not Mum herself, but the way she and I could never get on, even when separated by all the dark water of the Atlantic Ocean. It wasn't any different from how it had always been, the obstacles were the same. It had begun as small mutual childhood disappointments: hers that I was so chaotic and clumsy; mine that she couldn't laugh when I spilled a drink. Instead, she would purse her lips and sigh, and even from the beginning, neither of us knew how to say sorry. Silence is easy to live with, and to break it is as frightening as it would be to walk through a pane of glass. Mum and I had never managed to talk to one another. Both of us could talk to Lucy, both of us loved Lucy, and she was stuck in the middle willing us to get on. But she couldn't mend the fractured bond between us. In the end no one could.

I was all set up to go to London on the way to Denmark, dropping in from another continent just to have a stilted pre-Christmas lunch with Mum. I had talked to Lucy and we had agreed it would work best if she came too.

'I'll go and get her and bring her to meet you,' Lucy had said. 'That way there can be no ducking out.'

'I want to duck out,' I had blurted down the phone to my sister, but she wasn't having any of it.

'Oh no you don't. Just remember, you live far away and you only do this once in a blue moon. I am here all the time and it's not always easy.'

'But you're good at it, Lucy, you always have been.' A childhood memory floated past me containing Lucy with neat hair and clean hands brushing the cat, kneeling on the floor in the hall with sunlight shafting on to her hair. I was there, sitting next to Lucy, my favourite toy, a one-eyed doll named Blue in my arms, waiting for her to finish with the brush. Maybe it's not a memory, just a bad dream, but I think the next thing that happened was that the front door opened and Mum walked in. In my memory I held my breath, but I doubt I did in real life.

'What are you doing?' she asked.

'Nothing yet, but I am about to brush Blue,' I answered.

'Blue's got fleas, she'll ruin the hairbrush.' Mum picked up my doll by the head and, opening the door, flung it out into the garden. She turned and smiled, a small, sharp flash in her eyes as she looked at Lucy and me and sighed.

'Find something nice to play with, darling,' she urged, and walked briskly past us into the kitchen. I waited until she turned the radio on before I opened the front door and tiptoed out into the garden to find Blue and bring her back in. I hid her from Mum after that.

Lucy had sighed on the phone. 'Maybe one day you and Mum will sort it out,' she had said.

'I'll try when I come this time. I want us to get on, Luce, I really do.'

But Mum pre-empted my plan to see her, and let slip the vestiges of lucidity, sinking into breathless death behind her kitchen door on the day before I was to arrive. Lucy telephoned early. A call before seven in the morning can never be good news. Climbing out of sleep I heard the phone and I swallowed, a dry lump in my throat. I think I knew already when I heard Lucy's voice, brittle and tight, staccato with confusion and strain.

'Oh Grace. Oh God. Oh shit. The thing is, Mum died.'

'Oh.' I felt my heart stop for a beat too many, then race away, while a desolate bell chimed in my head. 'Good timing.' I realised I had said it out loud. Accidentally. Me and my big mouth. I found myself staring into the earpiece of the phone as if hoping my words would come back unsaid.

Luckily Lucy was still talking, she knew I hadn't meant it as it sounded. 'Yes, but the thing is, they found her all folded up and crumpled like she had fallen off a towel rail behind the door into the kitchen. She was very thin.'

My ear was hot. I pressed the telephone tighter to it, wanting to feel something solid no matter how insubstantial. I couldn't tell if the quaver in Lucy's voice was grief or laughter.

'Like Peter Pan's shadow,' I said.

'What?' said Lucy. 'What are you talking about, Sis?'

'You know, he kept it rolled up in the drawer.'

Lucy gasped. 'Oh, I see. Yes, I suppose so.' She began to laugh, I began to laugh as well, and somehow we were both giggling and gasping across five hours of time difference and our shock. Even when we stopped, the energy of laughing stayed inside us, propelling the first untested steps we had to take to begin our lives without our mother.

★ ★ ★

The taxi pulls up in an industrial part of the harbour. The sea glitters and slaps against the keel of a dark ship and the skimpy petals on the moon unfurl to cover it fully. It is as if a fall of soot has dropped through the cavern of a vast chimney and blanketed the surface of the sea. A moment of darkness exists, then a thin ribbon of light from further down the harbour brings back the dancing movement of the water. In that unlit moment, my skin crawls, and I shiver, the impenetrable blackness of night hooking me out of my reverie of displacement. On the street a taste of salt in the air hits the back of my throat, and the damp night is like a splash of cold water on my skin. Knotting the belt on my coat more tightly makes me feel pulled together. Better. Gazing around and stamping my feet to prove I am actually here in Copenhagen, I begin thinking randomly about corsets. Surely more should be made of the improvement to self-confidence that wearing them must bring? It is true, those women who wore them long ago didn't have to cross half the northern hemisphere, or at least eighty degrees of longitude, alone, so maybe they were never fully aware of how very good it is to stand up straight, take a deep breath in and walk tall. If—

My thoughts break into shards. The taxi has gone, the quay is empty yet romantic, lit with just a few street lights with pools of gold glowing beneath them. I turn my back to the sea and am dazzled by a lighting projection I was too close to see before. The Stettjens Gallery has a façade of exquisite purity. Or rather, it usually does; I've seen photographs of it in newspapers and design books, and among the paperwork that Hans Stettjens, the owner, has been sending me. Nothing has prepared me for the reality. The strips of steel and glass and concrete have inspired rapturous adjectives from the press and the architectural world at large and it is taut and beautiful. But it is not the building that is startling, it is the projection mounted on its façade. A huge green-lit screen covers the whole front of the building, and on it, slowly changing like a kaleidoscope, are magnified images of my work. It is like a giant window lit up at night with the figures I painted appearing huge, and slowly moving one after another like a giant shadow-puppet show. The effect is bigger than the sum of its parts. No actually, it's not. The projection is big, but so are all the parts of it. The thing that is small is me. It's a bit scary to see such a public representation of my work, but at least it's facing the sea, not a busy street. Probably no one will notice it. Anyway, this is the right place. I should go in.

Gripping the handle of my suitcase, I gaze at the shifting colours on the wall. It reminds me of a lava lamp. I can't go on standing outside for ever, but I also can't bring myself to go inside. So I hang around a bit, gawping up at the projection, unable to make much sense of it. I look across at the harbour mouth and find myself wondering what it would be like to be out at sea and see this vast projection. I haven't got an answer except that I'm sure it would be a lot better than being here in front of it as the accidental author. I am cold now, and I'm running out of excuses. I set off across the road and then stop again. Until I go in through the door and introduce myself, no one knows who I am or that I am here. This limbo feels the most comfortable place to be. No demands are being made of me, no expectations burden my psyche. This is a moment where I could vanish. I could hide, I could unzip the suitcase and get into it. As it has wheels, there is a good chance that I might roll off the harbour into the sea, and I would have to be Houdini to escape. Or I would float away, bobbing up the coast to another part of Denmark, maybe Elsinore. Vaguely I remember Elsinore is on the Sound. Wherever that might be. At school, Lucy and I fought like cats to be chosen to play Ophelia in the pantomime version of *Hamlet* which our English teacher wrote. Lucy won. It was so annoying, and I had to be Laertes in drag.

> '. . . *Was your father dear to you,*
> *Or are you like the painting of a sorrow,*
> *A face without a heart?'*

I didn't even know I knew these lines until I woke with them running through my head on the morning of Mum's funeral. And now that they have come back to me, they rush round and round in my head. I'd like to try to make a painting of a sorrow. It might be a painting of Mum, I don't know yet, but when I get back to New York and my studio I can start to make sense of everything that has happened since I left.

Until then I have to go wherever life takes me. I want to see Elsinore. I wonder how I can get there. Who can I go with? Suddenly loneliness hits me, and it is like vertigo in the way it swoops and grabs me from the guts and I wish like a howl that I had someone to go there with. Within the gallery the space is white. Dizzy, soporific white like being inside snow, except for the three large canvases hung at the far end and the paintings on both of the walls leading there. There is a sense of hard-won serenity in the room, a reverberating almost-stillness that I recognise as the aftermath of excessive action. It is like a stage set, and I can feel, though I cannot see, the last dust being swept from the floor, the papers and staple tucked away in a drawer and everybody smoothing themselves down, ready for the evening to begin. The warmth of the space flares and a vein on my temple throbs as loud in my head as a drum beat.

The gallery staff all turn round when I come in and the weight of their anxiety lifts and floats away from them to fall on top of me almost palpably. The pictures are mine and now I am here to speak for them. But I don't want to. I want them to speak for themselves. In the silence someone's bracelet or perhaps the metal strap of a watch hits the rim of a wineglass. The glass sings a pure note into the noiseless moment and the sound is renewing and spine tingling. I shrug off the anxiety I felt when I came in and it is like a coat slipping off.

To no one in particular I say: 'Oh, I love that. Wouldn't it be great if we had some music in here?'

There is a flurry towards me, a girl with wheat-blond plaits smiles and says, 'We often have music before the show, we just weren't sure you would . . .' she tails off, looking a little apprehensive.

I smile at her. 'Don't worry, you're very kind to think of it. I don't want to interfere with your preparations.'

She presses my hand between hers and the warmth of her welcome is physical, too, on my cold skin. I don't feel so stiff and alarmed now, the gallery is running smoothly, the show is hung and looks like someone else's work to me. I like the sensation of seeing it for the first time much more than I thought I would, and everyone here is overflowing with goodwill. A boy takes my suitcase and disappears with it behind a partition. Hans Stettjens comes across from the desk where he has been talking on the telephone and we shake hands. His eyes are long and narrow like flints, and his hair is a dusting of iron filings on his perfectly domed head. He bows over my hand. It is nerve-wracking. I cannot live up to expectation, I have never been able to. I can feel a wobbling expression forming on my face and I bite my lip to get rid of it as he speaks in beautiful English that makes me embarrassed that I don't know a single word of Danish.

'Miss Hart. I'm so glad to meet you. How was your flight?'

'Oh. God. I mean good. Please call me Grace.'

He has a sweet smile and is staring at me kindly. Like everyone I have seen in Denmark, he has a fine, chiselled face and nice clothes.

I babble on, filling the silence before it happens, 'Outside is quite a statement of – of— Well, it's certainly saying something. I mean—' I can't talk properly because I am trying to take Hans in; I am wondering if he will be an ally, and I'm not sure if I can allow myself to like the way he has hung my work, even though he has done exactly what we talked about on the phone.

I struggle with the silence again as his kind eyes regard me, and off I go in another peal of talk: 'I suppose it's like asking someone else to look after your baby – I mean having someone else hang your show.' I can't keep looking at him looking at me, it's embarrassing and I am getting hotter and hotter in the room. I tear off my coat and just stop myself chucking it on the floor behind me. Immediately the girl with plaits glides over and takes the coat.

'Thank you,' I whisper, and repeat it as she hands me a glass of water. As I drink it I surreptitiously look around the room at the work. It looks just as I would have hoped if I had dared hope anything. Excitement begins to bubble up inside me.

'Let me show you the hanging,' says Hans, guiding me around the paintings, his hand under my elbow so I cannot be surreptitious any more. I have to look and I will have to answer, there is no way out as he is beside me, his eyes moving ceaselessly between the paintings and my face, his expression still wise, thoughtful and kind. I do not know him, I am often hostile in a new situation like this, but now I feel his warmth and I begin to relax. In a comfortable silence, we walk around the pictures, and I begin to absorb what the show looks like as a whole. I smile at Hans without speaking, I am so grateful he has not directly asked, 'What do you think?' and that he is giving me time.

And the bubbling excitement I felt a moment ago is gaining ground. This is thrilling. I am so excited because I could never have imagined that all together, hung by Hans Stettjens, the pictures could look so amazing. And now I realise what someone unconnected might see and it is fascinating. Hans is clasping one waxy thumb and forefinger in a tight circle about the bony wrist of the other hand. He really wants to know what I think. It is a jolt to realise this. And he is nervous.

I want to reassure him. I open my mouth, 'I want to cry.' Great. That was definitely not what I meant to say.

'Oh no, that's not what I mean.' Appalling to say that, when I mean it is wonderful, and now I am crying, tears prick at the corner of my eyes and my nose tingles.

'They look great. I . . . I can't tell you. I'm sorry I'm not making sense . . .' How maddening. It is so easy to perpetuate a myth, to believe your own demons. So hard not to make the same mistake over and over again. Hans is anxious, his eyes contract into small black knots, he has one hand over his eyes, he swallows. He is a little theatrical, but frankly, so am I. Oh God. The show is about to open and we are all awry with one another and there is no reason for it. Shit. I press my palms into my eyes and take a deep breath. 'I love them.' Oops, more crying because it is true.

Hans puts his arm around my shoulders and we face one of the pictures, a big canvas with two figures entwined in the sea. I suddenly find myself wondering whether I should have given them gills and I giggle.

Hans's eyes brighten. 'Just tell me what is wrong and we will do our best to improve it right this instant. Yes. At this moment we will change it for you.' He flourishes a handkerchief, blows his nose, purses his lips and snaps his fingers. Two young boys arranging glasses on trays put down their tea towels and come over. I take a deep breath, and grab his arm, yanking his sleeve as he issues a torrent of instructions to these boys in Danish, during which they look at me as if I am an alien. Which of course I am, up to a point.

I make myself interrupt: 'No, no. You don't understand – I mean, I haven't made myself clear. I am not making sense. What I meant was, I love it. The pictures look incredible. They look so much more than they are. Or more than I thought they were. Oh, I'm making it worse, aren't I?' I wish I had made the effort to learn some Danish before coming here. I would love to be making an effort. Instead, I wave my hands and feel smiles bursting out on my face. 'Actually, I am stunned. It's so much more than I ever thought it could be. It's so exciting, I feel in awe. What I really want to say, though, is thank you, that's all.'

Hans relaxes, relief easing every muscle and bringing the blood back to his pale face so that I suddenly realise that his pallor has been reminding me of a vampire. He rubs his hand over his stubble hair and laughs too.

'Miss Hart, I mean Grace, it makes a big difference that you are here. I am so glad you like the hanging, it's been . . .' He trails off, and I can feel myself blushing, remembering the stilted phone calls and my endless faxed drawings which must have clogged up his office every morning as I obsessed over how far apart and in what order the paintings should be hung. How can I ever have thought I knew better than this kind, saintly non-vampiric man?

'You know, it would have been a nightmare for you if I had been here,' I confide, and Hans nods wholeheartedly. I still want to make up for causing trouble, so with a sense of climbing into a tumbrel and heading for certain death, I open my mouth and say, 'Is there anyone you want me to talk to? I know I said I couldn't, but if you need me to be interviewed or anything, I can. I know I can.'

His eyebrows ping upwards. Hans considers me then claps his hands, and I follow him as he moves down the room.

'Yes,' he muses, 'first I think you could do with eating something, you look as though you might evaporate. There will be a couple of people to talk to this evening. Your work has attracted a lot of interest in the press.'

We are in the back office now. Hans opens a small refrigerator and reaches into it. I am expecting a special Danish snack, but he hands me a tomato and a small carton of milk.

'That's pretty weird,' I can't help commenting, but he doesn't hear; he is bustling about the office putting things away and tidying. He has a tea towel over his arm and calmly polishes a glass before handing it to me.

'Of course there is food, but I always have something like this first,' Hans says. I stare gloomily at the milk and the tomato. I especially don't want the milk. He pours it into the glass. There is no way I can refuse, he is being so motherly, and apart from the grossness of what he is actually giving me, I am grateful for the thought.

Hans holds out the milk and, narrowing his eyes, looks at me. He grins half in embarrassment as he suddenly says, 'You have a look of the mermaid – the Copenhagen mermaid. I think they will photograph you.'

'What, naked?' I tease, but he is not really listening, he looks at his watch.

'Jerome Michaels, from the oil company, was scheduled to be here to meet you, but he's been delayed and will arrive later this evening. If you are happy to do press now, I think we should have you with him. Glacon is big money and the press is very interested in their new sponsorship programme.'

'OK, you just tell me what I have to do. I guess all artists sell out to commerce sooner or later, I just didn't realise I had done it already,' I joke, but the joke falls into space unnoticed. I don't mind, Hans seems happy and anything that can help me forget the glaring reality of my pictures on the walls must be good. I like Hans, he takes things personally. Hans squeezes my shoulders in an awkward hug. 'We just need to make sure this is not all too much for you,' he says, and tears sting my eyes because he is so thoughtful.

I wonder if any artist enjoys the experience of watching people looking at their work? I find it unreal, and dreamlike. Or nightmare-like, more often. I keep reminding myself that I am grateful anyone has turned up at all, as the gallery fills with people and flashbulbs explode like snowballs in the crowd. There is an unhurried yet insistent current as the guests mingle, greet one another and move through the gallery in front of the pictures. Often at a private view no one looks at the work. The ones I go to in New York are usually attended by friends and everyone stands in huddles, their backs to the paintings, drinking glass after glass of cheap red wine.

The Danish scrutiny is thorough and serious, and I want to run for cover, but there is nowhere to go and I am tensed for the critical equivalent of a bucket of cold water to be thrown over me. The air is full of energy, a combination of excitement and exhilaration, partly caused by people coming in from the cold, I suppose. It's exciting to hear the babble of other languages, and also to be among people who seem to be really talking about art. Of course, I don't know for sure, they could be discussing the plot of Denmark's leading soap opera, but I don't think so. This would never happen in London. My spirits are flipping up and up in the warm and unexpected welcome I have found in Denmark. In New York when it happens, it is always bound up with money. The atmosphere in an uptown private view only becomes charged when the show sells out. Copenhagen feels purer, but maybe it's just the drink talking. I look down at the ice in my glass, and decide not to have another vodka. Isn't vodka and milk a cocktail? I think it's a Black Russian. But that's when they are mixed, not when they are drunk one after the other in separate glasses. Looking around at all the unfamiliar faces I slump inside with the effort of doing this alone. Denmark feels very foreign suddenly.

When I won this award, I wasn't entirely sure if Denmark was nearer to Norfolk, where I grew up, or New York, where I live. Painting my way through the year towards the show, I secretly acquired Danish material, each bit revealing to me the depths of my ignorance. There are so many things I know nothing about, but it felt uncivil to know nothing about a country hosting a prize which had made such a difference to me. I think I thought they might take it away if they found out how little I knew about them. I liked the stuff I found out – the first king of Denmark was Gorm the Old, commemorated along with his queen Thyra by the Jelling Stones, two great rune stones planted in a churchyard at Jelling. He was succeeded by his son Harald Bluetooth. Knowing these things served no purpose beyond the pleasure of knowledge, and I filed the information away, telling myself that by the time I finished the work and got to the show, I would have met someone to share it with, someone who might come with me to Jelling and Elsinore. Someone to look over the harbour at the Oresund, the stretch of water that connects the Baltic to the North Sea. Someone who wanted to know what I know and what I feel. It was a measure of hope I threw up into the universe. I hadn't had a proper boyfriend for a couple of years and although I was scared to admit it even to myself, I wanted that to change. Now, all of a sudden, here I was, standing alone in the middle of the room at this exhibition, my own solo exhibition and the first since my degree show eight years ago, and no one I know is here with me, and there is no one specially here with me who wants to know what I feel. I'm not so sure I even want to know myself, though sadness is creeping into me like incoming tide. I look around, and my mind detaches and takes off, floating above me, separated by unchangeable circumstances from everyone else here: I made the pictures, and I am not one of the crowd. The warm welcome feeling evaporates and I feel like a deflated balloon, strung out with the strain of being on show, exposed and visibly alone. That is the most tiring part. Like a bride, I am at the centre of a party but also the outsider, the one person here with a different function from everyone else. But at a wedding there is the bridegroom too. And he is the other half of the bride. Another person also experiencing the aloneness, and thus sharing it. I love the idea that somewhere on earth each of us

32

has someone who is our other half. I wonder if we only have one, or if in all the millions and billions of people there are several with whom we could feel equally whole? It seems unlikely, but then so does the idea of there being even one. And it's just as unlikely that there should be none. What would be the point of that?

The point is that there is no point, one of the top three favourite arguments at art school. I never really went for it. How can we be put on this earth with all our instincts to yearn and strive and seek to find meaning if there is no meaning? And without meaning, how can there be love? And love is real. Often flawed and sometimes dangerous, but love is the spark that ignites us and burns through life. I believe that. I don't know what else I believe.

The motherly kindness of Hans Stettjens approaching now with a small plate of rolled silver-backed fish and three slate-grey capers, and the goodwill in the gallery is suddenly unbearable. I can't be the object of so much kindly focused attention for a moment longer. I feel the pressure building inside me; the gallery is filling up with an increasingly physical energy and it's like a giant blancmange or a pink cloud, benign, absurd, but engulfing and too much. The heat in the room presses against my temples and sweat breaks on my neck. I am near the door. It opens as more people come in, fresh air stiff on the folds of their overcoats. I turn my back on the room and step through the slice of space separating inside from out. I am suddenly free.

The moon has moved. It peeps from behind a church spire further along the front. A gilt cord of light loops away towards the church like a fishing line, but it is impossible to see the way properly or to work out where the sea ends and where the land begins. The breeze cuts through my dress, I am chilly now, and shivery after being so warm. But I can't go back into the gallery yet. I sit down on the low wall looking out to sea, confused and relieved to be outside gathering my thoughts. I am a long way from home. In fact, I am not even sure where I think of as home unless it's my studio. I am alone and I have forgotten my coat. Looking around in the dark, my impression of the city is oddly one of light. The streets are broad, the buildings set back on wide pavements. All the lines are crisp and clean, and the shadows of verticals and horizontals loom huge in the chiaroscuro of street lights. Along the line of harbour, tall multicoloured buildings like doll's houses stare through many windows at the sea as it stretches towards Norway, and somewhere much nearer is the mermaid, small and naked on her rock. These unfamiliar yet familiar elements of a city combine with my solo travelling and the grey shroud of grief for my mother which I forget and remember with the flashing regularity of a lighthouse beam. I feel as if I am the eye of my own storm, still, like the mermaid, at the centre of my own chaos.

2

The sound of a boat's engine is scarcely noticeable in the slap of water, the hushed whisper of chains undulating, snaking, weightless in the current. Above and overriding is the clang of metal on masts and the background breath of traffic in the town. When the engine cuts, the memory of its sound reverberates in the harbour mouth, followed by the slippery creaking of oars guiding a passage through the boats anchored in the oily water. A pause, almost silence. Then it begins again. More creaking, a whipping sound of a rope running through a fastening. Footsteps. Oddly, they seem to be coming from the water; my imagination leaps into a scene from a horror movie, where anything can happen as long as it's gruesome. My heart thuds and nervously I scan the surface of the sea in front of where I'm sitting, but nothing is visible. The footsteps stop behind me. I hold my breath, tensed for flight.

'Christ. That's psychedelic, I wonder if it's a bar?'

The voice that comes with the footsteps is not what I was expecting. It's English, for a start, and I wasn't really expecting a voice – maybe a club to the back of my head, or a chloroformed rag on my mouth, but certainly not a comprehensible English-speaking man's voice. Sexy, and with an owner who must be right behind me. Looking around in the dark I am disoriented and confused. And no longer alone. A man is standing in the middle of the road behind me, his head tilted back, looking up at the gallery. He has appeared from nowhere. The road was empty up and down, still is. I don't think he has seen me. I stand up and move towards him, still without him seeing me, and laughter and excitement tingle through me because it feels silly, a bit like playing Grandmother's Footsteps. I am so close now, and I still haven't been seen.

I am aware of stepping into the unknown when I open my mouth to speak. 'It's a gallery.'

He swivels to face me, and he is so near to me I could touch him, and I want to touch him, even though I don't know him. We look at one another, careful, like startled cats. 'You're English?'

'Yes. And so are you.' I can't see him properly, I don't know what he looks like, but he has an air of being stopped in his tracks. Slowly we circle one another, and it hardly feels like moving, but it is something to do, almost instead of talking, as we take one another in. 'I don't live there.'

'Oh. What a shame. I live in London on a boat.'

'Did you come here in your boat?'

He laughs and the frisson of tension leaps like a sudden kick of a pulse. My eyes are adjusting now and I can see him better as he speaks. 'No, it's moored in Little Venice, it doesn't go far. Though actually, I did come here on a boat, so in a sense you're right. But what about you?' He has a smile in his voice, and it has become a game between us because he echoes my words, 'Did you come in your boat?'

Somehow his words sound intimate, gentle, almost as if he is stroking me. I blush and press my fingers to my face over my smile.

'No. Mine was an airship. I'm working here, that's why I came.' I am playing with my hair, rolling a lock of it around my fingers. I am trying to have a straight face, but my grin breaks out in a flash.

He ducks his head and looks at me again, a matching smile all over his face. He is handsome and rugged, unshaven and tall. 'Me too, but I got distracted by something on the quay, and it turns out it was you.'

I gasp, laughing, excited. 'How did you see me? It's dark.'

'I don't think I saw you immediately, but I sensed you were here,' he says, and in the street light I catch a shadowy glimpse of smiling eyes. My heart thumps but I like it. The chemistry between us is exhilarating, I can hardly believe this is happening. Flirtation is instinctive; I catch myself flashing him a saucy look, and I giggle, excitement bursting out of me.

'You've got an instinct for finding people, have you?'

He is closer now. 'Not sure, really, but I must have an instinct for finding you.'

He is backlit between me and the building and it is like being in a movie, the two of us alone in the dark by the glittering water.

I like his voice. Maybe I have heard too many American accents, and he sounds familiar and English. I have a sense of warmth from him, and I love the potent intimacy of his interest in me. It's not what he has said, or not said, it's the feeling of being next to him, the sense of him near me. I could listen to him talking for as long as he likes.

Talking myself is more difficult: 'I'm Grace Hart, how do you do?' Oh. A nervous shiver slips out as a gasp and I bite my lip, staring at the ground. He holds out his hand and I put mine in his, conditioned for shaking a greeting. But, instead, he puts his other hand on top. He has a scar like a seam running from the base of his thumbnail straight down to his wrist. It's sexy.

'Hey, Grace,' he says, finally, 'my name is Ryder James.'

'Do you mean James Ryder and you are saying it the wrong way round like "Bond, James Bond?"' Laughing I pull my hands away. It is the most tantalising thing. Every nerve and fibre in my body is turning towards him. The breeze blows my hair in a curtain between us.

'No, I mean Ryder as in . . . as in . . . well, I can only think of Haggard, unfortunately, although spelled differently, and James as in . . . er . . .' He stops, looks at his shoes, glances at me and goes on. 'Well, as in *James and the Giant Peach*.' He closes his eyes, winces, and mutters almost to himself, 'Great, you would think I could have a better chat-up line than *James and the Peach* to impress a girl on a quay at night.' His words tail off into my laughter and our circling around one another has positioned him with his face completely in darkness. My breath is jagged. I want our conversation to keep going so we have no reason to leave.

'He wrote *She*,' I offer.

'Umm.' Ryder moves back, raises one eyebrow, and I feel he is teasing me. 'No, he floated off in a peach with some undesirables— Oh, you mean Rider Haggard. Yes, he did. I've never read it. Though of course my mother has, and, in an uncharacteristically romantic moment, named me after him.'

We are standing right in front of one another now, and it is so exciting. It feels as though something missing has been found. This is what I have been waiting for, but how can it be? In the silence between us I am holding my breath, which I don't realise until I let it all out in a rush.

'I'm not supposed to be here, we're leaving tonight,' he says. 'I should have been back on the boat, but I saw the lights – this place – and I wanted to find it.' He gestures at the gallery and looks from it to back at me. 'It's mesmerising,' he says. I don't know if he is talking to me or to himself.

The scar on his hand twists round to the underside of his wrist and disappears beneath his watchstrap.

39

When I notice it again, desire leaps within me and slithers into my core.

'Do you think so?' I can't believe I am responding so physically, or whatever this is, to a guy I have only just met. It's freaking me out and at the same time thrilling me. It's like driving a fast car or riding a horse at full gallop; the adrenaline pulses through me like a fix and I feel high. I might do something I regret. The thought makes me laugh and I twirl around and away from him, shy to look at him in case he sees more than I want to show him in my eyes. His gaze is on my face, touching me everywhere, along my throat and down the front of my dress. It makes me smile.

'It's an art gallery, not a bar.' I am just staying with the thread of our conversation but I am hardly aware of what we are saying, because all I can think about is how I'm longing to touch his skin. I have the urge to take his hand again and to trace his scar with my fingertip from its beginning in the curve of his thumb, slowly down the glinting metal of his watchstrap, and there to pause and press my finger under the articulations of the watchstrap and down the inside of his wrist.

What if he is thinking the same? What if he wants to touch me as much as I want to touch him? He is so close I am breathing in the scent of his body, his skin. It's making me feel dizzy. And his scar. I didn't know I was turned on by scars. Oh God. I am not thinking straight. I've got to come up with more to say; if there's a silence I am sure he will read my thoughts. Luckily he is talking, unaware of the state I am getting myself into. Now he is running his hand through his hair, looking up at the wall behind us.

'A gallery? Oh that makes sense. How great! Can anyone go in, do you think?'

'Oh yes.' Speaking breaks the tension.

'Your hair smells good,' he says, and it is like an electric shock when he touches it and it falls from behind my ear across my cheek.

Completely thrown, I gasp, 'Yes, of course anyone can go in.'

He looks at me and across at the gallery. 'Why do you think that?'

We are standing in one another's body heat. Or rather I am in his, as my body heat is around zero. No coat. I shiver. 'Because this is the private view.'

'Is it? How do you know?'

'How do I know? Umm. I was at it.'

I just can't say they are my pictures. It is too much of an exposure for this delicately balanced game; it will change everything. Really I am just scared. He touches my elbow and my nerves thrill as if he has run a feather along the inside of my arm and down the length of my body. I look back at him and both of us can't help smiling.

He takes my hand. 'Did you come with someone? They will be wondering where you are,' he says, then frowns. 'And why are you out here by yourself with no coat? Why did you leave the private view?' He laughs and squeezes my hand. 'And while we're at it, what did you say your name is?'

I laugh. 'Shall we start again? My name is Grace, I

can't believe you forgot that already, and I'm doing the same as you are out here, I'm standing around looking at the lights. You're right, it was a mistake to come out with no coat, and now I wish I had one.' My red dress glows like an ember but gives off no heat.

His voice is low and gentle. 'I'm sorry, I was looking at you and I forgot to listen to your name, I mean your surname, because I know you're called Grace.' A car hisses past on the damp road, and the quiet between us is as intense as any words. 'And I was just thinking what a coincidence it is that we met here, tonight. It's auspicious.'

'Is it? Why?'

He takes his coat off and holds it out on his finger. 'Well, for a start, you might be cold?' he asks hopefully. 'And if you are, I can give you this.'

I bite my lip, suddenly shy. 'Why do you think it's a coincidence? Isn't it just a random meeting?'

He shakes his head. 'No, I don't think so.' He shakes the coat, making me laugh.

'You look like a bullfighter. I'm fine, really,' I say.

'Oh really?' He swirls the coat around my shoulders and his warmth settles all over me. The coat smells of wax and oil and inside it I feel soft and safe.

'That's nice,' I whisper. My protective shell has dropped off. A random selection of soft, shell-less items float into my head, including an open oyster, a jellyfish, and an un-formed egg, its shell collapsed like the overused ping pong ball I found in the hen house at my Aunt Sophie's house when I was six. But these images only veil my true intent; I'm looking at Ryder's mouth and wanting more than anything on earth for him to kiss me.

I put my hand over my mouth to wipe away desire and hide the huge smile breaking from within me, as I stand cocooned in the coat as though in an embrace. Ryder wanders away along the sea front. His hair is dark in the night light, and he is incongruous in the winter street with no coat on. He doesn't seem to mind; he looks completely at home on the harbour. He is turning away, but he stops and is back next to me in a moment. 'Being chivalrous is the best excuse not to go back to the boat yet. I'm with a big ship, you see. We're leaving tonight.'

'How can you be with a ship? Are you a sailor?' Confused, I rattle through my thoughts aloud. 'Oh, and this is an encounter out of one of those old musicals. *Singing in the Rain*, maybe?'

He frowns. 'Yes. No. I'd prefer *On the Waterfront*.'

'Oh yes. That fits.'

Ryder lights a cigarette and inhales hard. Maybe he isn't feeling as relaxed as he looks.

'I've been in Copenhagen for a day or two, but mainly I'm working, and work is out there on a ship.'

'Are you a fisherman?'

His eyes are narrow through the smoke. I have a sense that he is looking past my face into my head and my heart.

'The real answer is pretty mundane,' he says lightly. 'I'm a marine engineer and I'm writing a report on the proposals to build an offshore wind farm here in Copenhagen.'

'That's not mundane, that's a real job in the real world,' I object, and maybe it's because he said he has to go, but I am sad that the grains of something precious are slipping away as if there was an egg timer tucked into the corner of my mind.

'Well, it's real up to a point. But making guesses about what might happen often feels like a nightmare, or an acid trip. But then reality is all relative, isn't it?'

I try to find words, but it is like a dream, nothing comes out of my mouth, even though desire to hear him and be heard by him tugs at my heart.

'I'm sorry, I've run out of brain power.' His presence is magnetic, distracting, comforting, singular. Even while my mind whirls with all these feelings I am aware that I will not forget him when he is gone.

And suddenly it is all too much. A rubber mallet has rained blows on my head ever since my plane landed, and now I feel flattened by exhaustion and I know I should be back in the gallery. 'I've got to go.'

'I'll take you.' He flicks the cigarette away and it rolls, glowing, into the gutter.

I shake my head. 'Thank you, but I can't go anywhere. I have to go back in there.'

Ryder is by my side, his face bathed in prism rainbow colours by the projected lights of the gallery. He touches my cheek. 'I'll come with you.'

'Thank you.' The hem of my dress swings against his knee. If he is coming in with me, I'd better tell him, that it's my show now. I tuck my hair behind my ear, embarrassed suddenly, and looking anywhere but at Ryder's face.

'It's my exhibition, you know. I mean, they are my pictures.' I wave at the façade of the gallery, feeling a bit futile. Would I feel any more exposed if I had unbuttoned my dress and stepped naked into the street in front of him? Probably not.

Ryder looks at me, whistles under his breath, and takes my hand, a wide grin on his face. His hand holding mine is a good, safe feeling. 'Wow. I'd love to come and see what you do,' he says. I feel numb now, but he keeps talking as we cross the road, easy chatter I can half respond to.

'I've never been to an exhibition with the artist before. I've never really wanted to,' he says. 'What would it be like to go round the National Gallery with Caravaggio, for example?'

'Scary,' I laugh, 'but it could be fun.'

'This is fun,' he says, opening the door for me, and his warm presence by my side is the thing I am most aware of as we walk into the gallery.

3

Ryder
Copenhagen
Five years later

The plane veers along the runway in a hiss of protesting brakes mixed with the applause of passengers. After a turbulent end to the flight, even the polite and usually implacable Danes are carried away with relief, and can't resist an impromptu party. Ryder squints out of the window, enjoying the comforting roar of wheels on the ground, gazing at the amber-lit evening and the bulk of the airport building ahead. A pea-green articulated bus passes, and as the plane taxis to a halt, Ryder watches people scurrying about. The outside temperature must be below freezing as dusk falls, and men in fluorescent yellow tabards move stiffly about the tarmac, circling awkwardly around themselves until the concentric nature of order takes over and they become still. The stillness lasts for a few moments then, slowly, they begin to spiral out again into more tasks and patterns and this part of the airport becomes busy again with spreading action while further over towards the runway, different people are turning different circles.

Is this all we really do in life? Ryder wonders as he folds his newspaper and stuffs it into his bag. One last clue on the crossword remains undone, so it is impossible for him to leave the paper on the plane. *A sweet bird descending, tree espaliered.*

He looks out of the window again and up at the yellow-white sky. Snow is coming, and suddenly he is pierced with a memory of the childhood Christmas tree and his family decorating it. His sister Bonnie standing on the back of the sofa, laughing as she tried to reach with the knitted fairy to the topmost branch. She must have been nine, her legs in blue tights, stretching impossibly long, teetering, her arms stretched out and the orange dress she was wearing like the heart of a flame against the forest-green of the tree. Her face was a pale oval lit with excitement, as she bit her lip in concentration and placed a glass ball on the tree, pulling down the branch to slide the loop on, then standing back to judge while the bauble bobbed and the tree settled again.

The window by his seat frames a scene outside; a long tier of steps rising into the side of a huge jumbo jet, a stretched white concertina filling up with first one or two, then a creeping flood of people. Transatlantic passengers, some of them very wealthy looking. Ryder grins, clocking a couple of sumptuous fur hats floating up the aeroplane steps on the heads of two black-coated men. On their way somewhere luxurious for the weekend, no doubt, or back home to houses with silk-clad wives and fragrant pots of lilies. Quivers full of finely grown children – Ryder can see it all, in the fabulous caricature that his brain conjured up for much-imagined ideas outside his own experience. The fantasy is made more sumptuous by the gap between it and his own reality. Though thinking himself into his girlfriend Cara's apartment isn't at all bad. Far from it, he likes the books piled high, the hiss of the gas radiators and the vague pleasure with which Cara greets him. Admittedly, he sometimes feels that she has forgotten he is coming, but better that than that she stopped her life to wait for him.

Cara, in fact, doesn't stop her life for anything, not even Christmas. 'They needed someone to cover at the office on the paper so I said I would do it and you know it's going to be easy to write because no one will call,' she'd told him on the phone a few weeks earlier. 'And I don't like Christmas, it's for people with children.'

Cara was single and liked it that way when she met Ryder two years ago. She came to interview him about the wind farm, and their affair began, based on a mutual restlessness and lack of commitment. Only now Ryder was beginning to realise that maybe the lackadaisical approach was more a symptom than a quality of their relationship, and he, for one, wanted more in his life. Christmas and children. Nothing wrong with that combination he feels, as he prepares to get off the plane on a brief pre-Christmas visit to see Cara and have a final meeting to sign off from the wind farm project. The green signs to unfasten seat belts flash along the plane and Ryder stretches and yawns, rolling his head on the seat back, hit by sudden exhaustion.

Through the window a woman catches his eye, or rather he notices the flash of a red dress. The hem flies up in a gust of wind from a jet engine, and his heart leaps. He looks again at the woman; she is walking up the steps now, carrying a coat over her arm and looking in her handbag, dark hair falling over her face. She raises her head and her face lifts towards him, and he whistles, or tries to, though it doesn't come out because his heart is in his mouth. And it starts racing like an engine. He can't stop staring, it's so unbelievable. It's her. The painter. The one. The one he met here. When was it? Five years ago. But it could be yesterday. The most amazing girl with whom he had the most amazing, intense evening. So amazing he remembers it still. She looks different, maybe thinner. Yes, perhaps it's thinner. Girls always seem to look thinner than before, but she also looks the same. Older, but who wouldn't? Actually, she doesn't look old. She is so familiar and yet exotic. She looks like a girl he might have seen in a movie or in a magazine, desirable and distant. Not his. He is leaning against the window now, his hand raised, ready to knock. She has paused at the top of her plane steps, and she looks back towards the terminal. At someone? Who knows. Anyway, she doesn't wave or smile. She tucks her hair behind her ear and though it is irrational, and untrue, he feels the gesture is something he knows so well it settles in a warm space inside him and he grins out of the window at her. Not that she can see him. She turns and walks on to the plane and the red dress flips and swishes through the doorway, vanishing from his sight but burned on to his retina like a hot kiss.

An air hostess coughs next to his seat. 'Sir, would you like to get ready to leave the plane? The doors will be opening in a moment and your hand luggage is obstructing . . .' she trails off, her smile peach soft and flashing now at the exasperated older man Ryder has not noticed who is trying to attract his attention.

Taking in the man's irritation, Ryder nods an apology and swings out of his seat to reach his luggage down. 'I'm so sorry,' he says to the air hostess. 'Yes, of course. I'll get out of the way. I just— oh never mind. Actually, can you tell me something? Do you know where that jumbo is going?'

She glances through his window. 'Oh, that's Dan Air's Copenhagen to New York flight. It's a bit late taking off this evening, they are usually away from the building before we land.'

'Are they? So it's just chance – a coincidence, I mean, that the plane is still here?' The air hostess raises her eyebrows, a silent judgement on the urgency of Ryder's enquiry, but she nods.

'Yes, it's just chance,' she agrees.

With difficulty Ryder stops himself gasping and smiting his brow like a ham actor in some ridiculous pantomime. He can't believe the air hostess is acting so normally. It's the flight to New York! This kind blonde woman is trying to see him off the aeroplane courteously without succumbing to this astonishing information. She is bafflingly preoccupied with her walkie talkie and uninteresting news about the door-opening schedule. But of course she is unaware of the enormity of the situation. That it must be her. It must be. The plane is going to New York. She lives in New York. It can only be the girl he met on the waterfront and whom he has never forgotten. She has a lovely name – Grace – and she is English, though she lives in New York. She is here again. The painter. The beautiful painter is back. Well, in fact, she's leaving, but she was here a minute ago. Here where he is now.

Suddenly Ryder is right back in time with her. There on the harbour wall in Copenhagen five years ago. It was so unexpected. Though what else could it have been? How can you expect to bump into someone you didn't know you were looking for? In his mind, Ryder is again standing with her on the harbour. This girl whose presence was so magnetic, that he wanted to put his arms around her and hold her close, even though he scarcely knew her name and it was so dark he couldn't even see the colour of her eyes. But he could see her smile and the shape of her face and her skin bathed in moonlight. And then, in the gallery, he lost her. Her world swallowed her up in a dazzle of flashing cameras and the white walls of the gallery which seemed to Ryder to do the exact opposite of creating a sense of space. One moment they were holding hands and then she was gone. He left without saying goodbye, though he left a note with the gallery owner: 'Dear Grace, I . . . you . . .' Crossed out. Rewritten. Crossed out. Finally, he just put his name and number on the match book in his pocket. She never called.

In the tedious delay while Ryder's plane doors do not open and everyone stands expectantly in the aisle, their briefcases and hand luggage gripped for the fray, night creeps across the sky above the orange glow of the airport lighting, and Grace's jet taxis off, twinkling like a decorated Christmas tree. Ryder feels wildly, absurdly elated. The connection he made with her is palpable. It may have been dormant for five years, but it has sprung up again and he is run through with it – the energy and the optimism of sexual chemistry surges in his veins and he is amazed. He has not felt this love struck for years. It's like a drug, but the drug has just got on another plane without him actually touching it. Finally the plane doors open and the passengers trudge off and out along miles of carpeted corridor. Ryder sleepwalks through the terminal. Why has she been in Denmark again? Who will know? How can he find out? In the queue for passport control he notices that the woman in front has an international edition of a Danish newspaper under her arm.

Without knowing what he hopes to find, he taps her on the shoulder, 'Could I look, please?'

She smiles and hands it to him. He smiles back. It must be a sign of something important that everyone is so nice, he thinks, flicking through to the arts pages. It is senseless to think the answer will be in the newspaper, but never mind, it's good to start somewhere. He is not sure what he is looking for in among the album reviews and interviews with illustrious film-makers. Not bad coverage, in fact, for a small-scale paper such as this. And suddenly, she is there. In a photograph with a lot of people.

Oh my God, thinks Ryder, I've lost the plot. This is like those moments in the tabloids when people find Jesus in a pizza or the Virgin Mary in an olive growing on an olive tree. OK, so this is in a newspaper, where information is generally supposed to be. But the chance of it happening . . . It's a million to one for sure. He shakes the paper and holds it closer. It's a terrible mug shot, the colour has run, and all the faces are pale green. Grace does not look her best, pale green, but undoubtedly it is her, looking unhealthy next to the Mayor and behind the right shoulder of the Queen of Denmark. She should never wear black, she looks like a ghost. Or else she should make sure she doesn't have green photographs taken. He must tell her. How can he tell her? He has not seen her for five years, he just saw her leave the country and he has no idea how to get in touch with her.

Ryder buys his own newspaper and gets into a taxi, his thoughts uninterrupted. It's usually a mistake telling girls that a photograph is not flattering. They do not take kindly to anything less than superlatives about photographs. A girl sees it as criticism, not realising that what it is, in fact, is fascination in every tiny thing about her. One of the things Ryder finds most difficult to come to terms with in breaking up with a girlfriend, and it has happened more often than is strictly desirable or necessary, is the sudden absence of daily female minutiae. He loves the intimacy of everyday life shared with a woman. Her cosmetics on the bathroom shelf, the ritual of her bathing and getting ready to go out. Her shoes kicked off in the hall. The subtle scent of her on her clothes and at home. It is his pattern to forget how much he loves these small things until they are gone.

Growing up with Bonnie, so tuned into her he could tell her mood from the colour of her clothes, he has never come to terms with losing this whole female element in his life. He misses it, yet repeatedly, whenever he has a girlfriend and they get to the stage of beginning to share intimacy, he begins to absent himself – cutting off from the very thing he longs for just as it is presented to him.

Not that there is any intimacy on offer here with Grace Hart. It's absurd to think there might be, but it's impossible not to dream. He is drawn back to the photograph. Better to keep it light. Look how lovely her eyes are, even appearing as they do here, slightly cross eyed. Ryder doesn't need the picture to remember they are beautiful, he has seen them in his dreams. So many times afterwards he wondered what might have happened if he had stayed. Walking into the gallery with Grace had fazed him. A crowd parted and then swarmed over them and Grace was taken from his side, passed on a chain of handshakes to a smooth-looking American businessman with eyes like a lizard and hair receding down the back of his head.

Grace stretched a hand back to him and he came to join her, but even though she introduced him, there was an insularity, like blobs of mercury sticking to themselves, that repulsed all hope of Ryder melting into the flow. He didn't know this world, he didn't know Grace, and he had nothing to contribute save his presence on this occasion. Jerome Michaels had his hand on Grace's back within seconds of meeting her, a big gold watch glinted from beneath the cuff of a pristine shirt, and the aura of money and power which surrounded him was as strong as the scent of a dog fox marking his territory. It was astonishing to think that this girl, who had been trembling in the cold on the harbour wall on her own, and who seemed as free as the moonlight dancing on the dark water, was big business for the City suits prowling possessively around her.

Ryder walked around the gallery alone. The pictures surprised him, not that he knew what he was expecting; they were so big and expressive. Ryder longed to pull Grace away from the American now resting a tanned hand on her shoulder so that she could tell him about her pictures. Without her he had no language to interpret them, and he felt pride in her that she had done all this. There was no hope of looking at them with Grace, however, and after half an hour, during which he watched her work for the gallery owner, Ryder accepted that the spark they had made outside together had burned out and he must go. He whispered goodbye as she was led to a chair to give an interview, and their eyes met in a moment he had recalled a hundred times, including now, as he stands in the taxi queue waiting to leave the airport.

Her eyes were beautiful, her skin was smooth. He can even remember the feel of her body, though he had only touched the small of her back through her dress. Otherwise all of the sense he had of her was from his other senses. Now, though, he is able to conjure the feeling of her with incredible urgency. Extraordinary urgency. Quick, better think of something else to stop the excitement, he thinks. It's definitely perverted to be in transit getting a hard-on about a green-faced person in a group photo with the bloody Queen of Denmark. The caption reads:

> The unveiling of the new picture wing of the National Gallery took place in the presence of Queen Margrethe last night. The Lord Mayor played host to international artists including Njenst Dinnisk, Luis de Corliune and Grace Hart, at thirty-two the youngest living artist to have work in the Danish National Collection.

Ryder looks at his watch. There should be enough time, it will be open for another hour. He gets into a taxi.

'National Gallery please,' he says, and blood is rushing, drumming in his head with the loud pulse of his heart.

Later, with the key poised to let himself into Cara's apartment, he changes his mind and rings the bell. It's not that he has met someone else, for of course he

has not, he has only seen her, but Ryder, with a poignant sadness, knows that he and Cara have reached the
point where it should either go further or end. His
work in Denmark is over.

Cara lets him in. She is wearing a long green skirt
and her hair glows in a pool of light from the sitting
room.

'You didn't use your key?'

'No, it's here.' He puts it on the table in the hall.
Cara looks at it silently. The apartment smells of a
smoky incense that clings to Ryder's throat. He sits
opposite her on a low chair, and in the faraway look
in her eyes he sees that she has moved on too. He
looks around the cluttered familiar space, wondering whether to speak first, wondering whether he is
making a mistake, the usual mistake. But maybe it
has never been a mistake, maybe it is just that he
has not met the person to share his dreams and real-
ities with.

'How have you been?' Cara pours him a drink. She
is wearing lipstick and a different scent.

'Oh good, thanks,' Ryder replies, stilted in his
manner with his glass, stilted in his voice. He rubs his
hands through his hair and moves over next to Cara,
putting his arms around her, resting his chin on the
top of her head. Two candles have burned low on the
mantelpiece and a blue scarf hangs off a chair, forming a pool on the floorboards.

'I know,' she says.

He squeezes her tight for a moment. 'I know you
do, I could tell when I walked in. I am sorry, I suppose

57

I never thought about what might happen between us when the work here ended.'

Cara wriggles away from him to reach for her drink. 'Oh come on,' she says gently, 'it's been nice, you and me, but we were never going to end up together.'

Relief and sadness hang in the air between them. 'I suppose I'm wishing we had known that from the beginning,' he says.

Cara stands up, and in a flashing moment Ryder realises she is going out and her actions are tinged with impatience. This makes it easier. Logs crackle in the wood-burning stove, and one cracks loudly. Cara throws her lighted cigarette into the fire.

'I've got to go, I'm meeting someone.'

Ryder gets up and hugs her. 'I'm sorry,' he says.

'Don't be,' she replies. 'Be glad we are friends and let's keep in touch.'

She crouches to stoke up the fire and they walk out of the apartment together.

In the street Ryder hails a taxi. He can hardly look at Cara because he is experiencing such an odd, weightless sensation. She stands next to him, delving in her handbag for her car keys. Ryder turns to kiss her goodbye, and, wanting to make a ritual of their parting, he suddenly remembers something he learned for an exam.

'You never knowingly do anything for the last time without a certain sadness of the heart,' he quotes.

Cara looks surprised as she considers for a moment. 'What?' she says.

The taxi purrs next to them, the words tumble out of Ryder: 'It's Oscar Wilde, and it's true. The idea that this is the last time I'll see you makes my skin crawl with sadness.'

Cara laughs and pushes him towards the taxi. 'Let's make sure it isn't, then. I will call you when I come to London.'

'Yes, but you never do.'

And he is in the cab looking round at Cara in the street. She waves her hand and walks towards her car. Shame leaps inside him as he watches her vanish from his sight because just as he never made the effort to learn to speak her language, so too he never made the leap or whatever it took to love her. And it feels like all he ever does is say goodbye to anyone his heart is touched by. Almost swept away by self pity, Ryder is stopped in his tracks as he realises the taxi is still stationary outside Cara's apartment block. Where is he going? He has no idea. Back to the airport is the best idea, but he has the meeting tomorrow morning in town. That's why he is here. Sitting outside this apartment is freaking him out. The empty street hits a spot of desolation very deep in his heart and Ryder taps the driver on the shoulder and gives the name of a hotel he has often had business meetings in.

The reception desk is a pale green slab of glass which reminds Ryder of Grace's paintings. Thinking of Grace at the same time as thinking of Cara is utterly exhausting. Actually, thinking of anyone is too much right now. Ryder opens the door of his room by pressing his hand flat on to an infrared pad, and enters. The room has soft grey walls and a carpet the colour of damsons. Glass surfaces appear to float without support near the walls; two on either side of the bed form little tables and another, positioned to the side of the window, is clearly a desk. On top of it is a cream-coloured telephone and a vase containing one twig. It does not even have a bud on it. Worn out, Ryder throws himself down on the bed, flat on his face, arms spread wide, surrendered. Stroking the silk shimmer of the bedspread, he wonders why the fuck he is alone. 'How does this keep happening whenever I am with someone? I want to be with someone, but when I am, I end up leaving. How can I change that?' he says aloud.

Having no answers, he gets up again, pulls the metal lid from a glass bottle of beer. He moves over to the desk and begins, for the thousandth time, his favourite displacement activity. He begins to draw the boathouse he wants to build. This time he finds himself drawing an actual house he might inhabit next to it. The house is on a chalk cliff. It sits facing the sea in a shallow bowl of grassland, framed by pine woods from behind, long and low and at a right angle to the sea; the rooms on either end of the house looking out at all aspects of the spectacular view. The diagram has ceased to be purely functional and is becoming an actual picture.

It is early in the morning, the sea is frilled with insouciant breakers, and the sun is rising on the horizon. With the chalky cliffs and the orientation, he realises this dream house he is conjuring could be in Norfolk. Ryder has hardly been back to Norfolk since Bonnie died. Maybe it's time for a visit now. Lying on the bed in a strange hotel, utterly alone, Ryder is curious and anxious that his thoughts have gone to Bonnie. They often do still, though sometimes it is a fleeting flash of recognition, an unspoken acknowledgement that he has experienced something she would have shared and seen in the way he saw it. This more than anything is what has kept Ryder from forming a lasting relationship. Can there be someone whom he can know and be known by? 'Why not?' is his thought when things are going well, but there are many more instances when he broods and thinks, 'Why would there be?'

Maybe all siblings have the closeness he and his sister shared. There is no way of knowing, and Ryder recognises this sadness tugging his heart now, when he yearns to pick up the phone and call her, to hear the perspective he trusted all his childhood. Bonnie never let him down. Until she died. Ryder pushes back his chair and stands up to stretch, his spine curving his back like a full sail. He has learned now, thank God, that his memories will not overwhelm him any more. And that it is possible to keep the past at bay. Some natural filter – perhaps it is sanity – allows only what he can tolerate to shimmer into focus from the shifting currents and unnoticed patterns of all that has gone before and remains unresolved and shattered. God knows what is forgotten for ever. Sometimes Bonnie is in his head; he can imagine her voice, and hear her thoughts as clearly as his own. At other times, she is a distant figure, walking away; she is weightless and evaporating and he cannot talk to her. Then grief tightens around his heart with the fear that he has lost her for ever. Even though this has happened more times than he can remember, and the sense of her has always returned, Ryder is still susceptible to the anxiety it brings. When he is not gripped by it, he knows that he has Bonnie and her memory tucked into his heart, and that she will always be there. The tie is blood. Can there be a stronger tie? Ryder has not found one. The family tie unbreakable, like being a parent; no matter how far a child goes, even into death, the place they occupy in their parents' hearts is theirs for ever. Or so Ryder believes from witnessing his own parents. For a long time he stayed away from them, from everything to do with his childhood and with children.

Norfolk, indeed East Anglia including Essex where he grew up, has exuded an anti-magnetic force for Ryder. Over the years any suggestions from his colleagues in marine engineering that he should go there have been met with ever more resourceful reasons not to. The job in Denmark was a useful diversion from a suggestion he might do some work on the gas platforms in the North Sea. It didn't take a rocket scientist to notice that working with the wind instead of fossil fuel was more ethical, too. Can man truly harness the sea? Ryder's work circles endlessly around this question, never accepting that the answer could be 'No'. Generally, he believes that the answers to all the pressing questions about what the planet can do for energy lie submerged in the ebb and flow of the tides. However, the route to finding them is as unfathomable as the depths of the ocean. Everything is possible and none of it happens, or so it seems after weeks of grey winter seas and too many sea birds smashed like exploded pillows in the blades of the wind turbines. Even then, the many projects that come up in Norfolk leave him cold. Secretly he knows he is afraid. Not of what he believes he will find in revisiting the backdrop of his childhood, but of what he fears he may not.

Marine engineering and, more specifically, energy conservation, requires a coastline. There is a lot of Norfolk on the sea, and increasingly a lot of Norfolk in the sea; Ryder had one reluctant trip there to photograph and measure an ancient wooden circle emerging from the shifting sands on the north-west coast of Norfolk. It was too extraordinary an opportunity for him to turn down – a wooden version of Stonehenge that conservationists were determined to remove from the sea, and Druids and the coastguards were united in believing should stay where it had been for thousands of years. Ryder saw it first at sunrise as the tide went out over the long shallow sand banks at Thornham Gap. The beach was silent but not empty, as grey dawn turned mauve and pink with the creeping arrival of the summer sun. Three figures loomed from along the shore beyond where Ryder stood at the water's edge, watching eagerly for dark shapes within the waves to transform into the circle. Two of the figures were fishermen, netting for sea bass. They nodded a greeting and strode on, incongruous in wetsuits on this ancient shore. The third was a Druid with a carved stick and a mane of dreadlocks.

'This'll show out in a moment.'

'Yes, the tide is dropping now,' agreed Ryder, trying to overcome his surprise that the Druid had a strong Norfolk accent. What was he supposed to sound like? Someone from *Star Trek*? Or the Middle Ages? And how had they sounded then, anyway? Probably like someone from Norfolk.

The Druid rested both hands on his stick and waded in with his jeans rolled up beneath his cloak just beyond where Ryder stood, also with his bare feet under water.

'That'll be a job to stop them moving it, but that'll be a job for them to move it, too. The tides at the summer solstice are big, and they've signed the papers to say they'll not move the circle until the next day.'

'Blimey,' said Ryder, more to himself than in response, imagining the chaos the whole operation could cause. The Druid looked at him measuringly.

'Are you from the conservation department, then?'

'No. I've been sent by the British Museum.'

The Druid tossed his dreads. 'Ah. Same thing. I'm part of a peaceful protest. We don't want this circle moved from the site. And we are concerned that in moving it, a whole lot of trouble will be churned up along with the sea bed. It's not a good thing to mess about with a sacred site. You don't know what spirits will be disturbed.'

Slightly dumbfounded, Ryder looked back at the sea, half expecting to see a serpent rise hissing and coiling towards the beach like the ones in the *Aeneid* which came in from the wine-dark sea and strangled Laocoön and his sons. Breathless with foreboding, he watched as something black and slippery emerged from the rocking water and, he saw, like Excalibur emerging from the lake, the bumpy tops of the circle rising as the waves fell. Black and ancient and extraordinary, it was more real every moment, and Ryder became lost in rapt contemplation. At last he put his hand on the Druid's shoulder and said to him, 'I agree.' The site was astonishing. In his report, he absolutely condemned the removal of the wooden stumps, and when he and those who agreed with him were overridden, he took it as a sign that he should not try to get involved in anything in Norfolk again.

Recently, Ryder had read that the circle had begun to decay in the salt-water tank in Peterborough, where it had been moved to, and no one had visited it. In the end the consensus of the Heritage Board had been to return it to the sea whence it came.

Stretched now on the bed in the hotel room, his mind feels clear and uncluttered. He picks up the pencil and reaches for paper again, frowning at what he has on the page so far. How will the boat get up the cliff? God knows, but what is more important is his house is suddenly there in his imagination and it has a kitchen as warm and friendly and colourful as his parents' one is cold. He begins to draw a room from inside, a low window, a deep window seat. He must be getting soppy in his old age, for now he is doodling a cat on a cushion.

He wonders if he should call Cara to see if she is all right. He can work up a bit of self loathing, and blame himself for leaving her, but the truth is she was moving on too. And today she was poised and accepting. He can give himself a break and just sleep for now. Respite. He has been looking for it for ever, or so it seems right now, and that is why he is habitually on the move. Buying time from his feelings, existing in a state of not yet. The timing of all this is surely no accident. The work in Denmark will be finished tomorrow. This chapter of his life is closing much more definitely than he imagined it would. And he is free. The trouble is, it feels more like a stay of execution than a state of joy.

The next afternoon, on the plane hurtling down the runway and up into the sky, Ryder's first airborne thought is that he wants to find a way to be free and yet connected to another person, and his second is that, given we can fly, surely anything is possible.

66

4

Grace
Brooklyn
February

Sometimes the need for air feels like a thirst. The temperature in New York has not risen above freezing for the past eleven days, or if it has, I was not present at the specified warm spot to enjoy it. Eleven days is a long time in a New York winter for the wind not to rise up howling from the East and hurl chaos through the wide grey winter streets of Manhattan, banishing moribund thoughts and this deathly cold. The air has been dense with ice particles moulding their shape on to the bricks of the buildings, swelling within the cracks in the sidewalk, containing the relentless chill which kicked in on Thanksgiving, changed gear with snow after Christmas and now seems set to stay for ever. The pressure drops in the atmosphere and is mirrored by the mood of mankind. No one is cheerful, and the small act of putting one foot in front of another is such a big deal that some days I don't get round to doing it and I just stay in bed.

The only way to breathe outside is through a scarf, for the chill damp of the air on the back of the throat is suffocating, and the whole population is coughing. It seems that the city has gone back one hundred years in time to the cloying, slow poison of coal-fuelled smog. I have been in a bad mood for weeks, and it shows no sign of lifting now as I let myself in to my studio, stamping my feet in pooled melting snow inside the main doors. The walk here from Jerome's apartment where I live now takes about twenty minutes, long enough for the chill in the air to penetrate to my bones. As soon as I'm in the building the tension of my body in battle with the cold drops, and I begin overheating as I climb the stairs, peeling off hat and gloves, unzipping my coat, weighed down by bulky annoying layers and the sheer volume of all I am wearing.

In the studio, a pale stillness sits like dust on every surface of the room, thick and untouched even on the walls. I haven't been here for a few days, and my absence fills my work place. The studio is on the fourth floor of an old warehouse a block from the Hudson, and has a jagged view between buildings of a sliver of Lower Manhattan and the vast river. This has been my own space since I moved to New York more than ten years ago and it has made it possible for me to work no matter what else has happened in my life. I wonder sometimes what would have happened if I had lost the space; I might have given up painting and got a regular job. Things might have been different, but I found it in my first week here through Dorelia, one of the girls I shared my first apartment with. She was a dancer in a club and her boyfriend worked in this building, running a business making rubber fetish dresses. I sublet from him and his partner Stephan and I painted the catwalk for their mad fashion shows for a few years. Somewhere I've still got a black rubber dress, dangling in my wardrobe as shiny as a pod of seaweed but smelling of the talcum powder I had to dust inside whenever I was putting it on. Unlike the dress, the rubber business is long gone and most of the spaces around me are offices. I lost touch with Dorelia's boyfriend after she split up with him, but Stephan and I stayed friends and he stripped every vestige of rubber out of his wardrobe, and his soul, or so I used to tease him, and started working in an art gallery. His boyfriend, Ike, and Jerome both work for the same oil company, so Stephan and I are in the same situation, as we often discuss. Stephan is always broke and relies on Ike to bail him out, and my rent for the studio creeps up and up and now I couldn't afford an apartment of my own if I didn't live with Jerome. It's not an ideal situation, but this studio is my security and I love it here. I guess I could move in here if all else fails.

I kick off my boots and light the gas stove to put on the kettle, each action blowing life and movement into the stillness. The gas flutters, the kettle sits silent for a moment and then, quietly at first but in an increasingly urgent crescendo, begins its slow cacophony of grunts and wheezes.

The phone rings as I unpeel layer after layer of outdoor clothing. I am almost down to the soft stuff – my actual clothes, thin and light and relevant to the shape of my body. Although the studio is still chilly, I find it hard to breathe as the furnace of my blood rushes to the surface of my skin, turning it lobster-red like a smack on the cheek. The innermost layers of my clothing, normally lovely silky garments I get a thrill just from the joy of having next to my skin, feel loathsomely like fur. This is a truly disgusting sensation – matted, sweaty fur. God knows why this morning I chose to wear a thin V-neck jumper over the T-shirt next to my skin. It itches like a hair shirt. Anyway, wrenching the goddam clothes off I grab the phone in a strop.

'Hello? What?'

It's Lucy, my sister, five hours ahead in England. She's a year older than me, and although I like to think of her as my inspiration and my mentor, the truth is that nothing she has done has rubbed off on me, and actually the dynamic between us is more that she glows and I try to shut my eyes to it. When she got married, I was meant to give a speech, but I couldn't find the words, and I burst into tears. I could not express what she meant to me, or how fabulous she is at all. It was so important and I couldn't do it. She could have done it for me, that is what I love about her; she will try anything and make a success of it. She could plait her hair and tie her shoelaces when she was five. She did mine too, so I didn't learn until I was embarrassingly old. I wanted to say that although I try to ignore her loveliness as much as possible, she is like the sun, and even when my eyes are closed, her golden warmth emanates through my eyelids, permeating my being, and that is what she is like with everyone who comes across her. In the end that was just about what I did say, and she stood up and gave a speech back that I wish I could remember about how she could not have been her without me being me beside her. On her wedding day it was a loving and inclusive thing to do, and that's Lucy. She is sunny and the world smiles with her. While I love that about her, it is sometimes hard to bear, and so is her unswerving belief that I will soon be experiencing what she is, in the way that she is experiencing it. It is nonsense, we are way too different, but she needs to think of me following the path she cuts through life; it's too big a deal for her to be doing it just for herself. Just now she sounds tired.

'Hey, Sis, how are things? I just heard on the news that they've closed JFK, your snow looks unreal.'

'Oh Lucy, hang on a sec, I'm so hot. How are the tiny girls?' With a gasp, I tuck the phone under my chin and wrench off the next layer, a dark green T-shirt, hurling it down. Even the way it floats to the floor is infuriating.

'Oh they're lovely, full on, but they're asleep now. God, I'm jealous you're hot.'

Now I am topless apart from my bra. 'God, it's so unhealthy to be living like this. It's wrecking the planet. We should get back to nature a bit and use fires instead of central heating. Then we wouldn't find the cold so freakingly COLD!' I am puffing now, and trying to put a different T-shirt on with the phone cradled somehow on my shoulder.

Lucy laughs. 'Yeah, you're not wrong, we should get used to the weather we have instead of trying to set ourselves up against it.' She pauses and sighs. 'But the reality of doing that is hellish, let me tell you. We've got no heating in this cottage, and in Norfolk by the sea there's nothing between us and the North Pole and boy, can you feel it.' The phone clatters as she chats on, I imagine her tucked up in bed in the wild weather of Norfolk, and it's sweet, like a children's story.

Lucy is still chatting, 'I seem to find every reason and fantasy not to get used to it – like telling myself this is only an illusion of cold and actually it's really boiling, or so Mac tells me all the time.'

'Is it?' I wonder what the geology lesson is leading towards. 'What are you on about?'

'The earth is actually soft centred. It's molten deep within, you know – but, speaking of boiling, how can you be hot for even a moment? How can you be hot in New York? It feels like the dawning of a new ice age.'

'I'm wearing too many clothes, that's how.' I am over my suffocation now and am gulping water from the bottle on the table.

'I wish I was hot here,' says Lucy, 'Mac is away and I've got three hot-water bottles to replace him, and they don't do the job when the draught is wafting the curtains. But anyway, we want to have a party and I really want you to come.'

'Yeah? I will, of course – if I can. When is it? What's it for?' My heart bumps at the thought of going back to England, and I know it's something I have been avoiding thinking about. But I should go. 'Sorry, Luce, it doesn't need to be for anything. When is it?'

'Oh, not for ages. I want to have it when the blue-bells are out.'

This is a long-term thing, the panic recedes a little. I don't have to go just yet. 'Wow. That's months away. You are amazing, Lucy, I haven't even planned next week. Or tomorrow.'

'Oh, I know, but you've got a career. How did it go in Denmark this time, by the way? Aunt Sophie sent me a cutting from the local paper in Norfolk. You were a headline on the front page, you know. Local girl makes good. She said the staff in her home had kept it for her so that she had two copies, one for her and one for me.'

I have a lovely cosy feeling thinking of Aunt Sophie. She is the only person I know who ever reads about me on the occasions where my work is mentioned in a newspaper, and she always keep the articles. It's a truly motherly act from my father's sister.

'That's nice. God, I must write to her, it's been weeks, I think. She's learned how to email, though, which makes things much more immediate. But yes! Denmark was good. I loved being back there. I can't believe it was five years ago that I had that show. What have I done with my life? But seriously, it was great to get away from here in the winter. Over there, they didn't even have a Valentine's Day theme, it was such a relief.'

I've got one leg over the sofa arm and I sit there astride for a moment then tip myself over into the cushions just for something to do. Then I slide down to the floor, flexing each foot, leaning forward over my outstretched leg, giving myself the illusion that I am doing some exercise while talking on the phone. Forward bends are beatifying, according to my yoga teacher.

'You know what, Luce, I'm really proud I'm in their National Gallery, but it's also a bit embarrassing, I feel a fraud. This visit was very different from last time. It was all so grand. I had to sit next to the Mayor. His name was Ginseng Jensen.'

She giggles. 'It wasn't! I can't imagine being so grand as to sit next to the Mayor, I have enough trouble getting books back to the library.'

I close my eyes, trying to feel Lucy's calm energy in the room with me. Her acceptance of life is one of her most restful qualities. I realise I haven't talked to anyone properly for ages. Jerome and I seem to pass one another on the stairs at the moment. Actually. I'm not sure that that's true; he's away and I've been away, so we haven't set eyes on one another for over a week.

'How's your love life, Sis?' she asks suddenly, and I know I can't get out of it with a flip remark. But it doesn't stop me trying. 'On holiday.'

'Is that good or bad?' Lucy is genuinely caring. She is so different from my mother; I can never understand where she got it from. Now she has children, she's even more loving. She also has a good memory. 'Does that mean you had a holiday romance? Wasn't that what happened in Copenhagen last time? Do you remember? It was when Mum died, and you were in a real mess. You hardly showed up to the opening of your own exhibition. Some man waylaid you. What happened to him? Is it him?'

'Don't be daft, I never heard from him again. I meant Jerome's away right now and it's all just bundling along as usual.'

Lucy is still talking. 'I remember you really liked that guy. What was his name?'

'Ryder.' Saying it out loud still makes my heart race – even now, when I haven't seen him or heard from him since that night, and probably never will again.

'Ryder. Nice name. Yeah, I always thought that if he had come to New York and found you again, that would be it. You'd be married with kids like me by now.' Lucy giggles down the phone and I laugh too. God, what if she was right?

'I wonder if I would? But he didn't, and here I am with Jerome.'

'How's it going, Grace? Did he go with you to Denmark? My God, did another guy turn up like before?'

'If only,' I sigh. 'No, Jerome didn't come; he was working, and I didn't ask him.'

I have a splash of cold-water realisation that I didn't ask him because I had secretly hoped subconsciously that I would meet someone else there – and I had wanted it to be Ryder. It's too crazy to share with Lucy, so I interrupt myself: 'But he's away and I haven't seen him since I got back. He'll be home tomorrow.'

'Are you looking forward to seeing him?' Lucy's questions are like arrows, they hit the bull's-eye and quiver there. I feel I'm under such scrutiny that I could be a laboratory mouse under microscopic surveillance. The only good thing – and it is exactly the opposite of what I felt a few minutes ago – is that she is on the phone in Norfolk and not here in New York. I hedge a bit by repeating her question.

'Am I looking forward to seeing him? What sort of question is that?'

'Not a very taxing one under ordinary circumstances,' says my sister gently. 'What's up, sweetheart?'

Oh God, it's always the same. These days, any human heart reaching out to mine makes me want to cry. I don't answer and she changes her tone, trying to make me laugh, and I know she's doing it because she's too far away to comfort me, and that makes me feel even sadder. Then she switches again and she does make me laugh.

'You didn't have sex with anyone this time you were away, did you?'

'Lucy! No, I did not. I didn't have sex with anyone that time either, actually.' I really miss my sister. No one teases me in New York.

'But you could have done?' No matter what the subject, the dynamic of Lucy and me has always been the same: she drives, insists and pursues, making the suggestions, while I hesitate, back off and remain non-committal, running away to avoid the spotlight of her caring.

76

Like now. 'Yes – no. Oh! I don't know. Of course I couldn't this time. Not that I could the other time, I never even gave him my number, he just vanished at the private view. Well, he said goodbye, but then he vanished. You are just winding me up and anyway, he— oh whatever. It's a long time ago now and I'm with Jerome.'

'Mmm.' Lucy doesn't need to be in the room or even on the same continent for me to know that she knows my feelings and thoughts better than I do. She is still on the trail and I can't bear it, so I try to create a false scent to divert her.

'I really loved being in Copenhagen, Sis, it's got so much. You know, fabulous architecture, artisans still working, and mournful poets all in a special bohemian area.'

'And cows,' interrupts Lucy dryly, in case I thought for a second that I had fooled her. I am more up for this now and I take the comment as it comes.

'Yes, and cows and such a richness of culture, but it's all quite undiscovered. At least, that's how it feels to me.'

'Mmm. Fish and silver is what it makes me think of; a bit like Norfolk, if you add some mud and sugar beet.'

'No silver in Norfolk. Just fish and fields of potatoes. Fish and chips, actually.'

Lucy laughs now. 'Oh God, I miss you, Sis. You've got to come over when we have this party to christen the girls and welcome everyone to the house. I need you to come. Come and have a summer holiday with us.'

'But the summer is a million miles away.'

I am so relieved that the conversation has swerved away from my private life. I need to look at the wounds I didn't realise were still so open, and to mend them in private before I can share my feelings with Lucy or anyone else. I left home a long time ago, and I have done my best not to think too much about what it is in me that has kept me away. I know Lucy wishes I lived in England, and when Mum died I thought I would feel some tug to draw me back to where I came from, but I didn't. Maybe one day I will move back. And maybe pigs will fly. I twist the telephone wire and lie back against a big cushion.

'But it's important to have things to look forward to. Will you come? Please? Grace?' Lucy's inability to be silent chimes with her hopes.

I move to the window, rest my head against the cool glass. Blocks of light make a modernist pattern across the façade of the warehouse buildings opposite, and beyond it, trickling between the sprawl of bricks and concrete to the Hudson River. Even the back end of Brooklyn in the snow – like all of New York almost all of the time – is familiar to me from films before it ever became familiar through my own existence there. One of the things that has kept me here is the unique unreality of living somewhere I know so well through other people's interpretation of it. I sometimes feel I don't even need to have my own experience of living in New York; someone is sure to have a better one which I can borrow, and I like the impermanence of that. I don't belong here, and for now that suits me. Sometime, though, I hope I will find somewhere I do belong. And someone I belong with. A huddle of clothing steps out of a door and down some steps just across from my window. Once on the sidewalk the bundle develops limbs and begins mechanically to shovel a mound of snow, stiff at first, but warming to the task until movement takes over and the figure bends, scoops, throws and bends again in a graceful flow like the articulated illustrations in a flick book of an animated cartoon.

'Grace?' Lucy is too impatient to ever hold on to a silence. She can't resist speaking first; she will always say anything to fill a gap. She isn't moody, so she doesn't need silence.

Even playing Hide and Seek as a child she was always the first to say, 'I give up, here I am.' Lucy isn't convinced anyone is listening if they aren't talking. It makes phone calls a bit of a problem for her.

'Yes. I'm here, I was just thinking.' My reflection is visible in the window, faint like the moon when it is out in the day, my bare arm a wishbone on the glass.

'God, I remember the summers in Norfolk when we were little. We used to go for tea with Aunt Sophie after picnics. I can remember going to pick cucumbers from those frames she made from bales of straw and panes of glass.' Shutting my eyes takes me there and I am six years old again. 'I can even remember the smell.' And the smell of the house, a mixture of lime marmalade and some kind of wax floor polish which I don't suppose anyone uses now.

79

'I forgot about the cucumbers. We used to make sandwiches with her. Do you remember, Luce?' The hall floor was made of wood bricks, or that's what we thought they were called, and we used to slide in our socks on it when Mum was late, polishing the wood for Aunt Sophie as we waited for her to come to pick us up. It was nice at Aunt Sophie's, she talked about Dad. Then we had to go home. I have a lump in my throat and it is everything I thought I had forgotten. The taste of my childhood; a mixture of toast and cigarette smoke, dust burning in the chimney and the salt of tears is in my mouth as if it were now. There is more than the lovely times with Aunt Sophie that I remember about being six. The rest of it is different and I was terrified. But with the terror I can also still almost taste my longing – a ceaseless, insistent yearning for it not to be frightening. I would willingly have gone through each day again in the hope that it might be different. And still now I have the same yearning; now it is to have had a happy childhood and a past I could love remembering. When I think about being little now, any salvage seems impossible. I see myself standing on the cliff with Aunt Sophie's house behind me and I am tiny at the chalk-faced edge. Much too frightened to jump.

'Oh Lucy, I just can't go back there. I'm sorry.'

Lucy is unflustered and unsurprised. 'I knew you would say that. Come on, Sis, if I can bear it, you can. And anyway, everything is better if we both do it. That's true, isn't it? It's always been true.'

I am agitated now, and I feel nauseous from being on the phone too long.

'Maybe. But no. Shut up, Lucy. You can't force me to come, you know, I'm grown up now. You've got your life there, and that was always on the cards because you found someone who comes from Norfolk. It's different for me.'

Lucy's reply is gentle. 'Hey there, come on. Calm down, keep your hair on. I don't want to make you do anything you don't want to, I just miss you.'

I press my fingertips against my eyelids and hot tears spill. 'I miss you too. I'm sorry.'

'Let's think about it,' soothes Lucy, and even though she can't see, I nod, nostalgia flowing, narcotic and frightening, in my head. When I put the phone down I light a cigarette.

There is no going back to rewrite the past, nor to repaint it, which, for a long time, I thought I could do. Instead, the pictures come like they always did, and some are wild and dark, with the wind pulling apart the neat little winter house we once lived in. Mum and Dad lived in the Old Bake House in a little market town in Suffolk when they met. It looked as though it was working between them from the outside; Dad caught the train to London where he was an auctioneer in a big art firm and Mum looked after her babies. But she was lonely, and she didn't like being stuck at home with two tiny children. She was too young herself, and she didn't know how to change her loneliness into domesticity. She slept a lot, and Dad came home late and some nights he didn't come back at all. Mum slept with us when Dad wasn't coming back. We had a big sofa in our room and she would bring a quilt and her book and read there in the evenings. Often in the morning she would still be there on the sofa, her glass empty by the open book.

Dad changed jobs and moved to Norwich and we moved to a gaunt house on the cliffs at Overstrand with a giant pine tree outside it and walls that looked as though pebbles had been thrown on to them by the sea. Doors banged and the wind howled through that house, and Mum was jumpy and sad even though Dad was home most nights. I really only liked home when Dad was there, then Mum could disappear upstairs and it didn't matter. At weekends he used to take me out into the garden where we would make bonfires and find insects for the aquarium I kept full of twigs and foliage. Once, when I was five, Dad found me a tiny jewel-green frog, under the water butt by the tap in our cliff-top garden.

'He may be a frog now, but that will change,' I said to Dad, squatting next to him looking at the small creature, jewel-bright on the ground.

Dad's eyebrows went up. 'Oh yes?'

'Yes. He'll change in my tank and become a lizard.' I very much wanted a lizard at the time.

Dad took me seriously; he nodded and picked up the tiny frog on a leaf and said to me, 'Look carefully, though, at this frog; he's already changing.'

I looked and saw a tail and, for a moment, I thought my dad had done the magic and was turning him into a lizard.

'Wow,' I breathed. Dad was smiling as he put the frog down gently and pulled me towards him.

'But he's changing into a frog,' Dad said, and he led me to our small pond and showed me swarming tadpoles. 'He used to be a tadpole.'

I looked at Dad and he looked at me and it seemed the funniest thing in the world to my five-year-old sensibility. I capered about, chanting. 'He used to be a tad – pole', and Dad dipped a net in the pond to find another almost-frog.

One day Dad came into our room very early before it was light and he whispered to me to wake up. His eyes were shiny in the half-light. Lucy climbed in next to me as he sat on the bed with his coat already buttoned.

'I won't be back tonight, girls,' he said, and his voice was gruff. 'And Mummy and I will still be friends, but I'm not going to live with you any more now. I'll see you on Sundays, soon.'

He said a lot more I didn't take in, about people changing, about loving us no matter what, but he was going, and then he went. And we didn't see him on Sundays, or, at least, not often, and the gap he left was jagged and painful. Mum said he was working in London again. That was her only explanation for him leaving. In his absence I floundered. Lucy was cheerful and uncomplaining and Mum's bitter sadness was a wall between us.

On the day of the storm, Mum picked us up from school in a bad mood, her coat flying like a purple kite and her hair tangled in her big hoop earrings.

'There isn't any electricity at home, so we're having fish and chips for supper and we'll have to light the fire and lots of candles,' she said.

Lucy danced in through the swinging gate. 'I like adventures,' she said, and in the shadowy grey kitchen she began gathering candles on to a tray and laying the table for supper. Mum didn't like the adventure at all, neither did I. Outside the kitchen window the great pine tree was bending wildly back and forth as if a giant had got hold of it and was trying to shake every needle off it.

I began to cry. 'I'm scared,' I whimpered.

Mum lit a cigarette and puffed on it fast then stubbed it out. 'Me too,' she said briefly and went up to the bathroom.

Lucy and I looked at one another. Lucy smiled bravely and went on pushing candles into candlesticks.

'Shall we call Daddy?' I whispered.

'Yes,' agreed Lucy, and we held hands to walk into the kitchen where the telephone sat on the window-sill. Daddy's number was written on the wall. Lucy dialled, and I held the receiver to my ear. The phone was heavy and cold next to my skin. It rang and rang but Daddy didn't answer.

'Maybe he's on his way,' said Lucy.

I wished I dared to ask Mum, but I didn't, and he didn't come. The wind was shrieking by bedtime, and the windows rattled in their frames. Mum was less scared after supper, sipping her gin and tonic and folding paper for us to stick in the rattling windows.

'Come on, girls, I'll sit with you tonight,' she said, and we went up to our room with the wind booming through the roof tiles. Mum curled up on the sofa under a big knitted blanket, trying to read with a candle, her drink balanced on the sofa arm, and my picture of her there that night is the cosiest memory I have of her.

In the middle of the night I sat bolt upright and found my mouth was stretched wide in a scream. I didn't know what had frightened me, but I was terrified. I was six, but I can still remember the abject awfulness in my heart as I became aware of hot pee creeping from under me across my whole bed.

'What's happened?' quavered Lucy's voice next to me in the dark.

Mum sounded as though her mouth was full of cotton wool. 'Dunno, I think something hit us. Hush, darlings, let me get a light.'

The flare of light in the darkness was shortlived, but as the match guttered and died in the draught, I screamed again. The window was full of glistening spikes and needles, and a shattered branch of the huge pine tree was wedged in the frame, the loo paper stuffed so thoughtfully by Lucy floating like a banner on the breeze. As Mum's match went out, I began to cry and, stumbling out of my bed, I climbed on to Lucy's, craving her closeness. Mum lit another match and then her candle, and the sound of her crying was more frightening than the wind that night.

5

I wake early in Brooklyn, secretly enjoying the peace while Jerome is away. It's a double-edged sword without him here; I feel guilty because I can so easily adapt to life without him and yet I am living in his apartment, supported by him, and he is kind and generous to let me, and I take it for granted. Or I sometimes do. It feels like a role. My life as his girlfriend has slipped from a mutuality of desire and intention into me feeling constantly pursued and guilty. He hasn't changed; I have. That's all. And it's sad. I walk to the studio soon after dawn. Today is a Copenhagen-coloured morning; this sky grey like duck down and snow is threatening to fall. Jerome is back today and I want to be pleased about it. Maybe if I can get my painting to go right, it will give me a sense of satisfaction that will follow on into seeing Jerome.

The painting I am working on is in limbo right now. I began it with an electric, tingling feeling two weeks ago and when I look at it now I can't resurrect the shimmering sense of vitality that lit me up and that I wanted to express and capture in the figure of the woman I am painting. Every mark I have made, every colour I have put down, looks just like that, marks and colours, stiff and superficial and no conduit of emotion or sensuality. Sometimes it gets like this, and the thing to do is just to lighten up. Walk away. If I'm alone, I put on some music and dance in the studio. I wish my friend Stephan was in town to meet up and muck about with. He never takes me too seriously, and although he works for my gallery, he teases me and laughs about my work and it is such a relief. Last time he was in the studio he nudged me, after walking around the pictures, and said, 'Look at that body you've painted, give her a make-over, lift her face and give her a Brazilian lifeguard as a boyfriend. That'll put the swing back in her step.' This morning, face to face with the painting I am stuck on, and with Jerome about to arrive, I don't dance, but I could scream with frustration. I want to run around madly like a headless chicken, doing a stupid dance like we did at primary school with a puppet and a rubber glove for a cockerel's comb. But Stephan is away with his boyfriend this weekend. Thankfully, before I start really panicking, a ripple of laughter runs through me when I think of what Jerome would say if he saw me freaking out like this, running in small circles. He definitely likes the idea of me as a sensitive artist, not a demented neurotic.

My phone shrills with a message: 'Hi, honey. I'm in the office, my plane landed early, and I'll be with you for coffee.' He had already left for Florida when I got back from Denmark, and I haven't seen him for over a week. It's like grains of sand crumbling in warning at the beginning of a landslide to realise I have not missed him. He must have got let in by someone downstairs, for suddenly there is a knock on the studio door. Then he is here, in my space, and his big, expensive smoothness rolls in with him. He gathers me in his arms, hugging me. I hug back, but it is like the painting behind him, it is just bones and flesh pressed together, the magic isn't there right now.

'Hey, baby, we missed Valentine's Day,' he says, pulling a cookery book from an airport bookstore bag and placing it on the table between us.

'Thank you.' I try to force my eyes down to it, and my lips into a smile. Bloody hell, I'm angry. What's sexy about a cookery book? Of course, anything can be loving if it is brought with love, but somehow, today, this is EXACTLY what I don't want. I wish I could rewind to the way he used to make me feel. Being with Jerome has been life saving and I know it, and even if I didn't he tells me and so do my friends. Especially Stephan. Jerome kisses me, and his mouth tastes reptilian. I bite my own lip until it bleeds, using willpower to stay within his embrace, his arms around my shoulders, while my instincts are screaming for me to leap back and wipe the taste of him away. I wonder how long before I know for sure if this is what it feels like – a lukewarm existence I can't face getting out of because moving brings the chilly discomfort of change.

The kettle begins its urgent shriek and I use the excuse to back away from Jerome, placing the scalding item between us while I search for cups and coffee. Jerome paces back and forth, eyeing the kettle with suspicion.

'It could be time for an electric kettle, honey,' he says, 'it would make everything a lot easier.' God, it sounds as though he is talking about much more than the coffee. I am fencing in the dark as I slowly answer. 'Easier for who?'

Unwrapping the croissants I bought on the way over, I decant spoonfuls of ground coffee into a jug.

'You mean "whom".' Jerome raises an eyebrow and smiles at me for a moment before returning his attention to the kettle. I find this so irritating that I could throw the coffee at him. In fact, I am twitching with the urge. And then I do what I always do and put it all away under a smile. I don't want Jerome to know he has the power to make me really angry. My best plastic smile is sugar coated. 'No, I don't mean "whom". I mean you. It's easier for you if I have a new kettle, because you are scared you might catch second-hand Weil's disease or something from this one.'

He has an incredibly annoying ability to raise one of his eyebrows. I used to find it sexy and now it's exasperating; it reminds me of the headmaster at primary school and it reduces me to being in the playground again.

'I come here every day, and you don't, and this is the place I work; it's my studio, not yours, I can choose the kettle I want. And I want this one. If I didn't, I wouldn't have it.' I have finished. I stalk away from him and open a window. Amazed and faintly appalled at having started a row, and half seeing the absurdity, I shake my hair back and raise a smile. The February fog-filled air seeps in from the street. Jerome looks at the window, at me, and raises both his eyebrows quizzically. He is not fazed by anything. He sits down, the picture of control, his elbows on his knees, hands loose in front of him, looking at me calmly. He is both provocative and reassuring, and we both laugh now, uneasily but at least it's broken the tension.

'Tell me about Copenhagen,' he says. 'Tell me what it was like to go back there as a national monument?' He is imperturbable. Like the Colossus at Rhodes. A wonder of the world. The ancient world. He is the monument, not me. I feel better, calmer, more cheerful.

'Oh, it wasn't like that, it was a huge show. Loads of people are in it. I wasn't unveiling a statue or receiving the freedom of the city or anything.'

Jerome's eyebrows look like caterpillars, curled at the ends with small knots of perplexity. He smiles, showing big canine teeth and moves the chewing gum in his mouth.

'So what are you kicking off on now, babe?' He strokes my hair. 'Did Denmark inspire you? I've got a boardroom which needs a new Grace Hart painting. Something big, with a sexy woman in it and a lot of yellow. I know you don't paint to order, but would you have time to show me an etching or two?' He is teasing me, and I smile and say something non-committal, but the truth is I really don't want him to be here. I know I can be overprotective of my work in the studio. I feel exposed when someone comes to see the work here; it's easier to take slides to show people or to put the work up in a neutral space. It doesn't matter whether it's my boyfriend or a collector, I don't want to talk about the processes of doing it, I like presenting a finished painting as just that. It shouldn't be necessary to have people inspecting the way I go about it.

Jerome knows I am annoyed, and he thinks he knows why. He thinks I am helpless without him, but that is not how it is. Do I really know him? He says he loves me, though I wonder if he means the same as I do by that. He likes to control what I do and how I do it, and the love is always conditional on my fitting in with what he thinks is the right way for me to be. For a long time I was flattered that anyone could be bothered to have an interest in the right way for me to be, and Jerome made a big deal about possessing me. He says he was sure from the moment he met me that he wanted me.

I didn't take him in that night at the gallery in Copenhagen. I was tired and fractured by the loss of Mum, and I was bowled over by the guy who came up from the sea, Ryder. But a month or so later Jerome called me up and took me out in New York and I loved the way he made everything easy, and how he never lost his cool. Most of my boyfriends were my age and struggling to find themselves and earn a living. I loved the fact that Jerome was older; I was flattered, and I wanted something steady to hold on to in America. I love his kindness and, mostly, I am grateful for how he handles me. But being grateful and being handled isn't a balanced relationship, and I want Jerome to let me be his equal. We have shared more intimacy than I have had with any other human being, and yet I don't want him at the studio, and I am defensive, though he has done nothing wrong. I see him, and it is as though I am outside my body, and the man I am looking at is a stranger. I cannot imagine walking side by side with him through life. With him it is about marching ahead, dragging me after him when I want to go somewhere else.

'OK, never mind the boardroom. Let's forget work and concentrate on you and me.'

I should never have let him come. It was an impulse of desire to share something with him, something important to me, inflated by his absence and my own. As I concentrate hard on washing up the cups in the sink, not looking at him, I realise that the trouble is that I don't want to let him in at all. Jerome in his blue shirt, his cufflinks gleaming, his every movement slick and expensive, is making me nervous when usually I feel safe with him.

He is by the window. 'You're very quiet,' he says gently.

Nodding, I wipe my eyes. He is in control again now, he knows how to deal with this. 'Grace, honey, if you want your work under wraps and a broken kettle, you stick to your guns,' he says lightly. 'I was just checking in case you'd like me to go around the corner to pick up a new one for you.'

'What?' Pretending not to hear is easier than arguing. I pour the water that has finally boiled into the jug and carry it, with the washed-up cups, dripping, over to the table. Jerome's skin is biscuit-brown from the trip he has just taken, a conference in Miami with other oil executives.

'Let's hear about your trip,' I suggest, putting my hand on his cheek. 'You've been lounging around getting a bit of winter sunshine on that so-called business trip.'

He flashes a smile. 'There has to be fun or no one would come on these trips. The next one is diving in Greenland, can you believe? It's to sharpen our team skills and take us into elements where we are unfamiliar.' He pulls a parody face.

I'm laughing now. 'It'll be FREEZING, who wants to be familiar with that?'

'I know, and in the presentation it looks as though we all have to wear black gimp masks with our wetsuits.' He grins. 'Look what you save yourself in this life of yours with just a studio and whatever is inside your head.'

His phone bleeps, he takes it out of his pocket and turns it off without looking to see who is calling. He does this to show the conversation he is having here and now with me is important. I have seen him do it with colleagues. I sometimes guess that he sets the alarm on his phone timer to make the point. But not with me; Jerome doesn't play games with me, and I'm glad of that.

In the flat north light of this New York winter morning, I notice the splodge of a liver spot and a wispy thinness to his hair and I am smitten with a pang of something beyond my frustration with him.

'Oh darling, it's awful when we pick fights, I mean when I do, I'm sorry.'

Jerome scans my face, his whole demeanour anxious, as if I have just been diagnosed with something worrying.

'Hey, honey, it's nothing. I guess sometimes it seems to me that you are so distant inside your head that I don't know how to reach you, that's all,' he says. We are sitting side by side on the sofa now, not touching and not looking at one another. It's a lot better for talking.

After Dad stopped living with us we hardly saw him. Sometimes he would come and pick me up from school, but he never explained why he left, or talked about that time; he just carried on as though the strange way we now lived without him was normal. The trust between us couldn't be repaired. It lay like a broken mirror whenever we saw one another. And all we did now was drive home from school with him which took an hour and meant we didn't have to sit face to face and talk. My father had nice cars – or cars that I liked, at any rate, because they had cracked leather seats and shiny wood and they smelled like him, of cigarettes and cedar oil. Being with him was odd. I always hoped he was coming to rescue us. I didn't know him any more; he left when I was six and I thought he'd left because Mum was always crying. But maybe she was always crying because he left. I asked him once on the way home from school, 'Why don't you live with us any more, Dad?'

He looked at me with tear-clouded eyes, and I shrank back against the door and wished I hadn't asked. Men mustn't cry, especially not Dad.

'I don't know how to come back,' he said. I wanted to bang my head against the dashboard, anything not to hear his sadness. I never asked again.

Mum cried a lot, but she also liked to have fun. Her idea of fun, though, involved bringing Adrian into our lives. Adrian arrived when I was seven, and Mum had moved with us from the cliff-top house to Norwich. It was fun being in the city, but our school was a long way away and Mum didn't have a car, so we had to go on the bus unless Dad came. Adrian arrived as a lodger, but that set-up didn't last long. Adrian moved into Mum's room and so did his collection of guitars. With him arrived a permanent smell of beer in the house. Mum stopped crying, but she didn't come and sleep in our room any more. She and Adrian stayed up late and she sang along to his guitar and it didn't feel like a family house should feel; it felt like a very embarrassing pop video. I never asked anyone home from school, and neither did Lucy. Dad never got out of the car to say hello to Mum, and I was convinced that if he did they would fall into each other's arms and we would all live happily ever after.

'If we could just get him up the garden path . . .' was the yearning secret wish between me and Lucy. Mum never knew, and I still don't know if she cared.

When Jerome leaves the studio I feel both relieved and bereft, and wander around with my arms folded as if I am hugging myself. I send Lucy an email, but the loneliness is intensified when I remember it is not even dawn yet in England. '*If this is long-term relationship at its functioning optimum, give me a shag pal and a bottle of oblivion.*'

It's tempting to write her a whole long letter, spilling all my heart out to my faraway sister, but I know I am just trying to put off my work, to displace the discomfort of doing it with a drama about Jerome. I stomp around the studio a bit; unless I give up and go home, or go into town and look at a gallery, the only thing I can do here is work. My big picture is still impenetrable, so to try to fool myself that I'm not doing anything much, I sidle up to a small canvas I have hardly begun and start painting. No form grows like I want it to. I put on Billie Holiday, and her mellifluous voice floats like a delicious scent on the air, and she helps a bit, but I can only ever get the work to flow when I can forget myself and the details of daily life and reach into my soul. I don't ever really know when that will happen, or even how it does. But the act of applying paint to a surface, of transforming the tangled images and feelings in my head into something tangible and visible is a life-saving process. I am not usually painting a picture for a reason, I am trying to make sense of something I cannot express any other way.

'I'll paint you all the colours of the sea.' I have no idea if I have read this phrase somewhere, or heard it in a song, or made it up myself, but it doesn't matter. Something tight unclasps inside me and suddenly I know what I'm doing. It could just be crap. And it could just be a pool of blue. Making a blue with powder pigment exploding in a puff like spores, reminds me of school and the mindless pleasure of holding my ink pen on blotting paper, watching the ink well out in a gently expanding circle, creeping through the fibres of paper which in turn begin to flow with the energy of the colour itself. Blue. Limitless blue, stopping at nothing, not even the horizon where the skin of the sea meets the sky covering all. Black-blue like the cloak of night in a starless sky, or a starry night when the sky sparkles and pinprick illumination radiates electric kisses from the wide, blue distance. Of course, it isn't the intensity of the coloured pigment that causes the ink to move through the paper; it is a combination of the absorbency of the paper and the penetrative quality of the liquid. Colour is irrelevant. How can colour ever be irrelevant? An hour of painting is like listening to music or making love – it's restorative. I'm not thinking, I'm being. Standing back to look at what I have done makes me want a cigarette, but I don't have one, so I bite my nails instead.

Jerome would be furious if he saw me. It's odd, or perhaps it's not, that the very qualities which attracted me to Jerome five years ago when we met at that very strange exhibition in Denmark, his calm assurance, his ability to keep order in the face of chaos, his belief that he could take care of me better than I could do it myself, are now the parts of him that make me want to scream and flail my way to an escape route. But at the same time, I've been such a willing slave to his velvet-fisted kindness.

My compliance lights me up inside with shame, like a potent secret. It is hot and dirty and reminds me of being eleven and letting Sandy Fletcher put his fingers into my knickers and then wiggle them inside me during scripture lessons in the top class of primary school. The third time he did it, I felt the flooding, tugging, flaring of an orgasm without knowing what it was. It took a while for me to equate the delicious honeyed sensation with what Sandy Fletcher was actually doing, as I was convinced that it was the result of something that happened to me by my thinking a certain sequence of thoughts.

I wouldn't dream of telling Jerome or anyone else about the fluttering excitement in my prepubescent body when an eleven-year-old boy touched me all those years ago, and neither would I tell him that now, in some twisted way, I am turned on by my own passivity, by the way I allow him to rule the roost at home. Not here in the studio. I have built a structure for my working life here in New York, because, even if I don't stick to it, having it makes me feel I belong in the world and have a reason for being here. Without one I don't always believe I exist. Sometimes I lose faith that the structure exists – it is hard to be convinced by something of my own making, when I have trouble being convinced by even myself.

When I was at art school I laid the foundations for all my work as I tried to express the solid physical existence of human beings on canvas. What I found was that it is incredibly difficult to keep people's feet on the ground. It certainly felt like a metaphor for life, and I was obsessed with the human form. I don't know when, or even if, it got better, but at first it was like a dream, everybody I painted, whether clothed or nude, seemed to be about to float out of their bodies. They were all irrepressible. Like helium-filled balloons, they kept wanting to float off out of the top of the canvas. All the great sculptors and painters from the Renaissance have addressed this – so many painters depicted their figures knee-deep in cloud, or like Botticelli's Venus coming out of the sea in a giant scallop shell, or surrounded by a pile of rumpled fabric. I fell in love with the fragile bones of the human foot. Finally, when I had left art school and started to paint on my own, I realised that the problem was in me; I approached all my work feeling unsubstantial and until that changed, I could paint my figures into cement bases or chain them to the ground, but they would still float away.

So now I've learned that it is important that I have a routine, even though it exists not to be adhered to. It begins with the walk to the studio, calling in on the Spanish bakery for a croissant half a block away. I really like the wink the proprietor Jaime unfailingly throws my way, no matter how crowded his shop is, or how loud the hiss of the milk steamer is. It's a moment of connection that I create in my day. Why is that such a big deal? It is paradoxical that the pleasure of being alone to think and do the thing I want and need to do more than anything else is also the part of my work that I find most difficult. No one talks much about loneliness in New York. Or their feelings, unless they have worked them into something malleable and acceptable with the help of an Upper East Side shrink.

Three years ago, my sister Lucy talked about the clanging sense of loneliness she experienced when Mac went back to work after their first baby was born.

'It was terrifying, Grace. When Mac left every morning, I heard the door shut, then looked at my house with everything I had longed and hoped for in it. I looked at my lovely baby, and then, suddenly, life was terrifying. In seconds I was climbing the walls. Actually, I started painting them. I needed an activity to stop the rising panic.'

Lucy had laughed, making a funny story, but there was fear in her eyes. We both remembered Mum's unhappiness, the way she crawled into our room when we were tiny, the way she cried when Dad left, and then the darkness that the drink brought when she met Adrian. What did she need? I don't know if she even knew herself.

'It is not our littleness we fear, it is our greatness.' These words are engraved on Mum's headstone. At first I did not understand them and felt angry that they had been chosen without anyone consulting me. Adrian had suggested them, and Lucy had agreed, and I did nothing when the fax came to me in New York asking if I could think of anything else. I couldn't. I was frozen. Even so, I felt a stinging sense of exclusion. The headstone was erected six months after Mum died, so I didn't see it until another eighteen months had passed, when I came back to England to see Lucy's baby. Lucy was different, she was pinkly triumphant and seduced by motherhood to a more sensual and gentle version of herself. I held tiny Bella in my arms, and when I kissed her head, the skin was softer than a peach.

'Look what you've made, Luce, she's beautiful.' I had never imagined that a baby could be so moving, or that Lucy, my sister, could create another being. And here she was, revealing new levels of competence, being a mother. Everything about her was radiant as she fed the baby; her voice was a soft coo, her gestures were all encompassing and flowing. Mac made us supper, and we ate in the kitchen with the baby in a basket at the end of the table.

'It's risotto,' he said cheerfully, adding, 'it's the only thing I can cook apart from bacon sandwiches. My Italian grandmother taught me, so Lucy's getting used to it on a daily basis. Aren't you, babe?'

He kissed the top of her head, but I was glad for her. It was way out of my league. The house was full of flowers and their scent combined with the sunlit smell of baby talcum powder, and an ambrosial loveliness emanated. It was delicious to be near to, and it felt as though it belonged to Lucy and she had earned it with all her sense and carefulness as a child.

Is happiness earned? It's definitely hard won. I saw Lucy with Mac and their baby, and I could see that I had nowhere near experienced the level of happiness she had. The birth of Bella was the moment I decided that I could have it too, and that I would.

Some things might have to change, though. At this point I was twenty-nine, and living in New York with Jerome. We didn't eat risotto, we barely ate a single carbohydrate, in fact. I don't know if I liked my life then, I just lived it. We went to a lot of parties. I got into my role as the artist girlfriend when they were Jerome's work parties. It was a relief not to be me, just to be a cipher. The artist girlfriend is a good mask, easily worn. With my friends, of course, it was different, and no one expected anything of me, but in the art world I felt the weight of expectation and I was convinced I could not live up to it. There is such an element of the Emperor's New Clothes in making a reputation and it has nothing to do with the work or the person. If Stephan from the rubber dress days hadn't turned up working for my gallery, I would have sunk without trace. Instead, I had collectors and an agent and a permanent feeling of fraudulence. How could anyone take me seriously?

I drove alone to Norfolk to visit Mum's grave the day before I flew back to New York. I would have liked to go with Lucy, but there was no way she could move with her newborn and, in a way, to go alone was better. March mist and rain clouds gathered as I approached the coast and the sea was a mess, blurred and hissing with churning waves, blue-grey like the gulls that wheeled above it. The wind spat raindrops in my face when I got out of the car and I leaned into it, hair whipping my face, my coat flailing as I inched through the grassy mounds and marble-edged squares of gravel to the windswept corner where Mum was buried. It was the only new grave in this part of the churchyard, where the tombs were mossy and the writing on headstones hard to make out, and it looked as though it had been brought in as a prop. No flowers lay on any of the graves save hers, just a few empty containers lolling like the remnants of a forgotten picnic in the long grass.

Hands deep in my pockets, I glared at the words on Mum's headstone. I had no idea what would be right, only that this was wrong. A part of me could stand back and know that in the bigger scheme of things it didn't matter a bit, but that thought only whipped the impotence into a bigger rage. What would have been right? What I knew, with aching clarity, was that nothing could be right when your mother dies of drink before she is sixty. I stared at the gold lettering in the flecked marble, my arms folded in front of me, rigid with pointless disapproval. The stone itself looked like a slice through a tin of jellied dog food, gleaming salami pink among the wrecked older stones at sea on the misshapen graves. Who ordered it? I had not known I had so many views on tombstone decor, or that it could matter to me so much. I had not really known that anything to do with Mum could matter to me any more. In a way I was glad. Not feeling anything had been so much worse. I sat on the grass and cried for Mum and the tears felt cleansing and good. There was nothing left to do now but learn to accept, and suddenly it felt possible. Back in the car, changing gear with gusto to speed my departure, I turned up the radio as piano music tumbled out, and I cried for all the losses and even more for the need to move on from them.

Poor Mum, I could suddenly see her greatness, it tumbled into my consciousness like sunbeams from a storm cloud. She kept a roof over our heads, although admittedly there was the time when it almost caved in thanks to that tree, but we survived. She loved us even though she hid behind Adrian and alcohol until we could hardly see her at all any more. But in the distance between us and Mum, Lucy and I became so very close and stayed that way. It is poignant now to think of her, living alone, though Adrian was never far away, and separated from her daughters. In her silent sadness, she missed out on seeing the greatness in herself or the joy in having us.

Returning to Lucy's small house in London I felt my spirits lift as I approached and it was painful to think that in the morning I spent with Lucy and baby Bella, more love and happiness flowed through her house than Mum had in all the life I remember with her. If I could slip through a shaft in time to talk to Mum, she has been dead for five years, I could tell her

I love her now. But it still isn't easy. My adrenaline is pulsing, with memories and the feelings they bring up, so the prospect of a holiday in Norfolk, returning to the place at the heart of my childhood, even with Lucy and Mac, isn't instantly appealing. I don't want to think about it now, I want to lose myself in work instead. I stand back from the canvas. Sometimes this is not the ordeal I imagine it will be. Sometimes it is a pleasant surprise to find that the painting is more coherent than I am. At best, a painting can illuminate a diaphanous thought, revealing it to be more lapidary than it seems, with roots into the past and wings to take it into the world and the future. Sometimes the thought is a new idea, or a belief, and sometimes it is just a fake, a mock-up that will not withstand illumination.

I often feel uneasy approaching something I have made. I never know what to make of it, and sometimes the work emanates a sense of having always been here, and it freaks me out that it is so permanent when I am not. Not every piece evokes this. More often than not there is a frustrating distance between my perception of what I am doing and what comes off the canvas in two-dimensional colour. Sometimes, though, if I keep going, allowing myself to observe whatever it is that is coming next, transformation can occur. The trepidation with which I come up against my work for the first time every day is not so much based on experience as the damping down of expectation – it would be too disappointing to come to it hoping to change the world every day. Better to believe anything might happen, and in that find a small glimmer of possibility or at least a dab of paint.

Later, at Jerome's apartment, I peel prawns for supper and try to suppress resentment. It's not aimed at Jerome especially, and yet it is. He is not the love of my life, but that is not a reason to be angry with him. He is giving me a home and he loves me. My part of the deal is not hard, I just have to keep things on an even keel. So why do I feel suffocated? His key in the door makes me jump. Here he is, right in the middle of my thoughts, and I haven't got them in order yet. Jerome is big and quiet like a panther when he lets himself into the apartment and puts his briefcase down in the living room, shedding his coat, letting it fall on to the sofa, walking around it, taking his tie off all without turning on the lights. Coming towards me in the small brightly lit kitchen his focus is scorching, his eyes intent on my face. My cheeks burn where I am caught by his gaze. We look at one another and there is welling excitement; the resentment inside me flares into something else, and I no longer feel invaded. Instead, I catch my breath with the thrill of being pursued. Neither of us speaks but the music has a bass line beating like my heart. I wipe my hands on my thighs and turn away from him. Pulling undone the strings of the apron I have tied over my jeans, I move towards the window to hang it on the back of a chair. Jerome blocks my way. Pinning me against the work-top he stands with one arm either side of me. It's a game I can either resist or surrender to and my body is already playing with his, so resisting is only another part of it. My back arches, and to stay standing upright with him this close to me I wrap my arms around his neck. He looks at me, his eyes flicking back and forth from my mouth to the buttons of my shirt. He doesn't say anything, I can hear blood drumming in my head, my breath a gasp in the silent kitchen, a song on a radio somewhere else. Still not touching me with his hands, Jerome bends his head and kisses me. I want to be turned on by him too, and I kiss him back. His tongue in my mouth is hot, he pushes one leg between mine, I am all up against him now, he presses against me right the way up my stomach and, through his shirt, I can feel his heart beating against me and the heat of his skin and the rise and fall of his breath. He pulls his body away and his fingers pull the ribbon fastening my top and it falls open. He unbuttons my jeans, pushing down the zip as he slides his hand down my stomach under my knickers. Still in silence, burning more and more electric, he strokes me between my legs. I feel liquid and my back arches more. He stops kissing my mouth and runs his tongue down my neck to my breast. He groans, or maybe it's me, as he undoes the hook of my bra, stroking me softly though the thin fabric of my shirt. All my nerve endings flare and yearn, I lean on to Jerome from the counter top, sitting astride his thigh with his fingers deep inside me, his tongue circling my nipple, and I am melting. Melting. My fingers yank his belt buckle undone and I am so intent on him pushing down his clothes fast and urgent and he turns me around to lean over the table. He whispers, his mouth against my ear.

'I've been thinking about fucking you. About touching your skin, your scent in your hair, your mouth, all of you. I wanted you all the time you were away.'

And he tugs my head back, pulling on my hair and my breath comes faster, harder and I gasp and swallow and in my body a pulse hits the base of my spine and radiates through me and another and another. And we move apart so I can turn around and I am lying on the table, my legs are wrapped around him and he is in me so deep and it's hot from the middle of me, intense wave following wave because he keeps moving and everything is electric, building up as we fuck, and the waves come together and we are both panting and breathless on the kitchen table. I open my eyes, smiling.

Jerome pulls his clothes back on immediately, not even looking at me, and getting out his wallet he flicks a photograph across to me. It's a coffee maker cut out of a magazine.

'What's this for?'

'I couldn't give up on you and your ancient *bouillardière*, so I ordered you an espresso machine and it'll be delivered tomorrow. Look on it as a love token for Valentine's Day if you can.'

'Enchanting,' I snap and I am angry. All the loveliness of sex has rushed away like sand in an egg timer and, disliking myself enough to scream, I do the only other thing I can and grab a sharp knife. Instead of acting like a crazy woman, which is incredibly tempting, I begin slicing mushrooms in a fast rhythm, my back turned to him, deliberately not doing up my top or putting on any other clothes over my knickers. It is all completely wasted on Jerome, because he has gone through to find his jacket in the next room, following the shrill command of his telephone.

Alone in the kitchen, I feel goose bumps rise on the back of my neck and prick me under the rumpled back of my shirt and up beneath my hair. I suddenly have a cliff-edge sense of what it would be like to step out of the safety of life with Jerome. I don't know if I can do it, I have traded so many absolutes to be with him that I don't really know who I am beyond the safe lasso of our relationship. Jerome's voice in the next room is a rumble; he has shut the door, he doesn't want me to hear. Most probably because he is talking about business and he likes the running joke that it drives me mad with boredom, and that I will think the less of him to hear him. But jokes only exist with some reference point, and here I feel that the foundations are set in truth. He is running the New York Marathon in November and is so fit his back actually looks as though he has the bubonic plague, so rippling and defined are the muscles strafing across it. He shouldn't have so many muscles, anyway, it's obscene. He's in his late forties, he should be slowing down. Something inside him is unresolved, though, and he is restless. He is obsessed with making money. I am absurdly irritated by this. It's time to move on, but being with Jerome is like being in the bath too long. Moving is uncomfortable, staying still keeps the temperature bearable. And hard as I try, I cannot take the passing of time seriously. I must be a bit backward, I haven't quite lost the belief that I am immortal.

Ten years ago the first show I completed was sold to a New York gallery. At that point I was unswervingly certain that I was immortal. Which meant that it was fine to drink anything that came my way, most especially vodka Martinis in the red-membrane light of the midtown hotels which were enjoying a mercifully brief, fashionable moment. I was reckless, then, in all areas of my life, and I pushed myself to experiences and encounters as acts of defiance first, lust second, and which had nothing to do with love or intimacy. Loneliness settles like a skin of sweat on my body because I am suddenly secretly certain that whatever there has been between me and Jerome, it has nothing to do with love or intimacy now, and I am not sure it ever did.

With frenzied slicing, I have created an unnecessarily large pile of pink-gilled mushrooms. I slide them into melted butter and turn down the heat, reaching for salt, sloshing in a splash of wine. I love cooking when it's like this, and I feel sharp edged with energy. Though ideally I would be more suitably dressed. Imagining what that would look like is useful for suppressing my thoughts. Ungainly and black, the realisation sits like a boulder emerging out of an ebbing tide: I am selling out. I don't like the work I am doing at the moment, I am painting pictures I don't really care about, I am living with a man I don't love, in a country that is not my home. I have been running for ever and getting nowhere because I am so afraid of what might happen if I stop. I have never once considered that it might be better. Everything might be better if I stop. I throw the wooden spoon into the sink and walk around the table to the window, reaching for a cigarette from the crumpled packet I left there when I got in earlier. Jerome hates me smoking. He often tells me it will make him leave me.

'So leave,' I always say, and I never used to mean it, and he never did. But now I really do mean it. With the flare of the match, the green light at its heart, the man I met on the harbour in Copenhagen suddenly appears in my mind. He is here, and I can see him as clearly as if it was now.

I close my eyes and I almost feel him touching my hand, his voice in my hair, saying, 'Come on, let me take you home.'

His name is Ryder James and I can remember everything about him as though he has only just left. His hand, the white ridge of the scar lit up by the moon, cupping mine. Holding my hand steady and protecting the flame.

6

Ryder
North Sea

Ryder is on the way to Holland to discuss plans for laying a new gas pipe between the Netherlands and the UK. Breaking up with Cara has left him feeling as if he is recuperating from flu, or rather not recuperating as the gloom and sloth are hard to shake off. And leaving his houseboat for yet another trip, even a short one, Ryder feels regretful. He would like to have time to cycle along the tow path all the way to Camden Lock, to pass the narrow boat village at Lisson Grove, where the world seemed to stop in the 1950s and where children play with hoops alongside the colourful boats with their tangle of hoses for gardens, and where dogs lie by the wall in the sun. It would be nice to be in London for long enough to meet up with his friends and to finish the bookshelf he started building on his boat last year. But on the other hand, another trip and another new project is always interesting. This time the appeal lies in the prospect of tulip fields and windmills and big skies to blow some vigour into him. And the travelling, which up until now he had firmly believed was ideal for a man on his own. Ryder wonders how he had failed to notice before that being a man on his own was frequently uncomfortable and depressing. And when did his rootless state change from being a pleasure to a pain? Perhaps it was to do with the fact that he has spent more time at home on the boat than usual, to the extent that the couple on the next boat came to call on him, bringing a hyacinth growing in an old tea cup. Ryder was charmed.

'Phyllis here keeps all the old china for her bulbs,' the old guy told Ryder with a gappy smile. Ryder stepped back from the door, welcoming them in.

'Pleased to meet you. I'm Ryder.'

'Arthur and Phyllis. How d'yer do?'

Phyllis didn't trouble herself with talk, she just pottered in behind Arthur and gazed at Ryder's minimally furnished home.

'You got a nice place in here,' said Arthur, 'though you've not got much to call home in there, have yer?' He stared blankly at the empty table, the sofa with its neat cushions. Ryder placed the hyacinth cup ceremonially on the table.

'No, but I think this might be the start of better things,' he said, and Phyllis nodded approvingly.

Landing at Schiphol Airport, standing in the green articulated bus and speeding off around the terminals, Ryder reflects that the magnetic force field around East Anglia has changed direction and has begun to pull him like the tide. His bosses in Holland want him to compose a paper on the costs and the problems for their gas supply links caused by the coastal erosion in East Anglia. So far he has resisted the pull of Norfolk itself but he has agreed to go out to one of the North Sea gas platforms.

The project kicks off in a prolonged meeting in a hotel near the airport in Amsterdam. Sitting back in his chair, Ryder is hit by stomach-churning torpor, the legacy of too much travel. The hotel bar is windowless and over-designed; it is red-lit, the ceiling glowing pink, the chairs like huge doughnuts, frosted pink and brown. It could be anywhere. There are businessmen alone at most of the tables, and two expensively dressed, carefully made-up women at the bar. Ryder tries to stave off sleep as John Shaw and Sveld Hegel, his employers, bat their beliefs back and forth across the low red-leather coffee table. Ryder lost interest some time ago when the question moved from one of sustainability to that of profit. None of it is for him, his job is simply to make sure that the work is done safely and environmentally well. To keep sleep at bay he recites to himself a selection of things he knows off by heart. These are neither many nor various. There is the Periodic Table for a start. 'Hydrogen, helium, lithium, beryllium, boron, carbon . . .' Boron should be the caption under these two guys. He could have saved them a lot of money and himself a lot of time by getting them to conference-call him while they sat together and talked in this airless room. Neither of them is interested in anything except the finances of the project.

Ryder tries to bring in an ethical question, 'But should we not be looking at some alternative energy forms that can travel? Volatility is the problem, of course, but then we're running into problems with transporting the fossil fuels we're using at the moment, and in getting them out. A lot of what we want in terms of oil is so deep digging for it is prohibited.'

'We will just have to get gas here for the best possible price,' sighs Hegel, leaning back in his chair and stretching so that Ryder has the full effect of his plump cushion-shaped stomach billowing from behind the buttons of his white shirt.

'It won't last long,' says Shaw, an anxious-looking man with, Ryder notices, a silver crew cut very like one of the older statesman-type space travellers on *Star Trek*. Shaw is still talking. 'Ryder, here, is right. We need to get a step ahead in this game. What's it going to be?'

Ryder has got as far as 'phosphorus' in his head. It is becoming increasingly difficult to get excited about money making for the sake of it. He wonders what else happens in the thoughts of these men. Hegel's most stressed button suddenly pops off. A blotched patch of stomach peeps out at Ryder. He rubs his hands over his face and wonders if he will manage to sit here for the rest of the meeting or if he will become possessed by the creeping desire to get up, walk out and never come back. Shaw is tapping something on to the key pad of his palm pilot.

'There's a lot of investment in turning coal into gas, of course. But it's not there yet, and we need results.'

Shaw drums his fingers on the table. 'It always comes back to the nuclear option. And the problem of decommissioning.'

The arguments float round and round and Ryder wonders if he could survive if he gave up this sort of work and got a normal job. Working in a garage, or being a postman. At the moment he seems to waste so much time discussing new ways of doing things and then continuing to do just the same. With this in mind, he leaves the meeting and is taken to the heliport, to the crew gate, to fly to the gas platform in the North Sea.

He is so near Norfolk he could spit and hit a breaker on the beach. The gas platform he is required to visit is a construction of steel and concrete six miles out to sea from Bacton on the windswept rump of the north-ernmost point of East Anglia. Coming from Holland makes him feel he is sneaking in, even though he has no plans for sightseeing in Norfolk today.

Ryder arrives by helicopter with the lads on the new shift. They will be here for four weeks, he will be here for two hours. No matter how bad it gets he would not trade his life for any one of theirs.

He suddenly thinks of Cara, and in an impulse of nostalgia, calls Interflora to send her some flowers. It's her birthday, and he is glad he remembered. Maybe he will visit her next time he is in Copenhagen. Out here in the middle of the sea is a lonely place. Ryder feels a need to have friends, and he would like to be friends with Cara. He suggests lilies to the girl on the phone then changes his mind. Lilies. The funeral parlour. What a bad idea.

'No, not lilies. Make that something more cheerful – bright.' At the church they had red and orange and pink dahlias for Bonnie, ranked in gaudy banks. They reminded Ryder of cancan girls in silk bloomers.

'Yeah, something colourful Oh well – yes, tulips would be great.' Fuck. More cancan dancers. Oh well, it's done now, and flowers are nice whatever they are. He switches off his phone and heads for the office block on the eastern corner of the rig. Fucking crap. Staring across mile after mile of iron-blue sea, Ryder's ears fill with the roar of the sea as its surface boils around the legs of the gas platform, and the vastness of it rises and falls in ceaselessly changing waves and troughs, and the notion of a bunch of flowers seems tiny as a token of friendship. He pinches the bridge of his nose, heaves a sigh, and mentally kicks himself. He must get on with the work he has been sent to do. Flowers and the bittersweetness of love have no place here.

This business is way beyond romance, even the romance of literature, though it might be interesting for a latter day Hemingway to write a rigger's novel – 'Gas Platform'. Ryder can almost see the gilt typeface on the cover. On second thoughts, maybe not. Why would anyone ever want to read a book about life on a giant Meccano set in the middle of the North Sea? Certainly, he will not be the one writing it.

There is no one in the office, the blinds are drawn and the desk is empty, tidy and unmanned. There is no one around to give him the information he needs until the platform manager returns. Outside Ryder moves to the railings. The sea snaps foaming jaws and seethes like a drooling mouth far below. From the platform he can make out the mauve fuzz of the coast-line. The sky is clear blue with clouds floating like dropped flowers and the sea is fresh and navy blue beneath the steely breath of the east wind and the rugged energy of the elements is tangible. Ryder reck-ons any marketing man could bottle the optimism and sell it to an aftershave company. He can see the giant golf ball poised on its tee at Mundesley, the early warning system which twenty years ago looked sinister, but now is just part of the landscape. It reminds him that the human heart can adjust to anything with time, and it brings a fragment of the past hurtling into his mind.

A summer weekend when he and his sister and a car full of friends drove from Essex and camped in the dunes at Waxham. There were seven of them, high on the excitement of an adventure in a car of their own – Jack, who passed his test before anyone else, had borrowed it from his parents. Bonnie was in her last year of school and she and all her friends were bursting out of life in the suburb of Colchester. Ryder rode along on the back of their wave of discontent.

'Actually, my parents don't know I've got the car. They went to France. On a sailing boat,' Jack confessed, tapping his fingers contentedly on the steering wheel in the beach car park. 'I thought they had enough to think about with the sailing so I didn't tell them.' A blue haze of smoke from a joint formed a loopy halo around his wild brown hair. 'Does that make it borrowed? Or stolen?' Jack had a slow delivery and a laconic way of speaking that hit the nerve every time, especially once the spliff was circulating. They drove down a narrow slipway at Mundesley first, and parked the car on a small tarmac shelf cut into the cliff and a little above the beach. The air in the car was fetid; too many people in a small space on a long drive, but they were all accustomed to being squashed up against one another, and were reluctant to move and break up the single entity they had become. With every inhalation of Jack's mind-bendingly strong Sinsemilla, Ryder for one became more and more convinced that he could not really get out of the car unless Jack, Bonnie and the others came with him, preferably glued to him.

'Did you know that a crab is exactly opposite to a human?' he announced during a sound break while James was trying to find his favourite Leonard Cohen track.

'How?' yawned Nat, pushing the front passenger seat back down hard so something gave way and it sagged almost flat on to the knees of everyone in the back and Nat's head was suddenly in Fran's lap. She stroked his face absently, and Bonnie traced the shape of his eyebrows and the outline of his mouth with her fingers.

Ryder thought he really might get out soon. 'Well, they have all their bones, which are actually made of shell, in their case on the outside and the soft stuff like the flesh and skin on the inside, and we have it the other way round with our bones inside our skin.'

Bonnie began laughing and the car became a pile of giggling bodies, arms and legs flopping over one another, skin touching skin, sensuously golden in the shafts of evening sun. No one was actually capable of getting out. Unable to get to the point where bracing air licked their soft bodies. They sat in the car, smoking, stroking one another, listening to Leonard Cohen and Lou Reed until the sun was almost down.

By positioning himself strategically in the right place in the car, Ryder achieved a long-standing ambition when he casually kissed Nicky Staples. Bonnie's best friend and the most prized trophy – an older woman by all of a year. This kiss, which he kept going for about half a Velvet Underground song, gave him the jolt of adrenaline needed to get him out of the car. He and Jack, who was also ramped up with testosterone over Fran, cast off their stoned lassitude and, throwing off their clothes, with much shouting and chest beating, ran naked into the sea. Diving under the first wave was a shock, heart stopping for a moment, and then exhilaration kicked in and blood raced around his skin, tingling against the cold water. Within a few minutes all the others were in too, their clothes strewn on the beach in a trail from the car, the music carrying on the still air off the cliffs and over into the water where they were lolling and splashing like seals.

Any song by Lou Reed can take Ryder back to that time in a flash, and now the memory has brought a song to him instead. In the North Sea now, on the bleak stage of the gas platform, wrapped in warm layers of clothing, Ryder shuts his eyes, his senses electric with the memory, 'Perfect Day' playing in his head. He remembers diving under a rolling wave, leaping up out of the spray, tossing back water-logged hair, his eyes and mouth and ears and nose all tasting of salt, all of him burning with the absolute physical realisation that he was alive. That was the night that he lost his virginity. To Nicky. A dream come true. It may not have been so great for her, of course, but it can't have been that bad, she stuck around with him for a few months – in fact, they only split up when she went to America to take up her place at university there. Ryder was heartbroken for at least a month – he even planned to go and visit her for weekends, ignoring the fact that the university was in Texas and it would take a week-end just to get there. In the end he got distracted by life and met Lila. Another story, but all of it is still so alive in his memory. 'Big summer,' he thinks wryly.

The platform manager, Geoff, is a dynamic, diminutive Glaswegian with a barrel chest and a Roman nose; he reminds Ryder of a bull terrier. Smoking a chain of un-tipped cigarettes, which he extinguishes by hurling them, red tipped and glowing, off the platform down into the sea, he rattles through his projections and observations without once looking Ryder in the eye. His eyelashes are pale, his skin a healthy pink. Very similar to the white bull terrier

Ryder's grandparents used to have. Rose was her name.

Geoff is in full dynamic bull terrier flow. 'So you'll find the budget strained around here and, I've got to be honest with you, for me' – and he jabs a thumb towards himself – 'the erosion is NOT, repeat NOT a priority. It's a nothing. Zero. OK, so a bit of Norfolk is falling into the sea round to the east, but it gathers in silt further west and what the hell – it's a big place.' He snaps his fingers and thrusts a folder of papers into Ryder's hands. 'You'll be taking off in a few minutes, I'd get your arse back in the chopper if you don't want to be spending the next stage of your life here with us.' He grinds his jaw, which Ryder finds a bit menacing until he notices that Geoff has exchanged his mouthful of cigarettes for chewing gum in a subtle sleight of hand in the last few minutes. 'So you can see the damage for yourself, we've arranged for it to take you right along the coast now, and then back to Holland.'

'Which coast?' Ryder has a sense that he is being thrust into someone else's schedule, and he hasn't got what he needs from this godforsaken giant hairgrip in the middle of the sea yet. Though actually, now he is thinking about it, what can he possibly need here?

Geoff the Glaswegian's flung arm is all encompassing and in no way clarifies anything.

'Where am I going?' Ryder asks again.

'The whole fucking East Anglian coast, the one that's falling into the sea, mate.' Geoff grins and, shaking hands with Ryder, he whisks himself back into the office and snaps the door shut.

Climbing back into the helicopter, Ryder dons the headphones and figures out the topography as the pilot floats the machine up and they turn north. He wishes he had someone to tell that he is looking at Norfolk from the sea, he wishes there was someone in his life who would care. These are the moments when Ryder feels lonely, time he previously filled with work and plans is now a space for someone to come into his life and share it with him. More than he allowed Cara to share it, which, in fact, was not at all. He went to see her when it suited him and otherwise she was in his thoughts, but she didn't disturb his life one bit. And now it is too late with Cara. But she wasn't the answer.

In the helicopter, Ryder has an eagle's view and an unearthly turn of speed, his body thrums with adrenaline. Although he has frequently travelled by helicopter, this is like being in a ride in an amusement arcade, or in a dream. Suddenly they are swooping around the haunch of Norfolk, where dregs of the North Sea end up in the Wash and Lincolnshire abuts, and the helicopter arcs like a falling shooting star and now they are flying lower. They have turned and for a moment are travelling straight towards the red and cream stripes of Hunstanton cliffs and the brighter red and white lighthouse on the western end. There is the caravan park, a few permanent residences huddled at the back hedge, other single caravans parked in random areas. None of it looks nice, which is just as Ryder remembers it from the childhood holiday when his parents took him and Bonnie to Hunstanton for one rain-drenched and never to be repeated week in a borrowed caravan when they were five and six. No one in the family had the practical skills required for caravanning, and his parents Jean and Bill did not have the sensibility to rise above this, and make it fun. From his bird's-eye view, above, and almost past already, Ryder cranes his head back to see the dark-fronted hotels and the rash of shops above the beach. He can hardly remember the town, he just remembers his mother sniffing, his father sighing and he and Bonnie whispering in their narrow bunks at night, too afraid of their parents' silence to be quiet themselves.

But now on, on in the rushing omnipotent bird's-eye view. On past the end of the cliffs, and suddenly the demarcations between land and sea blur and the past is heralded once again in the wooden druidical circle at Thornham, eerily confused, if the eye is untrained, with the twisted fuselage of the Spitfire aeroplane that nosedived into the sand during the war and has been left there as a solemn memento. Actually, neither the Druid circle nor the plane wreck are visible as Ryder passes, but he knows exactly where they are, and has a vivid recollection of the reed-edged path from the village and the pub to the beach. Well trodden by him and his friends on drunken summer days when they pitched their tents at different points right the way around Norfolk. They were carefree and hedonistic and completely stoned most of the time. It seemed to always be hot, which can't possibly be right, but no rain figures in Ryder's memories – maybe he has erased it because he needs it to be perfect. But what is certain is that with Nicky and Jack and often Bonnie and a couple of others too, he spent endless summers drinking and swimming and, whenever possible, getting laid on every Norfolk beach, every night.

There is nowhere without a memory. The blond expanse of Holkham, the inky blur of the pine trees, Gun Hill, Scolt Head, Stiffkey Freshes, Blakeney Point. He realises he has not returned all this time because it brings back too much of the past for him. It is not so much the pain of what he lost when Bonnie died that keeps him away from this place, it's the unbearable abundance of what he had, what they all had. It suddenly makes sense to him that his parents have closed down and hardly seem to live at all now, just existing within a small routine of daily life. Living fully is high risk. No one cares when they are young, and that heedless optimism is wonderful. Despite the black despair of living through Bonnie's death, and the unbridgeable gulf between before and after in his family, Ryder knows absolutely that he would not exchange the happiness he and his sister shared growing up together for a different outcome. Would she? Unknowable. And does it matter? Does it make him inhuman to wonder this? It is futile speculation, something he knows well, he has indulged in so much of it over Bonnie, and it brings him in a downward spiral to nowhere. Jean and Bill would trade any past happiness for Bonnie to be here now. Their longing for life to be different, for something to change that they cannot control, keeps them locked in sorrow.

The pilot has taken the helicopter incredibly low now, pounding over the waves only a tree's height above the surface. The churning sea mirrors Ryder's restless state of mind. New chapters seem to be coming at him at breakneck speed, or is that just the effect of a helicopter ride around his past? In it, though, he is aware of a glow of recognition; this is a place he loves. Not allowing himself back here for all these years has not dimmed his affection for this coast. He wonders what his parents would say if he told them that he, who has refused to live anywhere more permanent than a houseboat on the Thames, is thinking of putting down roots and living in Norfolk.

Not that this part of Norfolk is looking very permanent right now. As the helicopter swerves over towards Salthouse from the sea, the shingle shelf of the sea defence, usually a solid and visible land mark with a ribbon of beach between it and the tide line, is almost submerged by eddying, foaming water. In some places jagged gaps have been gouged out and the sea blasts through like a giant bucket of water thrown through the gap into the marshes behind. The salt marshes are peacefully green, cattle graze on the flat lowland towards the village, while beyond them cars glide along the narrow coast road. The sun floods golden light over the church and the village houses studding the hillside up to scrubby heathland a few hundred feet above the sea. This tranquil scene playing out on the inside of the sea defence is an opiate parallel universe to the maelstrom energy battering beyond the shingle wall. It is March, the tides are often huge, and it is for this that the dykes have been dug out, and the drains cleared in the marsh. The sea defence, built after the 1953 floods, is not a strong enough barrier any longer, and it never will be again. Ryder has studied this area enough to know that drainage is the only solution for now, but eventually the sea will reclaim parts of Norfolk. It makes the idea of living in a boathouse a lot more practical than Ryder ever imagined it to be.

The journey continues east. Ryder makes notes and from time to time trains his binoculars on the crumbling cliffs at Weybourne and Sheringham. A row of cottages at right angles to the sea have lost their gardens and a tumble of lawn dangles as if by a thread, over the edge of the cliff near West Runton. Beneath the dirty yellow of the cliff, boulder-sized stones clatter against one another and a snapped washing line festoons like tangled knitting wool. Further east caravan parks proliferate, forlorn, untidy rows in ragged fields. The countryside here is sullen and neglected, with scrappy woodland and a few churches the only elements breaking the monotony of flat farm fields.

It is not a place anyone is glad to come from, but here, in a white-timbered former sanatorium, Jean, Ryder's mother, gave birth to both her children, taking the old-fashioned view that a nursing home by the sea was the most appropriate venue. In many respects she was right – she was alone, her own mother and father had both died. Bill her husband was working, and anyway, Jean would not have dreamed of having him involved. What good would he have been? Better by far to go away alone, and bring the baby home to him a week or two later. Jean liked to be in control, and Bill liked Jean to be happy. It had worked like a dream for years.

Jean had never expected to have children. Ill health in her childhood and an historic family pessimism contributed to her belief that such a joy was not for her. She was a librarian in Colchester Library and heading resignedly for spinsterhood when Bill James came in asking for a copy of the *Collins Field Guide to Mushrooms*. It was April, not the season for mushroom hunting. The air of faint apology with which he excused this lack of synchronicity with nature, pleading an engineer's ignorance and need for help in the living world and the gleam of laughter in his eye won an answering, reluctant glimmer from Jean. They were married in the autumn. It was five years before Jean became pregnant, and when Bonnie was born, Jean was so delighted and dazzled by her baby girl, she entered her for the Miss Pears Soap competition, advertised in the highstreet chemist. Uncharacteristically for Jean, who was an unassuming woman, she fully expected her lovely baby to win. She did.

Jean put the £1000 in a bank account for Bonnie to receive when she was twenty-one. After Bonnie died, only the priest in the local Catholic church where Jean's conversion took place knew how Jean blamed herself. She believed she had cursed her daughter, shortened her life with too much love and expectation; she didn't make the same mistake with her son.

Ryder and Bonnie were born one day less than a year apart. Irish twins, such children are called, and even in the last third of the twentieth century, the community takes it upon itself to disapprove, Their parents are regarded as morally slack and unpleasantly fecund, unlikely epithets for Bill and Jean, whose efforts to be ordinary were only surpassed by their children's inability to be so. Ryder and Bonnie, both dark and curly haired, barely took a step apart from one another, before they went to school.

The inevitable question, 'Are they twins?' Which was answered wearily by Jean, 'No, she is a year older. Yes, they are very alike', caused raised eyebrows. Jean felt judged whenever their closeness was remarked upon, whether she was taking her babies for check-ups with the health visitor, or enrolling them in school. Every coo of surprise whipped her sensibility and left a welt of shame. She felt branded with visible disgrace. If she could have left Ryder at home, she would have done. Instead, though, he went everywhere his sister did and did everything she did. They shared an infant language, they shared their toys, and they rarely spent a moment apart until Bonnie went to school. Ryder could not accept being left behind. Not for school and not when she died. It was the same feeling to him. The desolation he felt at four years old seeing her go in to her classroom, looking back to wave, her smile, came back with renewed intensity at nineteen, forever playing back the last time he saw her.

There is no making sense of the twisting turns anyone's life path takes. As infants, Ryder and Bonnie tumbled right in the heart of each other's existence like puppies in a litter. With every age and stage the nature of their closeness changed, and their lives ran a little more parallel, a little less interwoven as they became children, then adolescents. But the essential thing about Bonnie and Ryder, as their mother observed with an ache of deep jealousy, was that they adored one another. They wanted to be together and they didn't really need anyone else. When they got older, became teenagers, and went to different schools, they remained determinedly close. Ryder played football for the local youth team, and Bonnie came in the car with Bill every Sunday to watch him play, and would hide her face and giggle at the admiring glances of Ryder's team-mates.

'Come on, Kid, you can do it,' she would yell from the edge of the pitch.

'Thanks, Betsy,' he would whisper, teasing her if she stood nearby at half-time. Ryder always called her Betsy as her cheerleading name, and she always called him Kid. They liked to tell their parents that they were the inescapable presence of the American dream brought to sleepy Essex by mistake. On the way home in the car, Bill smoked his pipe and drove, while Ryder and Bonnie talked, finishing one another's sentences, swapping absurdities, making one another laugh, symbiotically attuned to mood and moment. Bonnie had the use of a pony in the summer, loaned by a local riding school, and she rode to village gymkhanas in the neighbouring loveliness of the Dedham Vale. Occasionally, she persuaded Ryder to come with her, and they would set off early, when the shadows beneath the trees lay moon-blue until the sun poured through, and the leaves sparkled with early morning dew. Ryder was a little embarrassed to be trailing after his sister, but he was thirteen; it was dull at home with Jean and the small garden and the whole summer stretching luxuriously in every direction. It was better to go with Bonnie and, anyway, he was curious to see what the world she enjoyed so much held. Girls, was the gratifying answer. On one occasion Ryder sat on a bale of straw holding Bonnie's pony while she went to pay her entry money at the show office, an old green pony trailer with brown matting lining the ramp and inside the secretary, a woman like a human mountain, balancing a small table on her knees.

'Shit, we nearly landed on that! Is it your bike?' A girl on a tall chestnut pony bounced to a halt next to Ryder. He stood up, uneasy at the proximity of this snorting, prancing creature. The girl was pink cheeked and smiling. She looked sideways at Ryder, and her eyes sparkled with curiosity. Ryder rubbed his hand in his hair, 'Err, yes, it is. Shall I move it?'

'No, but I wondered if you would help me practise that jump?' She was blushing now and waving to one side. 'This is great,' thought Ryder, 'they want to talk to me.' Bonnie teased him later. 'Hey, Kid, I can't believe you were just all over Jenny like that. You're such a pushover for horsy girls. You be careful, they're fearless. Look at the mothers.'

They both collapsed sniggering as, perfectly on cue, a sharp-faced woman with blond wisps of shoulder-length hair strode past, a whip in one hand, the bridle of a white-eyed pony in the other. 'Come on, Sophie, for heaven's sake. Show some bloody phlegm!' she bellowed to the pale grey child on top.

Ryder shuddered in mock horror. 'Phlegm. Yuck, that's sick. Is she the mother? How can they be like that? She's meaner than our football coach by miles.'

Bonnie swung up on to her pony and bent down to whisper, mock serious. 'It's the cutting edge of competitiveness here at the gymkhana, Kid. Don't worry, I'll look after you. They're not all scary, I promise.' And she cantered off towards the practice jump.

In reverse, and more as they got older, Ryder looked after her. At the parties they went to through their teens, he was watchful over his sister. His nonchalant stance leaning against a wall, often late at night, was a safety net for Bonnie, who once kissed four boys in the same evening and blamed it all on vodka.

All these memories were never meant to have any more significance than their fleeting existence in the flow of passing time. Experience, hard won though it might be, is just experience; it contributes to growth, it harbours the capacity for reflection, but it doesn't wholly prescribe thoughts or behaviour. No one needs their past to become bigger than themselves, but sometimes it happens. There is no way of knowing when life will be overtaken by events.

7

Returning to London, Ryder cannot dispel a sense of emptiness and torpor. As spring moves forward, he broods daily upon the merciless quality of the sunlight as it pours in through the small round porthole by his bed on the boat, illuminating more than a few cobwebs. With Arthur and Phyllis determinedly guiding him, Ryder decides to paint the outside of the boat.

'It's a dirty job,' observes Arthur. 'This one hasn't been done in years, I think it was Edwin who last painted it and he's been dead this last nine years.'

'Or nineteen,' adds Phyllis, her voice muffled as she scrapes a curl of red paint off the window frame. It was Arthur's idea to paint the boat. He was smoking a cigarette with Ryder on the tow path, listening to the roar of traffic on the Edgware Road the morning after Ryder returned from Holland. Neat in his blue overalls, he narrowed his eyes against the light bouncing off the water and scanned Ryder's deck.

'It's been too neglected. Time it got a coat of paint and some care,' he had said, and Ryder, who had been gloomily not looking forward to anything, agreed, pleased to have a diversion.

'Yes, let's do it. Would you be able to advise me, Arthur? I'm new to this.'

Ryder had bought the boat from a friend who used it as a painting studio and, apart from furnishing it and building a bookshelf, he'd never got round to any decoration.

In the end it takes two weeks to scrape down the boat and repaint it, during which time Ryder and Arthur find a mutual interest in cricket, both of them *Wisden* disciples, and at the end of it Ryder feels that not only does he have a shipshape ship, but he also has two new friends. Returning from a trip to a hardware shop for yet more brushes, Ryder finds Phyllis on his deck, a radio murmuring Kiss FM next to her as she plants red geraniums in a pot by his door.

'I was potting them up and we always have too many and Arthur kicks them when he's getting his boots off,' she explains, clambering to her feet and wiping her forehead with the back of her hand, unwittingly spreading a smear of earth over her temple.

Ryder is touched. Having neighbours and being part of a community is something he thought only happened when you retired. His parents have it in Essex, where his mother does the flowers for the local church and his father does whatever he does with other old codgers, but Ryder had never looked for it in London.

Phyllis dusts her hands together and picks up her trowel. 'I'll see if I've got any more later,' she says, regarding her work. 'They do look nice here.'

'Yes,' Ryder agrees, 'they do. Thank you.'

At dinner with an old university friend and his wife later that evening, Ryder finds himself noticing the details of the room they are eating in; the photographs with curling corners tucked into the edge of the mirror over the fireplace, a sbag of pink knitting, clearly belonging to a child, spilling in festoons under a chair. Mike, now a publisher, has thinning hair and half-moon glasses behind which he wears an expression of dazed merriment.

'I don't know how to fit living into my life right now,' he says to Ryder in a tone of mock despair, when Ryder mentions getting tickets to the Oval for the Test match this summer. 'Solstice Books is about to be taken over by some huge American deal, so I'm going to have a crazy amount of work on, and Max and Nancy are turning five and they're a joy and I'd like to see them more. I'd love to go to the cricket, but can it be in a parallel life?'

Ryder walks home along the canal from Harrow Road to his boat at Little Venice and the silence echoes in the empty space. He wonders when he took the path that led him here rather than where Mike is. And, with a shiver of anxiety, whether it's too late, and he has missed the point of life.

★　★　★

It was the end of another summer, Ryder was just nineteen. Beaten-gold fields, drifting dust motes, and pigeons calling sadly to young already flown. Everything in the world had paused sleepily on the edge of autumn and he was restless. He had finished his exams in June, and had spent the summer loafing at home. Bonnie was there occasionally. In theory, she was back from her first year at university in Norwich; but in practice, Ryder knew she was always going to be somewhere else. No one truly comes back once they have left home to live somewhere else. She was changing now she had gone. She was full of her unique life and energy in her frequent long phone calls to Ryder and occasional one-night flying visits to their parents, where she talked ten times more than anyone else in the house, lit up with new-found independence and the myriad possibilities ahead of her. Ryder felt left behind, but he was not ready to go with her or to make his own way just yet. Like swallows gathering on telephone wires, all of Ryder's friends were near at hand that summer. They hung around, half poised for leaving home and half scared. Although nobody would admit it, there was not one among them who did not secretly wish they could turn back the clock and be children again. Of course, it was a luxurious wish, made in the full safety of the knowledge that this could not happen.

No one in their gang ever had to go to school again, with the exception of Ryder's girlfriend, Lila. She was a sliver of a seventeen year old from the year below with a curtain of palomino-yellow hair which she let fall, like Rapunzel, when she wanted something. She was not especially demanding, something Ryder liked about her, so the hair was tied up a lot of the time. She was exotic to look at, with pale brown eyes and creamy skin like a native Venetian, or so Bonnie, who was studying the painters of the Renaissance, said.

'You should ask her if she's got Italian blood,' said Bonnie to her brother after he'd dropped Lila home one evening.

'I have,' said Ryder, 'but she swears she was born and bred in Essex.'

'Like us,' said Bonnie,

'No, Betsy, we're the American dream, remember?' teased Ryder and they drove home talking in fake Californian accents and laughing loudly at their own feeble jokes.

Lila's parents restored violins in their higgledy-piggeldy cottage on the edge of the estuary. Lila hardly ever went home that summer; she had found a circus teacher through a small local festival and was training as a trapeze artist. This was another thing Ryder liked about her: she didn't expect him to make decisions for her. Her parents didn't know she was determined not to go back to school, and that she planned to join a circus in France in the autumn. They were expecting her to join an orchestra and were investigating having her impossibly flexible fingers broken and reset to make it possible for her to hold down the strings of a violin with her fingertips. Ryder was appalled that such mild and charmingly eccentric parents could be planning this degree of medieval torture. It awoke a wisp of chivalry in him, which grew into something like love. Lila put her hands together and the fingertips splayed out almost horizontally. He couldn't bear the thought of them being broken, it was inhuman. He could not let that happen to her. Never intending to have a big relationship, he found that he loved the air of ethereal peacefulness around Lila. She smoked roll-ups made of liquorice paper and when she did make rare trips home, lived in a tepee in her parents' garden, deaf to their entreaties for her to return to her bedroom.

'It's the endless creaking of cat gut,' she explained to Ryder when he first came back home with her. 'I can't live next to them sawing away with it all day, it twangs my nerve endings.'

'Sure,' said Ryder, having no idea what she was getting at, but fascinated by how she lived. In the tepee, Ryder lolled on Lila's bed, rolled a joint and toyed with the idea of asking Lila to marry him. It was the kind of thing that flitted into his mind when he was stoned.

Lila lay next to him, closed her eyes, and announced that she had been a squaw in the American Indian Blackfoot tribe in a past life. 'And you were my twin brother,' she announced dreamily. Ryder took her hand, gently pulling her impossibly bendy fingers.

'Either the weed is toxically strong or you are crackers,' he murmured, shifting on top of her, stroking her cheek with his thumb.

'Though actually, you do have cheekbones like an Indian, don't you?' His mouth brushed her eyebrows, her lashes, her ears, before he cupped her head in his hands and kissed her mouth. 'And I think it might be quite a turn on to fuck you in a past life, but I want to be me, not your twin brother.'

They both burst out laughing, quickly pulling off their clothes then diving beneath the heavy rug on top of the bed. In the dark under the blankets, laughter muffled, Lila's tongue was hot in Ryder's belly button, and hotter and so gentle running down the length of his cock. Ryder groaned and pulled her up to sit on top of him, arching his back to push up inside her, his hands on her waist pulling her hard down on to him. Fucking Lila was fucking great; he was deep inside her now and when she arched backwards her hair fell in a cool whisper right down her back, sweeping his thighs, tickling the soft skin between his legs. Ryder shifted position, turned her over so she was lying on her back, and looked into her eyes, pale brown eyes like an antelope. He took her hands, pressing them into the mattress, holding her down, loving her fast breath, the glazed desire in her eyes.

'You're so hot, Lila, your legs wrapped around me are pulling me into—'

A shout penetrated the canvas walls of the tepee. 'Lila, I've got Miss Reece, your old piano teacher, here to talk to you— OH!'

There was a blast of air and a stifled, 'Oh, for heaven's sake!' and Ryder looked up to see Lila's mother in the door of the tepee along with another woman who was wearing a hat like a tea cosy. The two women stared blankly across at Ryder and Lila, naked and making love on the rug.

'It's summer,' was his first thought, 'why does she need to wear that stupid hat?' He rolled off his girlfriend, who sat up, glaring, and pulled the rug up over them both.

Ryder knew he should feel embarrassed, but he didn't. A bubble of laughter floated out of him and he hid behind Lila, who was shaking with an anger which he hadn't known she could muster.

Lila threw one of Ryder's shoes at the two women. 'Fuck off, Mum! You have no business in here. Please go away,' she yelled, but the flap covering the door had already fallen again, and two voices began a stilted and over-bright conversation outside the canvas wall.

'Well, yes, I think we'll go and have a cup of tea. I've got a cake, I think.' Lila's mother was clearly trying to erase the vision in the tent as fast as possible from her memory.

Miss Reece went along with it. 'Yes, of course. Isn't it a lovely evening? We've been so lucky with the weather this summer.' It was as if they were on a gentle garden stroll.

Inside the tepee, Ryder, still laughing, pulled Lila down next to him, stroking away her stiff anger, teasing her into laughing too. Nothing their parents did mattered very much. Nothing at all mattered, in fact. Life and laughter were as limitless as the long slow summer days.

To any outsider, it seemed impossible as time unfurled that Ryder or any of his friends would ever do anything except smoke and listen to music. None of their parents had any faith that they would manage to galvanise themselves to go anywhere, or do anything. But steadily, subtly, they were cutting their ties, unknotting the heart strings that kept them close to home and hearth. The thing Ryder noticed was that in order to do this, girls seemed to argue with their parents a lot more than boys. He was adept at keeping the peace, mainly because his parents didn't worry about him as much as they worried about Bonnie. He was both grateful for this and sad. They never seemed to care what he did at all. He found the best way not to mind this was to get out of the house and out of his head. Life was so much easier like that.

On occasion, things got a bit out of hand. Ryder sometimes woke up with a shamefaced sense of being fetid. There was an evening at a pub up the coast and he and Lila and a group of friends were all staying the night with someone's granny in the local village on the sea. Of course, the granny wasn't there, but a whole lot of them were in her house. Ryder woke up early with pins and needles in his legs. In the half-light he could see someone lying on the bottom half of his sleeping bag and therefore on him. Moving any part of his body was impossible – the sleeping bag was one of those ones that tapers at the end – like a wedge of parmesan cheese, or so Ryder had joked when he got in it last night. It must have been a strong spliff because in the cold light of day the sleeping bag seemed more like a wind sock. Oh, what the fuck. It was Lila on his legs; curled up with hair all over her face, flopped forwards, her arms wrapped around her folded legs, and her hair like a pony's mane. There were ten people crashed in this cottage for the night. God knew where Jack's granny was. Playing golf, perhaps. Anyway, she definitely hadn't been there when they were in the kitchen making a bong and Lila smoked too much and went into a kind of trance that Ryder found very confusing. Frankly, it put him off drugs for a while. Well, a short while. Half an hour, to be exact. He had to keep waking her up and taking her out into the garden, and giving her orange juice to stop her shaking and crying. Someone said it was better if you drank it upside down, so they made her do a handstand which, even now, many years later, makes Ryder wince in sympathy for the poor, drugged girl whom he loved. He was sure she would feel better if he could get her to drink the orange juice. A straw was essential, but the sight of poor Lila, doing a handstand and frowning as she furiously sucked at one of those curly straws, tickled him and he got the most terrible attack of laughter. It was really infectious and everyone laughed except Lila. When she got better she threw the orange juice at Ryder and said the sight of him made her sick. That stuffy morning in the hot bedroom in a mysterious grandmother's house, Ryder also felt a bit sick. He put it down to the purple scratchy carpet right next to his face. It was nailed down to the boards, and Ryder must have still been stoned, because he found himself absorbed by speculation. Did the granny lay this awful carpet herself? Oh, for fuck's sake, did he have nothing more interesting to think? It was another morning, time to get up, but his head was wedged up against the wall. Propping himself up in the curtained gloom he could just about see that there were at least four people asleep on the floor. The big question was, which one of them had the weed?

Ryder looked back on that summer as a time when he was drifting in a slow-flowing current of intense and largely invisible energy, apathy loaded and laced with hormones. Slowly he was being propelled – in a haze of drugs – through the final bottleneck of confusion, until life as a dependent child was exchanged for life as a supposedly independent adult. The prospect was both alluring and alarming. Mostly, Ryder liked to shy away from it. It was amazing how days could follow on from one another and the biggest sum of his achievements would be rolling three joints and mending a bicycle puncture so he could get to the pub to meet Jack and Lila.

Bonnie was away a lot, principally because she was in love. Her boyfriend Mac was a third-year archaeology student. His finals were in June and in the autumn he would be embarking on his MA. She had never been so devoted to a boyfriend before and Ryder was conscious that something had changed for ever. Bonnie had someone else to share her dreams with now, and Ryder would not be the main recipient of her inner world any longer. Bonnie and Mac went to Greece where he was digging on a site for part of the summer. They came home after a month – brown, happy and skint. Mac got a job as a bouncer in a Norwich nightclub. Bonnie went to stay with him. Bill was quietly shocked and preferred to believe she was living on her own in Norwich, though this also offended him.

Jean was more loudly displeased. 'What will become of her if she lives with him? She should be at home now the term is over.' The voice of doom, Ryder always thought. Why would anyone want to be anywhere near Jean? She was a total killjoy.

'Why? She's grown up, Mum, and anyway, we don't belong to you, you know.' Ryder was speaking for himself as much as for Bonnie.

Jean twisted her wedding ring. Ryder could see her anxiety.

'Yes, but I'm responsible for you. Your father and I are— well, I just don't think she should be away all the time.'

Ryder gazed at her across the kitchen table as he slowly carved slice after slice of bread and spread it with peanut butter, ritualistically consuming the whole jar, reflecting that such was his hunger that this did not even touch the sides of it. He moved on to bread and cheese, and was on the third slice of that when enlightenment struck.

'Mum, have you dyed your hair?'

The look she flicked towards him was classic – guilty, and at the same time weighing up whether or not to come clean.

'No. Well, I mean yes. I haven't exactly dyed it, it's more of a rinse. Do you think it's obvious? I was quite hoping no one would notice, you see.' Jean patted her head on both sides, as if that might change something.

Ryder laughed and went over to hug her. His mother only came up to his chin now, and he felt protective when she wasn't being annoying.

'It's nice, Mum,' he said, and she laughed, grateful and pleased.

Ryder and Jack were hitch-hiking from Colchester to Norwich to see Bonnie and Mac that evening. Lila couldn't come because she was taking part in a moon-lit drumming ceremony in a wood just off the A12. Ryder was relieved he had already made plans and so didn't need an excuse to get out of going to the drum-ming ceremony with her. It had been planned to coincide with the full moon. Ryder and Jack walked to the roundabout to begin their journey under a scum-coloured mass of clouds. In the late summer evening light, the fields stretching beyond the Colchester ring road were dusty brown. No rain for the past weeks had shrunk the grasses to thin blond straws poking out of the bare earth, and litter drifted like tumbleweed.

'Doesn't look like there will be much moonlight for drumming,' Ryder said as they found their spot in a lay-by and he unfolded the cardboard sign he had made by using a strip of a shoebox and a marker pen for the word 'NORWICH'.

'What are you talking about?' The question was rhetorical, as Ryder knew full well. Jack had no inter-est in him answering.

Jack lit a thin one-skin joint he had pulled out of the pocket of his shirt and inhaled deeply before passing it to Ryder. 'It's so short sighted of my mother to have given Tom the car this weekend instead of me,' he groaned. 'Tom's not really going anywhere, so he won't put any petrol in it, and look at us!' He waved his arms at the surrounding trailer park gloom as a flattened polystyrene McDonald's box flapped wearily across the road. Jack kicked it. 'We're putting ourselves at terrible risk from perverts by having to hitch. I told my mum, but she just squawked something about me being ungrateful and drove off, so I couldn't even get a lift here.' He broke off to sway the top half of his body out into the road, thumb up, as a small brown car accelerated past. The driver, elderly with pebble glasses, didn't even glance in their direction. Jack slumped histrionically to his knees, groaning. 'We need a girl with us. You and me have no chance of getting a lift.'

Ryder flicked the butt of the joint into the dirty long grass and stepped into the road, his new shades a shield creating an Easy Rider atmosphere. Or so he hoped. 'Watch this,' he said, with a lot more conviction than he felt.

A camper van slewed towards them and stopped. A puff of smoke and a riff of Jimi Hendrix greeted them as the window was lowered. Grinning at one another, they climbed in.

Ryder hadn't much liked the idea of Mac at first. Bonnie was so into him it was disturbing, and Ryder felt excluded while also accepting that it was reasonable of her to exclude him. In fact, it would have been really sick of her to have wanted him to tag along the whole time.

'I don't want to be the third leg of the stool,' he said crossly when she invited him to come up to Norwich to meet Mac. 'I tell you what, I'll come with Jack.'

'OK, that makes us the four legs of a table,' replied Bonnie.

'Ha ha,' was the best Ryder could muster.

'He's a boxer!' Bonnie was trying to make connections, and Ryder was giving her no chance.

'I thought you said he was an archaeology student.' Tense with anticipation of dislike, Ryder could not allow his curiosity any small gleam of hope until he had met Mac himself.

Bonnie sighed. 'He is. He's both. Just come and meet him, I know you will like him. Oh, I mean I hope you will, Kid, I really do.'

They were to meet in a pub. 'It's called The Murderers,' Ryder told their driver, a flute-playing hippie with whom they had smoked three joints and had travelled a lot further in their minds than the mere two-hour journey between Colchester and Norwich.

Mac bought the first round of drinks, balancing a handful of plastic pint glasses as he wove between the tables in the crowded bar. He sat down next to Ryder and raised a glass to him.

'I am glad we've met at last,' he said.

'So, you box?' Ryder wanted to kick himself for sounding not only aggressive but also stupid. He realised how much he would cringe if his father had been here and asked that question. Shocked at his own surliness, he gulped the beer, a cold, sleek belt of alcohol, down his throat.

'Well, yep, but I'm a complete amateur.' Mac was low key, and friendly. 'I grew up in Lowestoft where there's a great boxing club and I'm still a member.' He grinned and Ryder liked his smile, felt himself warming up, and relaxed a little. Mac was still talking. 'My dad used to box there, my brother does and all my family. In fact, my grandma has never missed a fight at our club. Watching, I mean, thank God.'

He looked at Ryder, then asked, 'Tell me what you reckon for the European Cup line-up next week. Can I call you Kid, or is that just for Bonnie?'

'Only if you call her Betsy,' Ryder replied, teasing his sister, who was talking to Jack and pretending not to listen. She immediately spun round, shoving him playfully.

'Oh no – don't tell him that. He'll call me Betsy and it makes me feel about five years old.'

Mac laughed and stroked his hand up her spine to her neck, pulling his fingers idly through the hair falling down her back, a gesture full of quiet intimacy and love. A fragment of comprehension settled in Ryder. And acceptance. This was the real thing. He wanted this, someday, with someone.

Bonnie was leaning against Mac, laughing, and he was teasing, saying, 'You make a great Betsy, you know. I think it's a kind of mafia stooge, in Italy – oh no, that's a Patsy, isn't it? or a pasty. I'm never sure which.'

'No, a pasty is what you eat in Cornwall, if you're lucky and have any money left after the pub,' protested Jack through the laughter. Mac was impossible not to like. Mac and Bonnie together were like one being.

The closeness they had was potent and harmonious. Rare, Ryder thought as they walked through Norwich the next day, heading to the river where Mac had a friend on a houseboat. A girl who is loved, truly loved, is softer and happier. Ryder wondered if Jean had ever been like this, even in the early days with Bill. It was hard to imagine, but then she was young once, too.

'What does it feel like, you and Mac?' he asked his sister.

They were on the houseboat. Mac and his friend were dangling over one side, trying to nail down a curling length of flashing, and Jack had wandered off to take photographs of a collapsing warehouse further down the river. Bonnie and Ryder lay down to sunbathe on a small deck where there was a potted willow tree and a tiny fountain with a mermaid spouting water from her curled tail. Sunlight sparkled green over warped diamonds in the water and the air was heavy with the sound of lazy traffic and the smell of dusty summer trees. The morning felt as though time would go on expanding for ever, though that could have just been the effect of the joint Jack shared as they crossed the Cathedral Close and made their way down the path to the river.

Bonnie shut her eyes and raised her face towards the sun. 'It doesn't feel like anything else,' she said slowly, 'so it's hard to explain. It's something to do with knowing that we belong together, so it's inevitable. It feels like a magnet.'

'So what makes you know you belong together?' Ryder propped himself up on his elbow, squinting in the brightness of the day at Bonnie. Her eyes were still shut against the sun; she looked foreign and exotic, her bare arms brown, her hair almost glittering black and the yellow of her dress like sulphur against the silver green decking. 'Did you ever feel like this with any of your other boyfriends, Bonnie?'

She opened her eyes, and the look she gave him had a flash of fear in it. 'No. I never felt this. And what makes me know it's different is that when I am with him it feels real. Not like some happy-ending fairy tale, just real. I feel safe, but not bored. Happy, not crazily elated. When I'm not with him, I'm missing something. I keep looking round with that feeling that something is missing, you know?'

Ryder nodded, even though he didn't, but he wanted to. 'I think I've only had that when I'm hungry,' he said, needing to break the tension, and they both began giggling, rolling further into the sun.

Telling his parents that Bonnie was loving her life away from home gave Ryder a small sense of satisfaction. It was like opening a door to freedom, even though he was not quite ready to pass through it himself. He felt glad for his sister that she was away when he told them, and that he had done it for her, because Bill and Jean reacted with stiff resentment. In fact, when it was his turn to go, he thought he might get her to come back and tell them. Like startled cats they walked around Ryder in the kitchen where he sat at the table, staring at him, absorbing the tiny amount of information he felt was enough for them, with alarm.

'Nothing's really changed, Dad, it's just the next stage.' Ryder was finally goaded into speech, mainly to interrupt his father's tutting, pacing and nose blowing.

'We'll see,' said Bill grimly.

It was definitely the next stage, all right, when Mac came to stay. Jean's mouth folded like an envelope the morning after he arrived when she found Bonnie's bedroom door firmly shut, and the door into the spare room, where they had shown Mac the night before, wide open, the bed empty, the curtains not drawn.

Ryder felt really sorry for his sister. No one did that sort of crosspatch face at him when he brought a girlfriend home, or if they did, he had managed never to notice it. They were over-protective of Bonnie and it was suffocating to observe, let alone live through.

'I'm twenty, for Christ's sake, Dad,' Bonnie screamed at Bill when he began the tutting, nose-blowing routine over the fact that she was going away yet again. Mac was outside by the gate, his head under the bonnet of his car, which was making a high-pitched sound like a steaming kettle. 'I've left home. I live at – at – well, I don't live anywhere right now, but I will live somewhere next term. I'm going to look for wherever it'll be this weekend. Mac's found somewhere that sounds great.'

Jean hovered near her husband but kept close to the kitchen counter so that she could watch Mac out of the window. Two red blotches bloomed on her face as she noticed Mac, already quite unacceptably flamboyant on account of his long hair and suntanned torso, suddenly putting himself fully on show by pulling off his shirt and using it to protect his hand while undoing the radiator cap.

'How can you think that you know what you're doing with him?' she hissed at Bonnie, her eyes narrow slits of spite. 'It's all about sex, and you'll grow out of it and have so much to regret.'

Bonnie turned white. Even Bill stopped in his tracks and stood open mouthed, his spectacles and handkerchief studies of stillness in his hands as he gaped at his wife.

'Jean, really,' he muttered. 'I don't think you can say—'

Jean's knuckles gripped the edge of the sink, and if she hadn't just been so completely vile, Ryder would have gone to hug her, she looked so forlorn and frightened.

'I can say what I think,' she uttered in the same tight, high voice, her eyes on the floor in front of Bonnie's feet as Bonnie walked up to her and challenged her to look her straight in the eyes. Bonnie and Jean stood face to face for what felt like a thousand years, then Bonnie spoke.

'OK, Mum, it's true. You can say what you think. And you can think what you like. But I'm telling you that you don't know anything about me, you never have and I don't think you ever will. I'm going with Mac now and I don't know when I'll be back.'

She wasn't yelling, she didn't even seem to care if Jean took her words on board. She picked up her bag, overstuffed and open with clothes falling out of it, and left.

8

Grace
Brooklyn

It happens on a Sunday in April. Jerome is reading the Japanese stock market reports for the week on one of his many small beeping pieces of electrical equipment, and I clear away the breakfast dishes and put on my coat to leave for the studio. And as I lift my arms to pull the weight of my hair out of the collar of the coat, I look towards the window and see myself in pale reflection. I am almost not there. And that is how it is in life. At this moment the floating uncertainties that have been bumping about in my mind for months all slot together. Together they make something huge and certain. A reality. My life with Jerome, my five-year-old relationship with him, is over. It is like the end of a play, or a film you were just sitting through not especially enjoying but not hating, and then suddenly, irrefutably, it's the end.

With absolutely no finesse, I place myself right in front of Jerome and stretch out a hand to him. 'Please can you come with me outside? I want to walk somewhere with you.'

The look he gives me over his glasses shows me that he knows this is not just a walk in the park. Without saying a word, he takes off the glasses, reaches for his coat and his keys, and follows me out into the spring sunshine.

The street is bright and smells of diesel and cinnamon thanks to the baker's van passing towards the river. A pair of kids with a soft ball come by, their singsong voices snatched from the background roar of the traffic. Jerome and I walk up the slope and across the road to Prospect Park in silence. I can hardly feel my feet I am so disembodied, but in my head I have a thrumming rhythm, pulsing with life. All my senses are heightened and I am aware of everything that I encounter. Wondering if this is how Sleeping Beauty felt when the Prince kissed her and she finally woke up, I am surprised to find that I want to run and do cartwheels because I can suddenly taste freedom.

The rhythm in my head is saying, 'It's over. It's already over.' And the thing is that now I have to tell him which is awful, but beyond that the horizon is limitless because it's already over and I know it is.

We enter through the big wrought-iron gates that look like the balconies on this side of the park, and immediately I veer off the path, making an escape from the flow of human traffic. The park is the worst possible place to have come on a Sunday to end a relationship. The air is fresh, the sky bright with the flash of silver planes catching the sun as they float above New York and the sounds of happiness babbles like water over rocks in a stream. A jogging couple pass, just maintaining a conversation; the girl's voice is breathy, his answers steady, her ponytail bobbing jauntily as they head across the open grass expanse beyond the trees, curving to avoid the soccer games. They join the moving pattern of talking, walking, playing families and couples. Everyone seems to be with someone. What will it be like to be one instead of half of two? I begin to feel terrified I won't manage to say what I need to. My feet are wet in the long grass, Jerome is not paying attention, he is looking at his telephone, loitering on the tarmac, unwilling to get his shoes wet. It's all going wrong. As usual. Oddly, because the feeling of having got it wrong is so familiar, it paradoxically bolsters my belief that it is all very much right. Taking a deep breath I swing round in the shrubs where I have managed to bring Jerome by linking arms with him. He's still looking at his phone, and I know it's a shield; his eyes flicker nervously and he keeps licking his lips. I do not like this apprehension. Tucking my hair behind my ear, I launch into a speech I haven't thought about at all carefully.

'I have thought about this very carefully, and I have taken a long time to actually be sure, but I am now.' It's quite horrible meeting his eye, but I must. I know I must. It's more real if we are looking at one another, and I can't bear it if he doesn't take me seriously. The most unnerving hiatus of time happens when my voice simply peters out and grinds to a halt. I don't know what to say next. Jerome and I look at one another and I send silent prayers to all the gods that Jerome will say something. Can he see in my demeanour and appearance what I am feeling? Will he understand? He shifts from foot to foot and keeps looking away and sometimes yawning. He's apprehensive, and he's already building a barrier to protect himself. He's already escaping from the sadness. I blurt loudly, 'And it's over between us now, Jerome.' I feel both lost and saved by these words.

Jerome says nothing. I blunder on.

'I mean, I am over you.' It's not supposed to sound so teenage and sulky, but there is another horrible well of silence. I fill that one, too. 'I am sorry, Jerome, I can't be with you any more.' There is nothing else to be said. Is there? I haven't got the manual for this, and Lucy, whom I suddenly long to ask for help, is a long way away. Jerome's face is impenetrable. If I was a small child, I could now cast myself on the ground and sob. As it is, I dig my hands deep into my pockets and feel my mouth buckle. I can't stop crying once I start. I knew this would happen, it's a disaster. And of course, Jerome is really nice, kind and enveloping and he puts his arm around me. It feels wrong; I am betraying our time together already because when he does this I cannot respond, my body feels like stone against the stone of his body. How fickle and malleable is the human sensory system. Something can change from being comfortable and safe to being out of kilter and intrusive from one moment to the next.

'You've met someone else.' It isn't a question, to Jerome it's a statement of fact. Tears fall from my blurring eyes into the collar of his coat, but they are tears of frustration now. I am sick to the teeth with the frustration of misunderstanding.

'No! That's not it. It's this.' I grab his coat, yanking at his lapel. 'This is what I can't do, I can't hold on to you and be rescued.' I am yelling because I am so afraid I won't say it otherwise. It's like a nightmare where you open your mouth to talk and nothing comes out. 'I have to look after myself, I have to be on my own and to stand up for myself. I am suffocating with you, Jerome, because you are so sure of yourself and I am not. Except in my work. And that is sending me crazy.'

Jerome stepped back, not looking at me, looking over my head, past me, anywhere but at me. He takes my hand and begins leading me out of the park again.

'Do we have to talk about this here, Grace?' He raises his head and looks up at the sky, grey now, no blue between the clouds. 'It's cold, and I think it's going to rain,' he says.

'Yes. Or snow. It said on the radio it might snow, it's a freak low-pressure thing. Or high pressure. Oh, I don't know.'

I stop suddenly, desperate that despite all this, he's not taking me seriously.

'Please listen, Jerome. We DO have to talk about this here. Because I am moving out. I am going to go today.' Jerome gets angry. We are in the middle of the road, the traffic is going too fast past us, and a crocodile of slow-moving old people shuffles past us, back from the park to their residential home on Park View. One of them spits mightily and a slug of white phlegm lands in front of Jerome.

He swears beneath his breath, veins stand out on his smooth forehead, and he says, 'Of course it won't snow' contemptuously. Then, more contemptuously, he goes on: 'Look, Grace, you're being self centred and hysterical. Of course you can move out whenever you like, but this is not the way to do it.'

And it's terrifying how readily I'm able to accept this. At this moment, I want him not to be angry more than I want anything for myself. I feel manipulated and powerless.

'Well, how would you like me to do it?' It's as if I'm taking an order in a café – 'Eggs easy over and bacon on the side, and would you like your life turned upside down too?' What Jerome wants is usually what Jerome gets, and I am usually the one who supplies it. I am used to submitting to his will. We are halfway down the street and nearing the big brownstone house where Jerome's apartment is. If we go back inside, I think I might capitulate. Once back there, I will lose all the ground I made in the park. It's like a life-sized, life-altering game of Snakes and Ladders, and I am about to throw the dice that sends me hurtling back to the bottom of one of the snakes again.

'No.' I swing round to face him on the sidewalk. The flow of slow-moving Sunday families have to walk around us; or indeed between us: a child with a bobbing helium balloon darts through. 'I mean it. I am not coming back inside your apartment with you.' Gesturing across the street to Jerome's front door I take a step back. It is too near, I back away a bit more. 'I'm going to stay with Dorelia tonight. I'll come and get my stuff tomorrow.'

Jerome's mouth is like a small box folding in on itself. 'If that's what you want,' he says stiffly, 'but I'm not going to molest you or anything.' He knows how to yank me in. Every sentence is weighted. The only weapon I have left to help me is the frustrating strength about to explode within me because I can't get him to understand my point of view. He puts a hand out to me but withdraws it as if he has been burned. He gulps. 'And I think you owe me more than just walking out like this,' he says.

It is appalling that I find myself nodding in agreement. He is right, he is behaving well, and I am being a real bitch. The thought fans flames of shame.

'I know.' I drop my keys into his hand and slink away, feeling like a mangy cur dog, ashamed and guilty and not sure why I am leaving. I step off the sidewalk without looking and almost get hit by a car.

Jerome reaches me back. 'For Christ's sake, Grace, get a grip, you fool,' he hisses.

'Oh leave me alone.' I push him away and, desperate to escape, I shake his hand from my arm and run down the street.

This is not how it is meant to end. Nothing is meant to end like this. Or maybe this is how everything ends

– a slow murder of everything you ever loved about the other person, methodical and unstoppable. I can feel nothing.

The next morning I am still numb, and it has snowed. This hijacks some of the intensity and offers another focus. Dorelia, my flatmate of long ago, is no longer a dancer in a club and has left for Europe where she's attending a conference for research to help her environmental project in the Bronx, so I have the apartment to myself for a week. I walk naked through the empty rooms and it feels illicit to be on my own, and soothing to have the sun pour warmth through the huge windows while I know it's below freezing outside. There is a huge difference here from being at Jerome's apartment because there I was somebody's girlfriend. Now I am just Grace. Wondering if I am slightly perverted, I get dressed, but only in my underwear. Being here alone is charged and sensuous and I like that element of it. Also, I haven't really got anything much else with me. Yesterday I waited here while Dorelia went back to Jerome's and brought me what she could pack in five minutes with Jerome grinding his teeth and looking at his watch.

Dorelia's apartment is in an old storage warehouse down under Brooklyn Bridge, near my studio. The snow is dazzling – whitened light bouncing off the river, warm and insistent on my skin. It feels erotic because I want it to, not because of anyone else trying to turn me on. There is a packet of cigarettes in the fireplace and I smoke three of them in a row. They are stale, so the taste in my mouth is filthy. I make some coffee and eat a tomato. Dorelia only has vodka, lemons and this tomato in her fridge. I find some peanut butter and have a spoonful of that too. Single-girl life is very different from being half of Jerome's household. I feel unstable and fragile, but excited and alive. And very ashamed. I can't stop believing I am wholly ungrateful. Jerome was a perfect boyfriend and I am spoiled and will have a lonely life now. To escape this feeling, I go down to shovel the snow off Dorelia's steps. It needs to be done this morning. Dorelia left me a note asking if I would mind, and it seems like the perfect antidote to obsessing about breaking up with Jerome. I put on several layers of proper clothes, mostly belonging to Dorelia, and my coat and boots.

As a reward, when I finish, I will take myself to a diner for pancakes and bacon. It's important to have something to look forward to. There is a shovel propped by the main entrance, dripping water on to the door mat. Someone has been there before me. But outside it is evident that they have been extremely solipsistic. The dug path through the snow is one shovel wide and goes to a nearby parked car and then around it. Well, around the front of it. The earlier morning digger has scuffled about at the front of the giant pile of snow in which the black car is embedded and given up. The air is so cold it is like swallowing a frozen ribbon when I breathe. Raising and dropping my shoulders my skin rubs warmth into the fabric of my clothes. I think I will start on the bottom step. The spade scrapes down to the stone surface of the step and judders to a halt in the pile of snow. It is incredibly hard work. Snow is heavy and inert. Gasping, fingers frozen, the tips now without feeling, I try to remember about inert substances. Inertia. That's what has kept me with Jerome. Even the thought is like an injection of energy, and I have a few more heaps of snow off the steps. My nose has become a separate entity and my cheeks are steel plates on my face. There are ten more steps. It might have been a good idea to start at the top, not the bottom, then at least it wouldn't be so daunting. It would be a better idea to move up there now. Pushing my hat back on my head, I start again. I am becoming obsessed with the snow. It is heavy and recalcitrant, and the job in hand feels like a labour of Hercules. I start trying to remember the twelve tasks of Hercules and find this more frustrating than snow-digging. There was cleaning out the Augean stables, there was stealing the Mares of Diomedes, there was obtaining the girdle of Hippolyta. Oh God, why are there so many? At school I perfected methods for remembering things that were much more complicated than the list of things I am trying to remember. The methods were usually visual, so the twelve tasks of Hercules became a rainbow and the Augean stables were turquoise and the horses were yellow. By the fourth snow-stacked step I am in full flow and I can remember the first task – slaying the Nemean lion and bringing its hide back – and the second, which was another killing, this time a Hydra, and I feel very exhilarated. I am just trying to summon the brain power to recall a few more when I notice two small beings have manifested on the top step while I have been travelling through the possible tasks for the green part of the Hercules rainbow. They are both cocooned in layers of clothing, but between their hats and their collars, bright eyes peep out and big enveloping smiles are visible.

'We live here,' says the larger one, whose pink coat and purple gloves suggest to me that she is a girl. 'Mom said we have to come out and dig snow with you.'

'No,' pipes the other one. 'Mom actually said, "Get out from under my feet, you two, or I'll go spare."'

'Same difference,' says the girl with excellent dead-pan timing, but she is unable to resist giving him a spiteful push anyway. He wobbles like a skittle on the top step. Unconsciously, I drop my shovel and am ready to catch him. Ah yes – the pink task of Hercules; the tenth is stealing the apples of the Hesperides. Or something like that.

'Well, that's what I meant,' says the girl, looking at me. 'So what's your name?' she asks.

'I'm Grace, and if you feel like helping me, that would be wonderful.' I put out a gloved hand to shake theirs. 'What are your names?'

'I'm Brad Gallagher and I'm six and she's Tyler. She's my sister and she's nine,' says the boy, and he staggers down to the step where I'm standing to shake my hand.

'We don't have school today because the classroom has too much snow on the roof and we might sue the school,' he says, beaming at me. I beam back. He is so adorable. 'Shall we help you?' he asks. 'We've got stuff for digging.' He waves a small red tin spade. I reach out, but pull my hand back, and contain myself to just admiring it.

'Yes please. Gosh, I like the look of that shovel, it's the right size and not too heavy. Let's clear the steps and make a snowman.'

'Where are you from?' Tyler has plaits and the same shining brown eyes as her brother.

She slides a scoop of snow off the wall and holds it up heaped on her glove. 'Mmm, snow candy,' she says, sticking her tongue out to lick it.

'I'm from England.' I tip a big pile of snow down the steps, satisfied to see it puff and spill like icing sugar, enjoying the exertion.

Tyler runs down and, stretching her arms, falls back into a drift built up by the steps. 'I'm making an angel,' she shouts, flat now and flapping her arms up and down. 'Come and get me up so I don't spoil it.'

The last task is something to do with Cerberus. Maybe it's poisoning him with a bit of steak. If they had steak then. But of course they did because there was the cow task where he had to get hold of the cows of Geryon.

'Let's make a snow leopard,' yells Brad, flinging a snowball at his sister. Her plaits are bound with pink plastic hair elastics in the shape of wrapped sweets.

'You missed,' she taunts, and Brad sticks his tongue out. He has lost a front tooth.

'It happened last week, on my sixf birthday,' he explains in an impossible yet inevitable lisp. 'But it sucks because I lost the tooth and I never got to wish on it.'

I grin at him, 'Do you know what you would have wished for?'

'Sure,' says Brad. 'I would first have wished that I hadn't swallowed it. The rest is top secret.'

Tyler hums while she digs, and when she catches my eye, she peals with laughter. 'It's my snow song, I don't know the words yet, but if I hum it enough I might think of some.'

I hum too and feel like Winnie the Pooh with Piglet.

'Do you know the "Tiddlypom" song from *Winnie the Pooh*?' I ask them.

In an hour the steps are clear and we have remembered every verse about cold toes and the more it snows and sung them loudly, heedless of passersby. The snow leopard sits like a sphinx on the bottom step. Slightly in the way, but once it was started in the middle of the step, there was nothing the three of us could do about it. Pulling off my hat, I lean on the spade and contemplate our art.

'It's more like a dodgem car,' says Brad gloomily. 'Or a lying-down steer. It only looks like a snow leopard in my head.'

'But that's where it really matters.' I ruffle his hair and a catch in my throat sends tears to my eyes when he reaches his gloved hand into mine.

*   *   *

When Lucy calls that afternoon, I am in a mood to be won over by children.

'Anyway, we're having the girls christened in May and you've got to come over. It will be a lovely party, do you remember I said we would have a party? It's the twenty-fifth, I think. If nothing else, we need you to entertain Bella's long-lost godfather.' I'm lounging on the sofa in Dorelia's apartment, semi-naked again. All my belongings are scattered around the sofa in plastic garbage bags. I have just been to get all my stuff and now I'm back and alone. It is a low moment. Jerome's apartment still looked complete when I left, and these six bin bags contain all I own in the world apart from my work. It fitted into one taxi. How can I be thirty-two and still only own things that go in garbage bags? Why have I cared so little that this has happened? And what would I like to own? Lolling on Dorelia's sofa, with the phone, it strikes me that a large piece of furniture such as this would be a very good first purchase.

'How do you choose a sofa?' I ask Lucy, not wishing to commit myself to appearing at the christening or not.

'Well, before you choose the sofa, you need somewhere to put it,' my sister sounds unnecessarily tart. 'And you need to know which country you want your sofa to live in.'

I want to laugh and cry at the same time because Lucy knows me so well.

'Have you moved out of Jerome's?'

'Yeah. We broke up.'

'Do you miss him?'

'Well, it was only yesterday, but I don't really. I like my own space. Jerome took up a lot of room.'

Lucy laughs. 'Yes, well, that's why you can fit a sofa into your life now.'

'I guess. It's odd, though. He's been all of my life beyond my work for five years, it's got to take some getting over, hasn't it? And you know what? Right now I just feel relieved.'

'You know what?' Lucy's voice is a laughing mimicry. 'You're sounding SO New York these days. So come on, this will do you good. It must be the right moment, if ever there was a right moment. Do you think you will come?'

'Is this the summer holiday you promised me?' I suddenly feel excited about the thought of going to England, to Norfolk. The sun has gone behind a bank of cloud, and the snow has been melting all afternoon and now slumps in the grey evening. New York feels dirty and suffocating. There is a picture in my head, a John Piper painting with little children pattering on biscuit-coloured sand, mothers and nurses walking towards them, their skirts plumed and slender, billowing like sails. And on the horizon a real red-brown sail on a grey boat.

'Yup.' Lucy's voice is brimming with excitement. 'I want it for you and me as much as for my girls, you know. We didn't get it before, but that doesn't mean we can't now.'

Gazing down the Hudson River past glinting glass buildings and block after block of apartments and offices full of so many thousands of people, and on down the river out through the mouth to the sea, I am nodding at the mouthpiece of the phone. I can almost taste the freedom of being in Norfolk by the sea.

'I think you're right, Lucy. I've been looking at England from a safe distance for long enough. We can see off all our old ghosts together, can't we?'

'You bet,' says Lucy lightly. 'I've got to go, Mac's been holding the baby and she's asleep but I need to go and get Bella in bed. Love you, Sis.'

'I love you too.' I put down the phone, smiling. It is incredible that Lucy lives in this parallel universe of motherhood as if nothing else exists. I can't imagine it unless I equate it to a painting movement, but nothing, not vorticism, or any other obsession I have ever had, can match the absorption of the early years.

9

Ryder
Essex

Coming home is the problem. Of course, no one in their mid-thirties can reasonably expect their parents to run their household in the way that it was run when their children were growing up, nor, in truth, would they want it to be, but whoever said anything about being reasonable or speaking the truth? The train grinds to a halt. From the window the estuary with the tide out is the colour and texture of liver, and it almost feels as if the train is embedded in the mud. Ryder opens the small window in the stuffy carriage and the scents of salt and sea and thick cloying mud seep in and mingle with the dusty dry air of the heating system. The train judders into life for a moment then pulls up again before smoothly gliding on into green, open countryside. The smell of the estuary lingers, Ryder can taste mud in his throat. His sense of sinking down into subterranean layers of brown must be to do with where he is going. It's not home, how can somewhere you have never lived be home? And how can you begin to have a home when you have never lived anywhere except in other people's lives?

Finishing the crossword is easier than answering the sort of questions Ryder finds floating into his mind these days – '17 Across: "Result of a laundry-room short".' Tumble-dried? Probably not. He folds the newspaper and stows it in his bag. The train is pulling into Deepham and he waits for the doors to open, scanning the platform with mild curiosity.

Jean and Bill moved house nine years ago, and nine is about the number of nights Ryder has spent since then under the roof of their L-shaped bungalow over-looking the golf course. They seem happy enough there, it is half an hour away from Foxley, far enough to be a new beginning, but near enough to be famil-iar. To Ryder, the distance could have been one or a thousand miles; he couldn't bear the idea that they were leaving Bonnie behind. The difficulty of living anywhere, uneasy and unresolved, when Bonnie lives nowhere, has sent him around the world twice and kept him keen for change. Change for the sake of change, ceaseless motion to avoid the stark reality of being himself alone in the world. But in the end the self is unavoidable.

Ryder is alone on the platform. The train shunts away and the air is soft with the coo of pigeons calling in the spring evening. He walks across the level cross-ing and down towards the High Street. He could get a taxi, but the walk is only a mile or two, it's a lovely time of day and Ryder is in no hurry. He lights a cigarette and swings his bag over one shoulder. His phone trills. It's his mother.

'Hello?' She sounds surprised, although she is the one making the phone call.

'Hello, Ma, it's me, Ryder.'

'Yes, of course it is. I know, I rang you.'

'So you did,' he agrees cordially, wondering if there is any reason for the call.

'Your father would have driven to the station, but the car has been kept at the garage overnight.'

Ryder is absurdly touched. This is his mother at her most demonstrative. It is her way of showing she has been looking forward to seeing him. He flicks his cigarette away.

'That's very kind of him, but in fact I'm walking; it's a lovely evening for it.' Christ, does he really have to sound as though he's speaking to someone to whom English is a second language?

'Oh, that's such a relief,' says his mother. 'I'll leave your letter in the hall.'

Ryder turns to walk across the golf course, frowning, wondering if he has heard her right.

'My letter?' he says, mystified. Are they not talking? Is this the onset of senility?

'Yes. For you to open,' his mother says very patiently. Ryder grins, realising that she, too, feels the need to speak as if he knows no English.

'Flesh of my flesh, blood of my blood,' he mutters to himself.

'I won't be at home, you see,' his mother continues, 'I'm doing the flowers this week.'

'Splendid. Well, I'll see you when you get back. We'll have supper together tonight.'

'Oh no. Your father and I have just had a boiled egg. I've left some ham for you.'

Ryder's heart sinks. It's not that his mother was such a great cook that missing supper cooked by her is the end of the world, but the depressing image of a small plate of ham and one place set at the dining-room table does not excite him much.

'Oh well. I mean, that's great. Bye, Ma.' Ryder has had enough of the complete idiot role, yakking on a phone like a city slicker in his suit, stalking along the narrow margin of path past the fourteenth hole, where a pair of sprightly septuagenarians have alighted from their golf cart and are slowly creeping towards two nicely placed balls. The smaller of the two, curled like an autumn leaf in his zip-up jacket, pulls up his sleeves and grips the golf club. To Ryder it looks as if its weight is the only thing anchoring him to the earth, and if he takes a swing, he may well fly up and away. With slight regret not to be watching the rest of their game he walks on. Ryder has not been in the habit of wearing a suit, but that, like everything else, he has concluded, is changing. Last week a bag of his clothes arrived from Denmark, from Cara, whom he had not heard a word from since he sent her the flowers two months ago. In the case was a card with a picture of a cat asleep on a cloud, and on the back she had written:

Dear Ryder,

I hope you are happy. The flowers you sent were pretty, thank you. Jurgen and I are living together now. I didn't know how to tell you. No hard feelings, I hope, but I needed the space of your clothes! Come and visit us if you ever come to Denmark again, I would be glad to see you.

Love Cara

The clothes, in a plaid laundry bag, took up an unwarranted amount of space on Ryder's narrow boat. He sat on his bed, looking at them, Cara's letter in his hand, wondering how best to deal with the miserable sense of rejection that they had brought with them. And incidentally, who the hell was Jurgen? But the rejection was cured very nicely by getting Mike, his publisher friend, away from his twins and his work and begging him to come for an evening of Guinness and a pool tournament in Camden Town. Ryder and Mike won the tournament, and a stack of pints of Guinness to redeem at the bar. The healing process begun, Ryder began to find it possible to turn a negative into a positive. The next morning, slightly hungover, he got dressed in a suit and took the bag with all the clothes he hadn't missed while they had been sitting in Cara's wardrobe in Copenhagen to the charity shop. The reward for this was immediate – the girl serving him in the coffee shop next to his office told him that he looked like her favourite soap star in his grey pinstripe suit. That Ryder had no idea who the soap star was, or what he looked like didn't matter. In fact, maybe it was better not to know. If a girl liked the suit then he had pleased her, and she had noticed him – all that was good. Today he even has a proper shirt with it, though generally he interchanges three T-shirts. But his mother would like a shirt, wouldn't she?

Actually, Ryder realises, turning in at the end of the low brick wall, passing the tabby cat sitting smugly on the gate post, he has no real idea what his mother likes at all. And if a man with little interest in clothes starts trying to second-guess what a woman would or wouldn't like him to have in his wardrobe his life could become very frustrating. Anyway, on balance, he thinks, most mothers like suits. It makes a man look purposeful. And, since throwing out everything from Copenhagen, Ryder doesn't have a whole lot else to wear. As it turns out, it is his father who notices, opening the door of the bungalow with a caution that any Neighbourhood Watch scheme would find exemplary, but which maddens Ryder, who has already said, 'It's me, Ryder,' three times through the frosted-glass panes. Bill finally opens the door a few inches and looks cautiously at his son, then gathers his thoughts.

'Yes, so it is. Goodness, I haven't seen you in a suit since—' Bill breaks off with a stricken look that only makes Ryder more irritated. Jesus, are they ever going to get over it? he thinks. Can we not live a single day after eighteen years without the grief mountain in our midst? And if it's coming up in conversation, then for God's sake, bring it in fully, don't just break off leaving everything unsaid, nothing resolved.

'Hi, Dad,' Ryder says mildly.

Bill has slightly slumped over the door handle, and his body language suggests that he would really like to shut the door now and not deal with Ryder. Letting him in looks like the last thing on earth he wants to do, but with practised weariness he gathers himself up, and continues, 'Hmm. Well, any way, you'd better come in.' With a snail as his role model, he undoes the chain and opens the door. Ryder embraces the air close to his father's cheek, and breathes in the familiar whiff of pipe tobacco and shaving soap that is Bill's aura.

'Dad, it's great to see you.'

His father has got out his large handkerchief and is wiping his glasses. 'Ye-es,' he says vaguely, as though he can't remember if he agrees or not. Actually, he probably can't, Ryder thinks.

The hall is narrow; a spindly table sticks out into the plank-shaped space, the glow of much-polished mahogany incongruous on the pale blue carpet, against the peach walls. Furniture so much older than the house it inhabits, furniture with memories in a house with none. It's hard to work out what you are attached to, sometimes, Ryder considers, and whether belongings have any meaning at all. He has certainly made a virtue out of not attaching value to them, and has now got himself so few that life anywhere larger than a boat would be a challenge. But maybe it's a challenge he should be facing now. A net curtain hides the window above the table. Ryder pulls back the curtain, drinking in the prettiness of the apple tree in blossom beyond the window. He finds himself, as he always does when he gets here, looking around hopefully for the stairs. Not that he wants to go up them to any destination on another floor, it's just that he wishes they were there. A house without stairs and therefore without an upstairs, feels incomplete.

His father ambles past him. 'You've got a letter.'

'Oh, yes. So I have. Mum mentioned it when she rang me earlier.'

Propped against a silver hand bell in the shape of a lady in a crinoline, is a cream envelope, loopy pale green writing giving his name a pleasing edge of whimsicality. Ryder picks it up, and his heartbeat changes when he reads the postmark. Winterton-on-Sea. The name fits like Kiss Me Quick around the life belt-shaped red post office stamp. It can only be from Mac. Ryder holds it for a moment, mesmerised, then he rubs his eyes. How can time do this? It just telescoped through all the intervening years and took him back to the numb ache of the last time he saw Mac. It was winter. Ryder's first term at university. They had gone to a football match together, an attempt to keep the connection open between them and to put it on to an everyday footing. But there was too much sadness. Ryder could not see Mac as anything but diminished without Bonnie at his side, and conversations floundered uneasily as they both shrank from mentioning her. The wrong team won the match, and in the pub afterwards they played darts and became increasingly consumed by the difficulty of sustaining any small talk. Finally, Mac, having missed the board with all three of his darts, turned to Ryder with an empty smile. 'I miss her every day,' he said.

After that they got drunk, and Mac came back and slept on the floor of Ryder's room in the hall of residence. He left before Ryder woke up and though they talked a few times on the phone, they gradually lost touch over the next year or two.

Bill shuffles back into the twilit zone of the sitting room, and laughter like gunshot pings around the door frame from the old black-and-white movie he is watching on television. The trepidation Ryder feels is almost unbearable; he can't work out if he needs to gather his thoughts and strength before opening the letter, or if he needs to get on with it and face the nameless fear. While wondering, he opens it, remembering as he does so that it's always the best way to distract oneself from the fear and do whatever it is anyway. This, at any rate, is Ryder's philosophy. Inside the envelope is a folded card. Ryder opens it slowly, enjoying the unusual, sensuous experience of receiving a letter. Most post he gets these days is at best pedestrian. This is not a letter, however, it's an invitation, and written in the same fluid green as the envelope:

Please come and celebrate with us the joint christenings of Bella Bonnie Perrone and Catherine May Perrone at 3 o'clock on 25 May at All Saints Church and afterwards for tea at Chapel Farm Cottages, Love from Mac and Lucy.

Idyllic. Mac is married to someone called Lucy and they have a baby called Bonnie. For a moment he doubts it can be the same Mac, the impossibility of such life-affirming ordinary blessings being available to any of them has calcified in Ryder's thoughts. He realises that he has not given Mac a chance in his head, has not imagined him picking up the pieces and making his life whole. Ryder now really misses the stairs. And his parents' old house, his home. He really wants to go upstairs, he wants to take the steps three at a time and throw himself on the bed in his bedroom. He would like to be in his childhood bedroom, which he can conjure into being in his head in a flash and bring Bonnie back there as well, replaying the last time they sat there together. It was unbearable and uncomfortable for him to admit how often he had done that.

Bill is channel hopping. Ryder doesn't want to talk to him right now. He takes the invitation into the kitchen and sits down at the table. Without allowing himself to think, he dials the number on the letter. He has no idea what he will say, but it feels urgent and important that he makes the connection with Mac and his family.

A woman answers the phone.

'Hello?' she sounds nice. Ryder's heart stops pounding in his mouth and he sighs and relaxes his shoulders, he had not realised they were up by his ears.

'Hello, I hope this isn't a bad moment to call, I'm Ryder. I got your invitation just now. Umm. I'm a friend of Mac's. Well, you know – I – I— is he there?'

There's a silence, then he hears her smile. 'Ryder, yes, of course. I'm – I mean this is Lucy speaking.' It isn't that he is thinking this could have been Bonnie, it's just that speaking to Lucy now, Ryder has the sense of walking off the edge of a cliff. He truly believes in this moment that anything is possible, tragedy, triumph or a life full of ordinary happiness. No one has the monopoly on any of it. He wonders what Lucy looks like, and, meanwhile, he is talking to her.

'Hello. Yes, you had to be you. Congratulations on everything. I think I mean felicitations actually, that's what you say to girls, isn't it?' He laughs a bit. Oh God, he feels anxious, his heart is pounding, his shoulders have risen again. This is the wife of Mac, oh, get it right – Mac's wife. She's the mother of Mac's child, or rather children. She sounds sweet and gentle. She has called their daughter Bonnie. She's an angel. She's speaking again, laughing too.

'Oh. Thank you, yes. Well. Anything is lovely. How . . . How . . . ? Oh, I'm so glad that you've rung. Mac will be thrilled. Hang on, I'll get him.'

Buoyed by her welcome, not knowing what he expected, and dizzy with relief, Ryder realises his voice is booming crassly. He crosses the kitchen and goes out through a small dark utility room into the back garden. The tabby cat is in there when he opens the door, it chirrups as it passes him, curling like smoke around the door on the route back into the house. Ryder breathes in deep the spring air, and forgets to breathe out as a voice he had forgotten he knew comes on the line.

'Ryder, I'm so glad you rang. I wanted to call you, and I just haven't got round to it yet—'

'Mac?' Ryder's eyes smart. This is new, this feeling of generosity he is experiencing towards Mac and his sweet wife. Hearing him doesn't bring Bonnie back now, as he always believed it would. It brings a wish to know Mac and to see him again.

'Hey, how's it been, Kid?' Mac's voice is hesitant, and achingly familiar. No one has called him Kid for a long time. Ryder walks out through the back gate of the garden and on to the golf course. It's almost dark, the windows in some of the houses along the edge of the fairway glow, and the town looks cosy and safe.

'It's been good,' he says, surprised to find that 'good' is the word that comes first from his heart. He rubs his eyes, and bends closer over the phone. 'Well, you know, it's been everything you can imagine, Mac, and some more, but from where I am at this moment, it's good.'

Mac pauses, Ryder hears his breath hiss, 'Yes. I can imagine,' he says. 'Where are you at this moment, anyway?'

'On the golf curse – sorry, I mean course – behind my parents' bungalow in deepest Deepham, Essex.'

They both laugh. Ryder goes on, 'I had to call. I want you to know I am coming to your christening.

It's been a while, but on 25 May, I will be there in your lovely garden with you all, and lifting a glass to your baby girls. In fact, are they babies? I don't want to sound ignorant or anything, but I am – how old are they?'

Mac's voice is full of laughter. 'Not at all ignorant, how could you know? Bella is three and Catherine is nearly one. They can both walk all over me, literally and metaphorically.'

Ryder grins too. 'Yeah, I can imagine,' he says, and as he says it, he realises that he can't at all. 'Actually, I can't imagine, but I'd love to see you and meet everyone.'

'Come and visit us any time, not just the christening,' says Mac. 'I am so pleased to hear you. I hoped you would come, I'd love Jean and Bill to come too. It took a while to find out their new address. When did they leave Foxley?'

'Nine years ago.'

'It's a good thing, Kid, you know.'

Mac's voice full of empathy down the phone is like a big enveloping hug. Ryder takes a deep breath, and nods. 'Yes,' he agrees, 'it's a very good thing. They've got a life here they seem to like.'

'That's good,' Mac answers. 'And how about you, Kid? Married? Kids? Or life on the open road?'

Ryder grins. 'I live on a boat. Like that mate of yours in Norwich we visited all those years ago.'

Mac laughs. 'God, you mean Jules. I remember that boat. I'd be amazed if it's still afloat, it was riddled with holes and stuck together with putty. Man, we had a good summer that year. You and me and Bonnie.'

Ryder sends a silent prayer of thanks to somewhere that Mac has mentioned her, and even his posture relaxes now there is no taboo.

'We did. I must say, I haven't been in Norfolk much since, but your christening is well worth making the trip for.'

'I hope so,' agrees Mac, 'but Ryder. I don't think this is the moment, but when is the fucking moment – what the hell! I want to ask you if you will be Bella's godfather?'

'Bill and Jean may have to be chipped out of their concrete foot moulds to get them up your way—' Ryder is in relief mode, on rollicking overdrive. But suddenly he stops, mid-air, free-falling into what he has just heard Mac say.

'You what? What did you say, Mac?'

'I said, Lucy and I would like to ask you to be Bella's godfather. I hope it's not an imposition to ask. We wanted to give you time—' Mac stops, Ryder hears Lucy's voice murmur something in the background.

Mac comes back. 'Yeah. We don't want you to feel pressurised. Take a while and think about it. Please.' He pauses then speaks again. 'Perhaps I should have written to ask you, I don't know. But it's been a while, hasn't it, Kid?'

Ryder finds tears ache in his eyes. He doesn't need time. 'No. Yes, it has been a while. Too long, Mac. I accept, of course I do. I feel honoured. I would love that so much. Thank you.'

'Hey, Kid, I'm glad. It means a lot to me, you know that.'

'To me too,' says Ryder. 'I'll see you then.' He clicks the phone shut and walks back towards the night-lit houses.

The spare room in the bungalow is too hot. Ryder wakes gasping in the stuffiness and opens the window. A rush of birdsong and a breath of sweet air pour in. He lies in bed, the corner of the morning available to him through the gap in the small, stiff curtains is heavenly blue, and a lilac bush nods and rustles, scratching the glass of the open window and wafting in a scent of pure spring and a sense of stolen early morning time. Ryder yanks the curtain back without getting out of bed, and closes his eyes against the beating gold as the sun seems to double in strength and direct its efforts to warming him. The sunshine on his skin is blissful; Ryder floats into a trance, his body is a weightless vehicle for a syrup-like sense of well-being and, cocooned, he drifts away. When he next wakes, a breeze has got up and the cat has left a trail of give-away sooty foot prints on the windowsill and down the wall, and settled on the small of Ryder's back with its purr on full throttle. Ryder surfaces from a dream about motorbikes to find himself the victim of a rhythmical kneading assault. The well-being has departed, he can tell he has overslept by the height of the sun in the sky, and is instantly annoyed; he resents the bloody cat's assumption that he is a cushion. It seems to weigh a lot, it seems to weigh him down a lot. It gives him claustrophobia. He throws back the sheet and gets out of bed. The cat leaps on to the floor and sits by the door looking offended and meowing fatly. It bats the door, managing to make a lot of noise for something billed as stealthy. Ryder cannot remember its name, or rather he can, but he chooses not to, pointlessly making a stand of defiance which nobody will be interested in. At least he hasn't kicked it or performed any other act of malevolence towards it.

In the kitchen, he fills the kettle. No one is around, although the murmur of the radio suggests his parents are in the house. Piano music ripples, and Ryder could be seven again.

His father always played Radio 3 loudly enough to avoid conversation while he made coffee for himself and cooked porridge for Ryder and Bonnie before school. This only happened on the rare occasions that Jean went away to visit her mother, but Bonnie and Ryder always enjoyed Bill's moments of domesticity and the unchanging nature of his routine.

The radio beeps on the hour, and Ryder wanders through the house with his cup of tea. Although he doesn't recognise that he had a purpose, he stops when he comes to the door of the room at the end of the hall. He opens the door. The curtains are drawn and the room smells faintly of incense, a hint of patchouli oil and roses. The smell is utterly reminiscent of Bonnie and turns Ryder's insides upside down when he breathes in. He sits down on the red velvet bed cover. It is scattered with embroidered yellow suns in the middle of which are tiny mirrors, and it used to hang over Bonnie's bed, like the festooned ceiling of a harem. Or so he liked to tease her when winding her up. Teasing Bonnie never worked unless she wanted to play the game. Otherwise she just ignored him, rolling her eyes as she lit more joss sticks to hide the smell of cigarettes smoked furtively out of the window.

It is suddenly clear that the reason he has come in here is to find a present to give to his new god-daughter – his only god-daughter, in fact – as a memento of her namesake. Not easy, as he has very little experience of small girls and their taste, but they can't be hugely dissimilar to grown-up girls, and he likes to think he knows what they like, up to a point. He wonders if he needs to ask his mother if it's OK for him to have something from here, something of Bonnie's?

For a moment he has a sense of seeing himself from above. Here he is in Essex with his parents at this soulless house of theirs. It's not his home, it never has been, it's a kind of holding station for their grief. It's odd to realise that while his parents have kept everything that belonged to Bonnie, somewhere along the way he got left out. Perhaps it was because he has a house or rather a boat of his own that they, not unreasonably, didn't make a room or even part of a room for Ryder when they moved here. It's not that he resents it. At the time, he rose to the challenge that this brought, viewing it as freeing and independent-making to not have any ties in his parents' house but, with hindsight, it just seems oddly thoughtless, careless even, as though his feelings don't need to be considered because he enjoys the luxury of being alive. He can make his own way in the world whereas Bonnie is only a memory and she needs them to sustain her. On the mantelpiece in the sitting room there are his football cups, and in the loo there are photographs of him in teams, but his stuff, his paraphernalia, his football boots and leather jacket, his posters and the big green bean bag covered in a red-cherry motif, even his books have all vanished, given to jumble sales, thrown away, just gone. The way things do in life. The only things Ryder has retained himself is his record collection. This room, which in everyone's head is called Bonnie's room though no one says it, has been haphazardly arranged. Arranged in that the bed, the dressing table and the wardrobe are all in the place they would be in if someone used it as a bedroom, but the reality ends there. Black dustbin bags and boxes spilling books and peacock feathers, rolled-up posters, necklaces, clothes and curling photographs fill the floor space. The dressing table is stacked with small boxes and ornaments, there is no room anywhere for a person; the room is too full of memories.

More than anything, it looks like a film set; it has all the props to create a student's room, but none of the personality that inhabits it and brings it alive. Not sure what he is looking for, but trying to focus on something, Ryder opens the wardrobe door. Inside there are dresses and a long dark green coat; they have hung there for years without being looked through, without being pulled out, tried on, chosen or rejected. They have a look of inauthenticity about them and, pulling a flounce of a black-and-white-striped dress, he remembers Bonnie wearing it to his football team's 'Graphic' party. It was one of many parties held in that long-ago last summer. Parties given to mark the end of the lives they had all led as teenagers. Most of the football team was going to university, and Ryder and two team-mates had made an invitation they were very pleased with, showing graphic sex. Or bits of it. Of course, in the end, it wasn't at all graphic, but they had a lot of fun doing it nonetheless. Most people had taken this, not art as the theme. Bonnie was just about the only girl with clothes on, the rest were wearing skin-coloured bikinis. Lila had come to stay that night. She didn't often come back to his house, because he found Bill and Jean too embarrassing. 'What about my parents?' Lila countered. 'They only pretend to be laid-back hippies; underneath they're probably more uptight than yours are.' Lila had drawn a very pretty nude body on to a suede dress. And even better, as Ryder knew, she had a very pretty body under the suede dress too. In the living room, before Lila, Bonnie and Ryder left for the party, Bill hardly looked up from the news on television when they walked in to say goodbye. Jean, however, leapt from her chair as if she had been scalded, and threw her handkerchief at Lila.

'Oh, thank you.' Lila was surprised, but she took the handkerchief and held it. Ryder looked at his mother in astonishment.

'You're mad, Mum. You were trying to cover her up, weren't you?' Lila and Bonnie burst out laughing at the absurdity of the idea, but Jean blushed. Ryder felt a pang of sorrow for his mother's unease. Bonnie drove them home after the party, chatting to Jack all the way, until they dropped him at the end of the track where his parents' farmhouse was. Bonnie was on form. She was always quite happy driving and not drinking, and, Ryder honestly felt, though he never said so, she was not suited to drink – it made her maudlin and seemed to erase her judgement entirely. He sighs now, nostalgic for a time when life was effortless.

All the dresses hanging up in this room were put here by Jean, though they once belonged to Bonnie, but it's not surprising that they look so uninhabited. Can that be the right word for a dress? It's certainly the right word for the room. A whiff of the dry, acrid smell of mothballs curls into the gentle muskiness in the air. Ryder shuts the wardrobe door again. As it swings shut he sees his mother's reflection in the mirror on the door. She hovers on the threshold of the room, the fingers of one hand clasped in the other, anxiety driving lines up her forehead and on through her hairline. Staring at her, Ryder notices the ripples in her hair carefully created by the local hairdresser. He reckons they are more a manifestation of his mother's state of mind than personal adornment.

'Darling, there you are.' She has a way of speaking to Ryder that comes across as if she's from a parallel universe and very surprised to have bumped into him in this life at all. Her eyes meet his briefly, but she doesn't come into the room or invite an embrace. Ryder feels a rush of sorrow. He has never thought of his mother as small before, and now she seems to hardly fill the doorway, and her expression is fearful.

'Morning, Ma, I thought I'd find something of Bonnie's to give to Mac's daughter for her christening.' There is no point in beating about the bush, Ryder feels caught with his hands in the till, and frustrated enough to be direct; it is his mother who has created this set-up. Last night when he mentioned Mac's children's christening, his mother had said, 'I just don't see how we can go,' in a voice of such practised martyrdom that he decided not to discuss any of it further.

Jean moves forward into the room, she puts a hand out, twisting the edge of the curtain, and glances again at Ryder, her eyes moving ceaselessly on around the room. 'I just didn't know what to do with all her things. I thought when we moved they would somehow be dealt with, and they never have been.'

Ryder shuts his eyes, he doesn't want another anguished conversation. There have been too many over the years and they add up to nothing. No one goes anywhere except round and round in confusion.

'I know,' he says, and waits for the next bit apprehensively. But suddenly he is opening his eyes in surprise, as Jean goes on, her voice level, not unhappy or strained, and even a tiny bit warm.

'You know, Ryder, I haven't been stuck in the past as much as you might think. I've accepted that Bonnie's gone. A long time ago in fact.'

Ryder waits, Jean looks at him openly at last, and he sees that the distance in her eyes, a shifting unapproachable element that he has always known, has changed. She is still talking. 'And yes, I think that's lovely – find whatever you think would be – would be – well, yes, take whatever you want for Mac's daughter. And it's time for me to go through this room properly.'

'Don't do it on my account.' Ryder says the first thing that comes into his head. Jean sits on the bed next to him; she smells of china tea and lemons. He thinks of Leonard Cohen suddenly, and the lines where Suzanne feeds him tea and oranges. On a houseboat, come to think of it. He sighs and wonders why he has to be such a fucking idiot to throw back something so fragile, so long awaited as his mother's attempt at building a bridge between them.

But Jean squeezes his hand, her touch is soft and giving, not brittle as he expected. Then she takes both his hands. 'I don't quite know how to say this to you, and I'm very ashamed I didn't say it before, as it's so important.' Her eyes swim, she bites her lip. 'I don't think I've ever told you that I'm glad you didn't die. And I am. Very glad.' Jean gets up and leaves the room, closing the door behind her. Ryder slides down to sit on the floor and his head lolls back against the bed. He has believed the opposite for the last eighteen years.

It takes him a long time to get up off the floor. Long enough for the cat to come back, climb insolently over him and settle with its thrumming purr on the red velvet bedspread. It sounds like a pneumatic drill; Ryder scrambles up and takes the box in front of him over to the window. He knows what he wants to find, and it is just as well he has a specific purpose, for ten minutes of sorting through the folders and notebooks, Bonnie's letters and photographs, is bewildering and transporting. It becomes hard not to see all that there is in her room through his own, very young, grieving eyes from almost twenty years ago.

Beneath a slide of records and an old record player decorated with stickers of rainbows and hearts, is a wooden box inlaid with an intricate mother-of-pearl pattern. Bonnie bought it at a hippie fair in Suffolk, the first time she and Ryder went off on their own together. Ryder was seventeen, and it was for him an initiation festival – he ate hash cookies, learned how to roll a joint, and drank magic mushroom tea. Thanks to Bonnie, he did not make the mistake of doing all these things at once, but over the three days they were there he seemed to be always putting himself where drugs were, thus rendering himself increasingly depraved. He got into trouble on the first night with his sister for having forgotten the ground sheet for their tent. They had to find somewhere else to go in the middle of the night. Ryder remembers trying unsuccessfully to lie on the sharp golden straws of the stubble field, mud clods in his ears, while Bonnie tried to stamp down the stalks of corn, cursing crossly.

'We're giving up. Come on, we've got to find some-where else to sleep.' She yanked him out of his sleeping bag.

'You're like the bloody Princess and the Pea,' Ryder muttered to his sister as they stumbled out of their tent and across to the lighted tepee further along the campsite. Bonnie somehow decided that the lost ground sheet was directly linked to Ryder's soft-drug consumption, and she lectured him all the way home in the car the next day on the evils of addiction.

'Fair enough,' Ryder pointed out to her, 'except you've got three ready-rolled joints from that astrologer bloke who fancies you.' Bonnie giggled, and tried to look innocent, but Ryder knew they were stashed in the wooden box Ryder had at his feet in the car.

Now the wooden box is on Ryder's knees. He opens it, his head full of what he will find in it. He knows it with some conviction as he had put Bonnie's trinkets in it when she died. What else was he to do with her jewellery when it was given back to the family by the police?

'You put all this somewhere safe in Bonnie's room,' someone said, and the jewellery was suddenly in his hands. They were just flimsy beads, a necklace and her special bracelet, but they were what she had been wearing. It was not difficult to know where to put them. It had been difficult to forget them.

It only takes a moment for Ryder to find what he is looking for. As soon as he opens the box it is there on top, the C-shaped silver bracelet Bonnie always wore. It is tarnished dull grey, but its purity and prettiness shine through. It has a tiny silver mouse engraved on the ball at one end, and an apple on the other, both now mistily obscure, but Ryder rubs the bracelet on his shirt and the mouse appears. Magic. Not knowing much about three-year-old girls, he can't be sure, but he reckons there is a good chance that Miss Bella Bonnie Perrone will like this.

Bonnie didn't tell Jean and Bill she was planning to live with Mac, and that they were hunting for a house that summer. She didn't want to expose him to their disapproval, and she didn't want to discuss her boyfriend with them.

'I'll tell them when I've seen the house we're going to live in,' she whispered to Ryder after a row because she had said she was going away again. She said that there was a party she wanted to go to.

'There's always a party,' grumbled Bill.

'Well, what do you expect?' Bonnie yelled at him. 'That's what everyone does at our age. You may have forgotten, but you were young once, Dad.'

Ryder realised that she was fighting his battle for him, breaking away with all the directness and courage he loved in her.

'Chhrrriiisst! Dad wouldn't know a party if it crept up and jumped on him!' Bonnie exploded into Ryder's room, bracelets jangling, her long hair a tangle of curls and five mini plaits she had started undoing and then forgotten about.

'Look at these rat's tails,' she wailed, pulling at them distractedly, 'I was trying to do a *Ten* head. You know, like that film? And I got distracted and forgot I started. Oh bugger. I'm going to miss the train. Or maybe I'm not. What time is it?' There was a stream of thoughts and questions, no answer was needed, Ryder knew that, but she needed him to be there. He loved that mercurial energy that was uniquely his sister's. It was so much easier than having any energy himself. He sighed and lay back, staring at the ceiling, pleased with his new poster of a girl with long brown legs, walking away from the camera, her arse caught mid-swing in orange hot pants, her head turned, her mouth an 'O' of surprise. Cute. Very cute on the ceiling. Or was it oppressive? Ryder was bored and missing Lila. She had gone travelling, and he knew although they hadn't talked about it, that the bubble of their relationship had burst. He felt impatient for the rest of his life to begin, Bonnie suddenly seemed to be so many miles ahead of him.

She was still talking. 'Anyway, it looks stupid to do those tiny plaits if you aren't blonde.' She broke off, noticing her brother was now horizontal on his bed. 'Are you listening?'

'Mm. Definitely.' Maybe the poster would be better on the wall next to the shrine? Maybe there was a good reason why people didn't usually put posters on their ceiling? Lying there, Ryder decided he was not enjoying looking at the orange hot pants. They were definitely in the wrong place. The shrine was so called as it was a collection of black-and-white posters of dead people – Jim Morrison, Sid Vicious, Jimi Hendrix, Steve McQueen and Janis Joplin, in various states of decay. Steve McQueen was the one he most wanted to be. In *The Getaway* with Ali McGraw. She could be on the ceiling in any clothes she fancied and she would never be an oppressive presence.

Bonnie scanned the room. 'God, Ryder, you've got very retro taste. Have all the festivals we've been to turned you into an old hippie?'

Ryder threw a cushion at her and didn't bother to answer. Bonnie bounced up on to her feet and was craning to see herself in Ryder's mirror, most of which was obscured by graffiti drawings of the Jefferson Airplane logo.

'I think I'm going to cut my hair. It looks like a wig. It's too much,' she announced. 'Shall I?'

Ryder nodded, looking deliberately very sensible, then reaching behind himself on to the floor, he grabbed hold of a purple afro wig nesting in a jumble of old fancy dress under his bed. 'And then you will look like this!' he said, putting it on and pouting and stretching in his version of girl posture. 'We can be matching.' He grinned.

Bonnie pulled the wig off him and chucked it out of the open window. 'You're stoopid,' she protested. Giggling, they both looked out to see the wig in the top of the apple tree.

'Oops,' said Ryder, 'better go and get it.'

'No,' Bonnie had her hand on his arm, eyes gleaming mischief, 'let's leave it. It can be like one of those urban myths – you know, how on earth did that mysterious purple wig get there? Like the diving suit left in a tree in the African bush.' Her eyes were shining with mischief. 'And let's have a bet how long it will be before Mum and Dad even notice.'

Laughing, Ryder picked up a cushion and biffed her gently on the head. 'Listen, Betsy baby,' he said in a mock-Chicago gangster voice, 'there ain't never gonna be an urban myth about our back garden. Dream on, princess.'

She biffed him back. 'I hate that Betsy crap. Ooh, look, I've got to go.' She sighed and ruffled his hair. 'Oh, Kid, I wish you would come too.'

He shut the window and stretched. His hands brushed the ceiling, and inevitably the arse of the girl in hot pants. Now that was quite fun. 'Can't. I'm going out with my mates, everyone's leaving next week and this is the last Saturday. I'll come another time next term.'

'OK.' She was wide eyed in the mirror again, drawing kohl in a purple smudge at the corner of her eyes. 'Take me to the train, then. I can't bear to have Dad fussing all the way to the station.'

'Sure thing, Betsy, when d'you wanna go?' Ryder coughed and swaggered in his imaginary Raymond Chandler coat.

Bonnie scrabbled in her bag for lipstick and ran it around her mouth fast and practised as she headed out of the door, swinging back in, mock serious, to add, 'Don't get cute with me, Kid, or I will leave you out of all the fun.'

He drove her to the station with the music up loud. They worked out she would make the connection in Ipswich.

'If I miss it, I'll hitch-hike.'

'Don't be stoopid, not on your own,' said Ryder.

196

Bonnie grinned at him. 'Oh, you're as bad as Mac. I do it all the time, it's fine. Anyway, you do too.'

'Yeah, but I'm a bloke.'

Bonnie made a face. 'Stop it, Ryder! I'm sure I'll get the connection anyway.'

At the station she kissed his cheek and swung her bag on to the train. When she pulled down the window to look out, he blew her a kiss through it and shouted, 'I'm coming up there next week, so get everything in place for me, Betsy.' And she threw him a key on a blue velvet ribbon.

'It's the back door at Mac's – it's always open to you, Kid,' she yelled. Ryder waved her off, his big sister, pretty enough to turn the heads of three guys waiting on the platform and the station guard as she waved back, her mane of curly hair shining as she smiled the same wide grin she smiled when she was four years old.

A familiar sound at an unfamiliar hour is disorientating. The drilling of the door bell was urgent, intrusive like a warped alarm clock. Ryder swam up from deepest sleep, reluctant to return to consciousness, pushing his head further under his pillow until, irritatingly, the pillow wasn't there, and his head was burrowing against the cold plaster of the wall. God, who could be making that fucking racket? Some road workers in his parents' garden, maybe? Digging a road to nowhere? The unreal sense of having a hangover pulsed through his veins and his head swam as he attempted to raise it from the mattress. The horrible bell stopped for a moment, and now there were voices, or maybe it was just the echo in his head of the pub last night. Then it was rattling away again, more like a chainsaw than a drill, Ryder thought, but that might have something to do with the flayed state of his senses. He groaned. Regret is such a frustrating emotion. Too late now to say no to the tequila slammers lined up on the bar. Or to throw cold water on the really stupid race he had sped through with Jack to chase the pints with a couple of vodka shots. The drinks were all downed through a game of pool and no supper, though Ryder dimly recalled a stop at the kebab shop a bit too late at a point of no return last night.

Oh fuck. Maybe life would improve with some breakfast? Definitely life would improve if the drilling noise would stop. He felt vaguely omnipotent for a moment as, in answer to his wishes, the drilling stopped. It was immediately replaced by an episode of *Z Cars* turned on much too loud.

'BEEEP – calling car 274 on the corner of Beechcroft Avenue, come in please – BEEP.'

'Officer Blaine, have you located the household? Residence of a mister – BEEP.'

'Turn off the sodding TV!' Ryder yelled, unable to bear the pain his parents' insensitive behaviour was causing him. In desperation he burrowed further into his bed and wondered for a moment if a cigarette would help. Probably not, but he may as well have one anyway. He reached an arm out, feeling across the floor for the packet he hoped might be lying there. Before he found anything, he heard thudding footsteps in the hall and his father's voice outside his bedroom.

'Ryder, the police are here.'

Panic tasted like metal, solid like a box in his mouth, ramming fear down his throat. In less time than any thoughts left his brain, he found he was upright, out of bed, guilt chasing through him like a flame. What did he do last night? No, not the stuff he had just been remembering, but what did he REALLY do? With whom? Oh fuck, how stupid. At least he didn't drive home. And he wasn't that drunk. Was he? Every nerve ending in his body was screaming panic. Ryder knew he was overreacting, but sweat broke out on his upper lip and he succumbed to the state of paralysis that shock brought. He could not retain a simple thought in his head. He tried to concentrate on suitable clothes to wear for meeting the police. Fuck. What sort of clothes could they be? And if by some miracle it wasn't him, who the hell was in trouble? Dad? Mum? Ryder was pulling T-shirts out of his drawer like a mad man, rejecting the Sex Pistols one, and the New York Dolls one, in favour of the one which said, 'Jesus loves you, but I'm his favourite'. Pulling denim out of the cupboard he hurled all his jeans on the floor. Not a single pair without holes, and holes look criminal. Shorts might be more suitable as the uniform of the upright citizen.

Oh man, he could do with spending a minute brushing his teeth or his hair, but instead Ryder grimaced, rubbed his head to try to boost some circulation, and headed downstairs.

The scene was more surreal than any late-night pub experience. Ryder stopped short in the hall and stared at the disruption of his parents' home. The doorway from the hall into the kitchen was full of people, his mother at the table in her dressing gown, his father standing by the window, and two policemen like cartoon cut-outs with curling wires exuding from their pockets, hairy arms sticking out of their short-sleeved shirts. Their colonisation had extended to the kitchen table, where their black hats sat awkwardly among the cups, milk jug and toast rack. The kettle was shrilling on the stove. No one turned it off. Everyone in the room turned to look at Ryder. Ice ran beneath his skin. He suddenly knew why he was scared. He looked wildly at each person in the overheated room, hoping for a way out. Reality was hurtling towards him and his head pounded. He had not done anything wrong last night; the police were not here because of him. Ryder was afraid because he had nothing to fear. He saw his mother was crying, and comprehension flared bright then dimmed to nothing, like a lamp extinguished inside him.

His voice came from a long way off and it was a whisper. 'It's Bonnie, isn't it?' he said.

Nobody moved, his mother's face was blotched and red, frightening. Ryder walked across and lifted the screaming kettle off the hot plate. Then he turned and unlocked the back door and stepped out into the garden.

Everything he had ever felt in his whole life was jammed in his chest and his throat trying to come out. All the rage and joy, the hope and despair, the love and regret writhed and got stuck. Ryder's skin felt as if it was stretching over and no sound, no tears, no anything came from inside Ryder. The apple tree where Jean hung bags of nuts for the small wild birds was studded with small vivid green apples. And with the purple wig. Ryder walked under heavy branches to the smooth tree trunk and sat down. The dew-soaked grass tickled his bare legs and drenched his shorts and the tree dug into his shoulder blades. Moments passed. They were not real. Nothing was real for a long time again.

In the local paper the photograph they used, apart from the Miss Pears Soap 1970 one, with baby Bonnie looking cute sitting in some cow parsley, was one of Ryder's. Bonnie with her dimple and her eyes lit up, making a daisy chain in the garden with her friend Nicky. Ryder had taken it with his new camera, it was his first roll of film. He had dropped it off to be developed earlier that week. The local camera shop delivered it back free of charge, posting the envelope through the letterbox early on Monday with a note saying, 'With our condolences to you and your family.'

That was the day the police asked for a photograph of Bonnie. But it was worse than that. They asked for a photograph of 'the deceased'. Numbly biddable, Ryder gave the one on top in the envelope. Bonnie was looking up at the lens, her face heart shaped, enquiry in her clear eyes. The colours of the picture, the blue of her eyes, the red of her mouth and the pale gleam of her skin were vivid like a stained-glass window. Her immediacy, the lustrous life shining out of her, was at once both uplifting and stomach churning. Ryder felt his heart clawing up in his chest and up to his throat and a sob trying to escape with the urgent need to rebalance the lopsided wrongness of life without his sister in it.

Staring at the photograph, his tears falling on it, brushing them off angrily, kicking hard fury against the kitchen door, all made not one jot of difference to what had happened.

Ryder couldn't look at the rest of the pictures yet; the first one had swirled into his senses and swallowed up all the courage he hadn't realised he was holding on to. He was still staring at it when the police telephoned. There was no time for him to put up any resistance; he was malleable and compliant.

'Yes. I've got one. Yes. It's here. They're coming now? They're outside? Oh. OK.'

Opening the door to police officers was becoming more normal than anything else. Ryder's aunt Felicity, widow of Jean's brother, had come to stay expressly to prevent the family from suffering these domino-effect experiences, and she clasped Ryder's arm with her small cold hands and shook her head.

'Dear me, let's see,' she fluttered.

Neither she nor Ryder thought to ask what the photograph might be used for. Plump yet delicate in her white dressing gown, Felicity reminded Ryder of a dandelion clock. He never really felt she was there, even the next morning when she stood, stepping back and forth, one arm across her bosom, the other hand pinching the bridge of her nose, her eyes shut but her head bowed over the newspaper. Bonnie was on the front page. Ryder's picture of Bonnie was staring out from the front of the newspaper.

'TOO BONNIE TO DIE' was the headline. And yet she had died. And the local newspaper had all the details.

In a freak accident last week an American car, a Mustang, hit a stag on the A1065 near Brandon, killing outright the passenger Bonnie James, 19 years old and former Miss Manningtree and Colchester Beauty Pageant winner two years in a row. The stag was also killed, and the driver, Tony Mail, an aviation worker at the nearby Lakenheath airbase, was concussed. Darren Parden, 22, from East Tuddenham, was the first witness at the scene. He reported no passengers. Miss James was not found immediately. Her body had been thrown from the car by the impact, and it was not until later on the same evening when Tony Mail regained consciousness in hospital and told the nurses that he had been carrying a passenger, a hitch-hiker whom he had picked up in Ipswich, that a search party returned to the scene of the accident and her body was recovered from the forest.

Reading it, Ryder's mind whirred through the information like a football rattle, juddering loudly to cover anything he could not bear to imagine or did not like. Most of it. Flicking his restless eyes across the printed words, he ended up obsessing about the stag. Where was the dead stag when the car was found? It was unacceptable and impossible that a stag crossing the road on a summer's night could provide the brick-wall ending to a life. Ryder had not believed it was true from the moment he was told. But now he knew better, and he knew that every local hospital has a mortuary, and that Bonnie was in the one in Thetford. Thetford, for God's sake. What the fuck was she doing dying anywhere near Thetford? Why did she hitch when she knew she shouldn't? What happened with the train connection? Why the hell had he not gone with her?

Ryder had not realised how many imaginary conversations he had always held with his sister until he was having them for real with no follow-up. When she was alive they were echoes of things they had talked about or reminders to himself to bring some-thing to her attention. Especially once she was away at university. Ryder always remembered better if he said things out loud, and it was more likely that some-one else would hear. Even if they are dead. She needed to know, for example, that the ribbon on the key was just right for putting over his head. She needed to know he wore the key round his neck, she needed to know Ryder had talked to Mac.

They met him at the mortuary. He had asked Ryder by telephone to ask Bill if he could come too. Bill had cleared his throat, looked up from the newspaper he had been staring at. 'Mm? Yes, of course he can come,' he said mildly.

There were stilted discussions about what she should be buried in, but it was just conversation, painful and halting, something to fill the screaming space. It had no practical purpose, as the truth of the matter contained no Sleeping Beauty corpse to mourn and kiss goodbye. 'Are you coming, Mum?' Ryder asked Jean when he was off the telephone. Jean shook her head. Her smallness in her chair made Ryder shiver. He wanted Lila to come back from Europe, but even more he wanted Bonnie to come back from wherever she was now. She must be somewhere surely?

Bonnie was not laid out pale and perfect in a glass casket to be mourned tastefully. She was smashed to pieces on the A1065. '*A bracelet of bright hair about the bone.*' The line was all Ryder could think of. It had to be metaphysical. Reality was unspeakable, unthinkable.

The police gave the plastic sack with Bonnie's jewellery and the clothes from her overnight bag to Mac. They couldn't give it to Bill because he had walked back out to the car and shut himself into it. He had gone into the hospital morgue alone to identify her.

Ryder wanted to go too, but a doctor met them when they arrived, and after pushing his spectacles up, shoving his hands into his pockets, twisting back and forth on his heel as if stubbing a cigarette into the shining floor of the room, he beckoned them into a room and said, 'Of course, there's no rule to apply here, and you're free to see the – umm your – your sister, I mean.' Small beads of sweat appeared on his forehead. Ryder, who could feel nothing except a creeping numbness, glanced at him then stared at the floor. The room was insufferably hot. 'But I must inform you that the body has suffered considerable trauma.' The small, muffled noise that Bill made was like a red-hot spear to Ryder's soul.

Bill reached a hand out to Ryder and squeezed his arm. 'Ryder, you stay here. Doctor, I'm ready to come with you.' Bill stood by the door, his glasses reflecting the pale green of the floor. Ryder was glad not to see behind them to his eyes. He had a knowing hollow in his stomach, a permanent unease and a sense that something was missing. And the person he needed to get through this with was Bonnie. Left alone, Ryder felt as if he was melting into the ground. He went back outside to the car park with Mac who had been waiting in the entrance lobby. Beside him was the bag of clothes. Neither of them spoke as Mac picked up the bag and carried it to the car. The car was locked, Bill had the keys. Mac and Ryder stood waiting, one on either side of the bag. Ryder shivered in his T-shirt, Mac lit a cigarette. The air held the first bite of autumn though it was still only late August and the sun shone. Pigeons clattered their wings as they moved branches and settled again, cooing in the summer afternoon. A passing car engine on the road swelled then drifted away in pursuit of ordinary business.

God knows how much time passed before Bill returned. He walked towards them and Ryder could not bear to meet his eyes so he shoved his hands into his pockets and moved back from the car, praying that Bill wouldn't speak. He didn't. He fumbled in his pocket for the keys, and when he found them he stood for a moment looking back towards the mortuary building.

'Would you like me to drive, Bill?' It was Mac who spoke, mildly. And out of the corner of his eye, Ryder saw Bill's face shining with tears. Bill nodded.

Ryder stared at the bag of clothes all the way home, terrified of what it contained. And of what it did not. There was neither the yellow T-shirt nor the black skirt Bonnie had been wearing when she left. He was glad he hadn't seen her body, but his thoughts returned to her face smiling at him, and tears poured down his face as they drove home, and he let his desolate mind linger on his memory of Bonnie waving from the train the last time he ever saw her.

PART 2

'I want to know if you will risk looking like a fool for
love, for your dreams, for the adventure of being alive.'

'The Invitation'
Oriah Mountain Dreamer

10

Grace
Norfolk

Although it is May, and I left New York in a heat-
wave, here in Norfolk an early morning breeze plays
and the smell of the sea is uplifting. Diamond raindrops flutter and chime against the glass of the
window and the tiled roof, and small petals of white
blossom whirl like wet confetti in the air. This house
is developing by stages into Lucy and Mac's home,
but the bathroom is still more like something from a
Barbie Doll set from 1955. If they had Barbie in the
Fifties, which I don't suppose they did. Apparently
the whole house was a hymn to coloured plastic and
wipe-clean wallpaper when Lucy and Mac moved in,
but they have been stripping it back to an older state
– more of a cow byre, to be honest, with whitewashed
rough walls and huge exposed plank-like floor boards;
wonky and curved as if reclaimed from ships' hulls.

The bathroom is the last outpost of kitsch. The bath and basin and loo are all made of sky-blue plastic and the floor is the same colour, as though the whole thing came out of one giant mould. The mirror, mounted in a frame of yellow bakelite shards, like plastic razor shells, reflects my eyes. Huge pupils flaring like ink. Something to do with jet lag, I suppose. It is four o'clock in the morning.

The warmth of my body is flowing out through my feet, into the pink- and grey-scalloped lino, then through into the concrete and then, I suppose, on into the earth as this bathroom is downstairs. My warmth vanishing into the ground. And chilliness coming up in its place. It is so early it almost counts as late last night, and I seem to be stuck on New York night time. I've been here a week now, I'm going back soon after the christening, and I have seen the dawn every morning. This gives plenty of time for cleaning, and Lucy says the house has never been so thoroughly scrubbed.

Today the bathroom is my project, and I gain deep satisfaction through squirting blue-liquid cleaner in a wavy line around the bath. Lucy and Mac are away, they left for London last night after putting the children to bed, so I am in charge.

'Don't feel you have to do any more cleaning,' Lucy cautioned before they left. 'Looking after the girls is more than enough, thank you so much.'

But as I wandered in here, wide awake and energetic, the bath seemed to me to be crying out for a scrub, and anyway, it's so therapeutic. And this whole trip to England is proving very therapeutic. I miss

Jerome. Even though I didn't love him and it needed to end, there's a big gap in my life, full of silence, and every so often I turn round to see he's there, or think of calling him to talk something through, and it takes a moment to comprehend that he's not there any more. I don't know how long it takes to accept this, but coming away from New York has helped shrink the sadness back into perspective. After all, it was and is the right thing to do. We could not go further together without mutual willingness, and I was suffocating. The truth is that I feel alive now, and most days I am thinking about work. I love the quicksilver state of inspiration and the rush and spark of ideas, and in time, everything heals and it isn't really a big deal, it's just life.

There is a painting by Brueghel I first saw on a slide in a lecture at art school more than fifteen years ago. The painting depicted Icarus falling to his death – his dramatic final moment unnoticed by various people, including a farmer and shepherd going about their normal business – his defining tragedy nothing to them. I met Dad for a drink after the lecture. We didn't meet often, and this occasion was memorable because we had a really good conversation. He told me that W.H. Auden had written a poem about the painting, and he said that humility comes when we can accept that human beings experience suffering and miracles in the midst of ordinary life. He was just as he always was when I saw him, quiet and thoughtful and contained. We sat in a pub by the river, at a table outside.

Willow hung low over the green-black water and a swan glided past on a surface so smooth her reflection was symmetrically clear beneath her, the whole pattern like folded origami. Her feathers plumed cool marble-white as she sailed on. I watched her disappear behind the willow and thought her beauty was a million miles from poor old Icarus and his overheated wings. Dad got up to go, and we hugged one another tight. His cheekbone bumped mine as we kissed goodbye and when I looked after him, the sun dazzled and the swan's image burned against my eyelids. I didn't know that Dad was ill, nor did I know that I would not see him again until he was in hospital; it was just as he said, an invisible tragedy no one knew was happening.

The bath is pristine now. It looks too good to pass up but the last thing I want right now is a bath. I get into it anyway without undressing. When I was first in New York I slept in the bath in Dorelia's room for two weeks until another room came up for rent. Mind you, a bed was not an urgent priority, I don't think Dorelia and Stephan and I ever slept much, we were always propping up the bar in the clubs that are open when everything else is closed. I loved the anonymity and the acceptance of everyone I met. I was just Grace, and no one asked where I came from, no one cared if I had parents or a past, all of us were high on the energy of the city and wanted to cram as much experience as we could into our waking hours.

Through the warped window panes, day is diluting the sky and the blue is tinged with pink-velvet softness. I should go back to bed but I am still not tired, and then the children will be up and I must give them breakfast. To fill in the time until then the only solution is more cleaning. 'Turn crisis into virtue,' I pant to myself, letting the hot tap in the basin run. Doing the cleaning really helps, it always helps. I hope it's not all I am good for in this life, but if it is, it's not the end of the world.

Honeysuckle is bursting through the open window, only recently unsealed and seemingly a kind of motorway for nature to enter the house. I catch a spider on its thread and waft it back outside. Jerome pops into my head again, accompanying me through the early hours and saving me from being on my own, just as he did when I was with him. He will not be on his own now, he keeps his life very full. Sport and work are parallel obsessions and he plays a lot of squash, has a twenty-year-old personal best to beat of 3 hours 17 minutes for the New York marathon, and keeps abreast of his deals, his metabolism and his blood pressure through various bits of electronic technology more or less implanted on his hands or ears. When I was with him, the only time he was not on his mobile phone when he was awake was when we were having sex, although, as I told Lucy over a bottle of pink wine in the garden a couple of evenings ago, 'It's only a matter of time before he finds some sex toy he can use on whoever he is sleeping with now that also communicates with his office.'

Lucy snorted and spilled her wine, Mac caught the glass as it rolled off the table, and raised his eyebrows.

'I'm beginning to think sisters should come with ratings like films,' he said. 'The combination of you two has got to be an 18.'

'Or X-rated, but definitely adult,' said Lucy, satisfaction ringing in her voice, echoed in her flushed cheeks, her dishevelled hair. She was in the mood for letting off steam. As she said herself, most of her evenings are spent putting away small children's clothes, or endlessly putting and re-putting to bed the small children themselves. A couple of glasses of wine and a lot of laughter were unlocking memories for her of being a grown-up and having fun. I didn't see that we were acting like adults myself, I personally reckoned we were being as infantile as three-year-old Bella blowing raspberries on her arm in the bath. Mac stroked Lucy's shoulder as he replaced the glass on the table, his fingers brushing lazily across her skin. Lucy poured more wine and tilted her chair back, raising her glass in a toast. 'Mmm. Sisters,' she murmured. 'Actually, any relations apart from parents are welcome.'

'But you haven't got any parents,' Mac pointed out, teasing, leaning his elbows on the back of his wife's chair and twisting a strand of her hair around his finger. Lucy rolled her head back towards him and she smiled up at him. Her look of love pierced my heart. Whatever it is Mac and Lucy have got looks good to me. I wonder if I am anywhere near getting it for myself? Suddenly, in the bathroom, I have a sword of Damocles moment as I realise that the answer lies within me.

Something ticklish and damp brushes against my leg. I shriek and turn round. I may have learned to love spiders, but not every creature on God's earth.

'Urgh, what is it?' England is not supposed to be full of large creepy crawlies. In America I am familiar with assaults from roaches and moths and beetles. I wouldn't say I accept them, but they are in films and often they are around the places I have lived. Fair enough in Brooklyn or Long Island, but there is no place for them in my sister's bathroom in Winterton-on-Sea.

'It's me, not an it.' Bella's voice always surprises me as its huskiness suggests a cigarette habit a three year old cannot hope to achieve.

'You're up. Great, I was getting lonely.' Bella grins, adorably rumpled in her pyjamas, her eyelids heavy with sleep, her hair a light nest with straws sticking out. She pats my bottom, which is at her own head height, then looks me up and down slowly.

'Why are they orange?' she asks, squinting at me, and waving a hand towards me that encompasses my naked flesh and the orange knickers that are my pyjamas.

'Oh. You know . . . some things are.' I don't have a good answer, I am preoccupied wondering whether Bella has noticed my rubber gloves. Is it disturbing for a small child to find their aunt vigorously cleaning the bathroom at four-thirty in the morning in her bra and knickers?

Far from it. Bella seems very happy with the status quo, and pushing up her sleeves she grabs a flannel and begins wiping the floor with it.

'Your gloves match. That's why. It's work clothes. I'm doing it too.'

'Oh yes.' The mood is much cheerier now in the bathroom. I give up on the wistful notion of removing the gloves and getting a dressing gown on. Suddenly Bella hurls down the flannel and with a deft twist, removes her pyjamas. 'My pants are green,' she says. 'I need green gloves. Do we have some?'

'I doubt it,' I reply and, giving her my gloves, I perch on the side of the bath to talk to her. 'Why are you up, Bella? It's practically still last night and we've got all day, haven't we?'

'It's good to start now. You have.' She seems to have all the answers, and nimbly she climbs on to the corner of the bath, and begins squirting the mirror with the glass cleaner. Through the open bathroom door I look down the landing and have a sudden flash of being at home in Mac and Lucy's colourful messy house. When I arrived here I was on a high of excitement from a week in London, and I was in no mood to be daunted by the pouring rain, though the reality of being in Norfolk where so many demons of the past lurk for me was nerve-wracking. I told Lucy I was scared of the idea of all our ancestors sucking me back into a life here. She gave me a long, steady look then burst out laughing. 'You are such a nut case,' she laughed, 'the demons are here, all right, but no more than anywhere else, and they are only in your head. It

218

doesn't take long to see past them, babe.' The dimple in her grin was unchanged from our childhood. And Bella has inherited it.

'Right, Aunt Grace, in the bath! You first.' God, she's bossy. And she pops up from under the veil of a towel hanging beside the basin, and climbs on to the side of the bath to boss me around.

'More squeeze?' Bella proffers the glass-cleaning spray, both hands round the squirter, adorably careful and polite. In the goldfish bowl of life she has moved on from wanting me to have a bath, thank God. The soundtrack outside the window has intensified with clattering from some bird, mad chirruping from others, and a poignantly sweet song I didn't know I knew was a thrush until now. Hearing it takes me to a memory of being with Aunt Sophie in her garden when I was about seven. 'There is never a true silence in a garden,' she told me, 'or a stillness. Everything is growing and changing, it's just that you can't always see it or hear it. And one of the joys of being small, like you' – she poked me gently and smiled teasingly – 'is that you can notice it all if you want to.' I certainly chose not to notice any of it for a long time by living in New York, but now, with the honeysuckle scent mingling with bath cleaner and the dawn chorus ringing in my ears, I have no choice. Bella gives me a calculating look and squirts herself with the purple glass-cleaner.

'Just a bit dirty on my tummy,' she says, dabbing herself with the cloth. Stripping off her rubber gloves I twirl her into the bath.

'Oops, let's wash this off and go and get Cat. She'll be awake soon.'

I am in charge of the girls until tomorrow when Lucy and Mac will be back with Mac's aunt who is staying for the christening. So far childcare is more of a joy than I ever imagined it could be. Mind you, it's now five-thirty in the morning, but I like being up early. I reckon the trick is to sleep when they do; is jet lag the perfect foil for toddlers? I follow Bella out of the bathroom, and we meander to the front door and out to inspect the day.

'It's not raining,' she says, as if it has been, which it has not.

'Good,' I take her hand, 'we can have breakfast in the garden.'

'I'd like olives,' says Bella. 'Olive pie.'

'Right.' I can't imagine what she means, I just hope it isn't what she says.

Breakfast in the garden is so much more difficult than I imagined it could be. The logistics are impossible. How do you hold down a baby, limber and slippery as a landed salmon, while trying to cut bread for olive pie which is actually going to be a sandwich?

Cat's belly is stretched into a curve, pale pink like the underside of a mushroom. She is so delicate, with her tiny fingers laced in my hair and her cheeks the most kissable curves, her existence is a miracle. I don't know how something so ethereal can live and breathe. I panic that she should have sun cream on her, that she might eat a worm, that I might put her down on something sharp and that I should hold her all the time. Where is the sun cream and how is one supposed to apply it? She is slippery enough already. Cat has writhed out of her dress, out of the small wheeled trolley I tried to wedge her in while making the breakfast, and out of her tied-on sun hat, with the easy contempt of Houdini under-using his skills on a pair of shoelaces. Lubrication would render her lethal, and wholly unmanageable. The eggs have been boiling for ages, Bella has laid the table outside the back door with ketchup, multicoloured sprinkles and a tin of corned beef. I am suddenly hungry and exhaustion hits me, blanking the earlier joy, and my common sense. I wonder if they are as hungry as I am? They are certainly bearing it with more aplomb. It's not even seven o'clock in the morning and I have no idea what I should try to persuade the children to eat and what is just table decoration. Bella slides a plate full of olives on to the table and, sitting down with a teaspoon, begins to eat them. She knows what she wants. But is it good for her? Does it matter when you eat olives? After all, we eat loads of olives on holiday, who is to say that breakfast olives are less healthy? Not me. Cat is determined not to do anything that I want her to. She purses her lips and turns her head away from the spoonful of cereal as if she is Lady Macbeth and I am administering hemlock. She waves her small hand in protest and accidentally slaps me in the eye. Or is it an accident? It's awful to admit that, at this moment, I hate Cat.

'There is a screw-on chair,' announces Bella, spitting an olive stone across the table. She could be a torturer, so emotionless is her tone of voice. A white pick-up truck slows at the gate to the road, the engine idling while another car passes on the narrow lane. Squinting in the dappled morning, I see the driver looking up the slope of the garden to where we are sitting at a table which appears to be floating on the long grass. The man half waves, or maybe he's adjusting something on the open window of the truck, but a smile bursts out of me, unexpected like the sun wheeling out from behind a cloud. The truck is still hovering at the gate. As the man changes gear to drive off, the wheels spin a little on loose stones. He looks down and away. The angle of his head, the shadow of his temple, the shape of his jaw, all of these subliminally observed elements tell me he has seen me and I suspect he is smiling.

It's an infinitesimal non-exchange, but it feels like being given a bunch of flowers, or a glass of champagne. Stumbling back inside the house, I am blinded by the darkness of the kitchen after the sunshine in the garden. My head spins as I butter the toast. I have been told by Bella that it's got to be soldiers, which completely confuses me.

'What sort of soldiers?'

'White ones,' she says coldly. The toast is brown. Buttery cavalry soldiers? Artillery? Desert Rats? Humming a fragment of Lou Reed's 'Perfect Day', which is definitely one for my desert-island disc list, I rummage in the bread bin and find some breadsticks. Perfect soldier material – bayonets, in fact. Balancing them next to the now overboiled eggs, I find I am absurdly buoyed up. Sunshine, a man in a truck, the beautiful day, all contribute to my sense of excitement, and the frisson of sex, and with it a sudden whiff of fantasy and fun which career through my veins at a galloping pulse. No longer interested in food myself, the focus on feeding the tiny nieces vanishes.

I suddenly remember something I learned from a Native American on a trip Jerome and I made to a Reservation. The whole thing was deeply embarrassing, I felt like a crass tourist and was so ashamed of my white skin. I only spoke to one Indian elder, and he gave me a piece of paper with a prayer on it. I gave him a fifty-dollar bill and got lectured by Jerome.

'He'll only spend it on booze; they're all alcoholic,' he scolded, his palms somehow epitomising superiority as they rested flat and fat on his knees.

'You know what? I'm sure you're right, but it doesn't matter what he does with it; that's up to him.'

Jerome smiled and hugged me. 'You're right, honey. It's up to him, and everyone deserves their dignity. Show me the poem.'

It was beautiful, and I learned it off by heart. A bit of it runs through my head now:

> *It doesn't interest me to know where you live or how*
> *much money you have.*
> *I want to know if you can get up after the night of*
> *grief and despair,*
> *Weary and bruised to the bone,*
> *And do what needs to be done for the children.*

I definitely feel weary and bruised to the bone, and it's the children that have done it to me. This is not coming naturally to me. Plopping the eggs on a tray, the sulphurous smell of the hard orange of the yolks hits the back of my throat with a slug of nausea.

Only Cat is sitting where I left her at the table, Bella is out of sight somewhere near, I can hear her humming.

'Your eggs are done,' I yell, and try to push the breadstick into one. It is not happening, the egg has morphed into yellow playdough. Mum always used to overboil eggs – that's clearly where I learned my cooking skill, and I also remember that what she used to do was decant them into a cup and announce, as though delivering a huge treat, 'Look, darlings, Irish eggs!' I try this on the children, without much conviction in my voice. Not surprisingly, they push them away. Bella eats another olive, this one dipped in sugar. I decide I didn't see.

I am ridiculously disoriented by the non-encounter with the man in the truck. Desperate is the word that springs to mind. Though any link, no matter how tenuous, with a strange man is a welcome surprise. Jerome diverted all my pheromones for so long, and finishing with him stamped the last embers of them to ash. To find a whole fountain of desire and sexiness and possibility leaping into being at the sight of some bloke in a white truck is intoxicating and seems almost illicit. The way I was hooked by Jerome, who reeled me in from my low-rent life in my East Village apartment and took me to Brooklyn Heights where everyone moves in and lives two by two, ready at the drop of a hat to go forth and multiply like species from the Ark, involved no effort from me at all. Just a lot of gratitude. I was truly grateful to be looked after, and too busy working to think about making an effort for myself. Sometimes I just felt I was living out a script. I stomped around making mountains out of molehills and building castles in the air until the spool ended almost halfway through my three score years and ten. There doesn't seem to be a script for the next bit.

Running the show here in Winterton for the next twenty-four hours is a little daunting. It is hard to imagine how the rest of the day will pass. Will it pass? Or will time just stick for ever? I have been much too afraid of losing out to time to ever think about what it might be like to come back home to England and marry someone. Nothing has yet convinced me that I want or am capable of spending my days with small children. At the moment, time is too precious and yet too ephemeral, and that is how I like it. Bella climbs on to my lap, leans back and sighs. Her body emanates warmth like a hot-water bottle and I love the way she has flopped on to me as though I'm an armchair. Kissing the top of her head, I wonder if it's possible that her hair can actually smell shiny, it's soft, spooled silk beneath my lips. Like a distant boiler firing up, a tiny adjustment occurs inside me; the difference between being lonely and loved seems as simple as putting my arms around Bella. She twists to look up at me, and waves a pair of goggles.

'When can we go swimming?' she asks.

We are on the edge of Norfolk, there are miles of beaches, and I haven't been to any of them since coming here. We will go where I went when I was small, and see how it has changed.

11

Ryder
Norfolk

It's the day before the christening, Ryder is driving to Norfolk. Mac had invited him to stay, but Ryder has some work further north on the coast. And he is nervous. Turning up tomorrow will be enough time there. Seeing Mac will be strange. Or maybe it won't. Anyway, tonight he will stay with Ed, a guy he met a few years ago on a salvage project in Iceland. Ed is a boat builder, married with four kids, and he has a brusque exterior easily pierced with a joke. Ryder likes his dry, straightforward approach to life and his easy silences. He and Ryder have kept in touch, with boats as the common language deepening their friendship, and Ed has extended an open invitation to Ryder to visit. Now is the right time for sure, and seeing the four children will be a good warm-up act for the moment of meeting his god-daughter.

Ryder leaves London early, he will probably make Red Lodge for breakfast. He is excited and the world is full of possibility. As well as the bracelet, now polished and wrapped in a box with a bow, he has a basket full of foil-wrapped chocolate ducklings and two Barbie dolls. He is especially pleased with the dolls, and grateful to Anthea, the secretary at the gas company headquarters which currently employs him, for giving them to him.

'If you have god-daughters, you will need Barbies,' she had told him at the beginning of the week, and the next morning he was in the office, she winked and pulled out a small floral bag from under her desk.

'Here. My daughters are out the other side of this stage now, and they are much better handed on,' she said. Bemused, Ryder peered into the bag, It was full of small explosions of nylon and plastic. Anthea leaned forwards across the desk on her elbows and her bosom filled the whole space between her shoulders and the desk top.

'Little Mermaid Barbie and Fantasy Miss Barbie are in there,' she said.

Ryder raised an eyebrow. 'Are you sure it's suitable?' He grinned. 'And will they really like second-hand ones?'

'Oh yes, they love quantity. They will already have hundreds, I expect, but they will like the kit from other girls, honestly.' A colleague of Anthea's walked past and paused to pick up a package. 'Oh, Barbie, excellent,' she said.

Ryder was amazed. 'Is it a secret code?' he asked.

'For little girls, yes,' Anthea told him.

The road swings through a new chalk cutting, a scattering of feathery grasses and clumped thistles like old ladies' hats have grown on the moon surface surrounding him. Yellow and pink smudges tint the sky ahead and the tarmac gleams blue-grey and empty. On through the early morning landscape. Ryder is listening to the radio. A song he doesn't know comes on and the lyrics stir in him a longing for intimacy. Having no girlfriend is an unfamiliar state for Ryder, and he misses warmth, a female voice on the phone, the soft thighs in his bed. He misses sex and hot skin and laughing with someone you have made love to. It's been a while. Apart from a brief and actually quite potent encounter in Paris with Sophie, the girlfriend in his life before Cara. She was married and it was never going to be more than a remembrance of things past, and they met by chance and of course he shouldn't have done it, but he was lonely and so was she, and we all have animal needs and – oh, that's no excuse and guess what – if he was trying to fix anything within him, it didn't work. Ryder turns off the radio and pushes in a CD. 'Sexual Healing' by Marvin Gaye. Why not?

It doesn't take an expensive shrink in St John's Wood to figure out that the long line of girls Ryder has not been prepared to love have been at best pain-killers for him, at worst chimerised versions of Bonnie, doomed from the first moment he is attracted to them not to live up to the memory of his beautiful, beloved dead sister. Lila was the first casualty when she came back that autumn. Ryder could remember his sense of separateness when he saw her. He could not reach her.

And now it doesn't work for him any more. The emptiness of a random encounter, the low, creeping boredom that he has let come into all his relationships, killing them with stealth like mustard gas, is not what he wants. But.what could there be instead? His unruly heart pounds. This is the big question. And speaking of a pounding heart, there is never a morning when Ryder can wake up without his heart leaping in his throat, hammering him awake so he starts from sleep. Will it ever be different? On the plus side, it means he gets up early. That's when he runs, or walks, anything, but he has an urgent daily need to go somewhere and subsume his racing heart. Today it was into the car and on to the road. It's still not quite eight o'clock, and he is sweeping off the Thetford bypass and into the Red Lodge truckers service station.

It's years since he's been here, or, in fact, to a proper old-fashioned motorway café, though he remembers them from childhood holidays driving to Norfolk, and the noisy friendliness of the atmosphere after too many hours in the car with Bonnie hovering on the brink of vomiting and their mother fussing. There are not many of these places left now, most have been consumed by petrol stations with huge shops selling coffee and tea from machines and rubbery microwaved sandwiches. Ryder feels the passage of time in his own life suddenly and it is uncomfortable to find himself troubled by change and nostalgia, just like his father. Red Lodge is off the Newmarket bypass, and its strength is that it has been forgotten by everyone except the lorry drivers, and no one cares whether it is there or not. So, in defiance, it is. Thus it has not needed to modernise. Inside it is the same as it ever was. The steam from the espresso machine hisses, the windows are all shut, creating a good fug, and the walls are covered in black-and-white signed photographs of boxers, singers, glamour girls and Eurovision song contest winners.

Ryder orders and sits down next to a window overlooking a field of horses. Buttercups glint like gold in the grass and a foal lies flat on its side, sleeping close to its mother, as she swishes her tail and grazes. Above the horses an oak tree is unfurling its leaves, and the shade from it spreads a purple blanket into the field. Ryder's coffee arrives, and he sits in a daydream, staring out at the day. The foal's ear twitches, it lifts its head, which looks like a big effort. Ryder wonders if horses have a lot more in common with giraffes than he had previously noticed. The answer would seem to be yes, as a moment later the foal begins to unpack lengths of limb and arrange them as awkwardly as possible in a bid to stand up. He makes it and immediately frisks off around the field as if on a lap of honour, prancing, half ungainly, half floating, and reminding Ryder of a seahorse. A golden sense of well-being pumps through Ryder as he watches the foal playing. Breakfast is good, too. And it slowly dawns on him that it is actually quite easy to feel happy. He heads back to his car. His meeting is in King's Lynn at ten. Ed wants to show him a boat and to take him for a pint at lunchtime. The sun is shining and the day is his. The boathouse he is forever building in his mind needs a piece of ground. Or rather, it needs water. The house next to it needs ground. It could be on the marshes up near where Ed lives, on the footings of an old barn. Maybe today he will find what he is looking for somewhere in Norfolk. For the first time in a long while, Ryder believes that anything is possible.

The meeting in King's Lynn this morning was both brief and successful, neither of which Ryder was much expecting, and Ed sounded relieved and slightly manic when Ryder called to say he wanted to drive along the coast for a bit.

'Sure, I'm scraping *Susannah*'s underbelly and looking for leaks,' he shouted into the phone, and Ryder could hear the whine of a drill in the background and the jaunty metallic pulse of a pop-radio station.

'Is *Susannah* enjoying it?'

'Well, she bloody well should be. She'll sink like a stone if I don't sort this, and if I do, I've got a buyer who'll hand over thirteen grand for her tomorrow.'

'Why, what is *Susannah*? I thought she was an old crock?'

Ed gave a crack of laughter. 'She's rare,' he said. 'I'll show you later.'

It is mid-afternoon, Ryder is sitting outside a café on a cliff in a seaside village where time has done no marching on at all. His sketch book is open, but he puts down his pen and looks around him. Everyone seems to be asleep, and the café awning flaps blue and white, shrimping nets and windmills in a basket by the door. Ryder has bought two of the windmills for Bella and her sister, and he goes back in now to buy a whole lot more for Ed's children. In the café he orders another cup of tea and chooses a postcard for his parents. The picture on the front is a tinted photograph of a ruined tower, poppies flickering around it and along the edge of the cliff like flames. The lack of space more than anything is what drew Ryder to the card, and he reads the small-printed paragraph on the back:

> Clement Scott brought popularity to the Cromer coastline when he christened this area Poppyland and wrote his famous poem 'The Garden of Sleep', which contains the lines:
>
> O! heart of my heart! Where the poppies are
>   born,
> I am waiting for thee, in the hush of the corn.
> Sleep! Sleep!
> From the Cliff to the Deep!
> Sleep, my Poppy Land,
> Sleep!

It's an Ealing comedy. He wonders what his mother will think of the appalling whimsy of the poem. It's nice to have a joke with her, that's for sure. It may be slight, but it's a beginning.

233

Dear Mum and Dad,

You will remember this place, I think you told me you came here when you were first married. It may have been a resort then. Frequented by poetry lovers, perhaps? Now it is not. Back to see you later this month and find out what on earth you did here. On second thoughts, maybe not. But seeing you for sure.

Love R

His mother will remember Poppyland; will his father? Ryder realises with a pang that he doesn't really know them at all. He would like to change that. Voices float up from the beach; it's the family he saw down there earlier, little girls playing with their mother. Their voices ripple and flutter towards him on the breeze and he lights a cigarette and moves over to the railings. Without thinking, he flicks the cigarette away over the cliff. He has leisure to regret this as it plummets inexorably towards the woman and the children kneeling in the sand beneath him. He closes his eyes.

'Oh,' she cries, and Ryder forces himself to look down. She lunges at the baby, rugby tackling her away, as the burning ember lands next to them. The woman picks up a stone and grinds it into the sand then sits up, brushing her hair away from her cheeks and glares at him from behind her sunglasses.

'Bloody hell. You threw your cigarette at us. And it was alight.'

Why had he thrown it? Why didn't it get blown off course?

He opens his mouth to apologise as she takes off her sunglasses and her face becomes visible.

It's her. Ryder's heart crumples. It's her with small children. Grace. The girl from Denmark. She's got children. If Ryder could step back at this moment to observe his reaction instead of churning with it on the edge of the cliff, he would notice that while he has accepted her presence in this remote spot without a blink, but has focused keen disappointment on her circumstances, she hasn't recognised him. He feels as if he has been shot, without knowing what that feels like, but his heart is pounding, his mouth full of the metal taste of adrenaline. Has she forgotten him? Or is it the sun in her eyes? God, is it not really her? She is not looking friendly; her eyebrows curve like a question mark and she has pulled the children towards her in instinctive protection. He wonders if he should introduce himself, but it doesn't seem like the right moment. She is looking a little like a mother tigress protecting her cubs. He rubs his hand through his hair. The only thing to do is to admit responsibility and apologise.

'Yes. Sorry. It was a mistake.' Odd to be able to talk as though he is standing beside her, when she is a hundred feet beneath. But the vantage point of the cliff is not giving him any helpful moral high ground. She seems pretty annoyed.

'What do you mean it was a mistake? We're the only people on the beach. There is nothing for miles.

Could you not throw it somewhere empty? Or even maybe just stamp it into the ground, or put it in an ashtray?' She shrugs, steps back, and looks up at him again. 'I don't understand which bit is the mistake, when you deliberately throw something at someone. Or several someones. Us, in other words.'

God, she is going on a bit. Ryder becomes aware that he has a big grin on his face now, it can't be helped. She is very lovely. Girls like this are rare. It's a good thing she doesn't recognise him.

'Er. Maybe you're right; it wasn't a mistake. I meant to hit you with a lighted cigarette,' he says to tease her. It comes out a lot more combative than he means it to.

She can raise one brow in an arch while the other stays still. She can't know how captivating this is to him, nor that he suddenly doesn't want her to recognise him. There is a gleam of laughter in her eyes, a spark of joy, and he's certain she hasn't recognised him. She might be flirting with him. Or is he imagining it? It is over fast, and she looks away with her smile.

'Oh,' she says. It hangs in the air like an invitation. Or that's how Ryder interprets it. He doesn't want her to recognise him now. He doesn't want to hear that she is married, though the evidence is squatting next to her in the sand, unpacking the picnic basket she has put down. Maybe it isn't her. Maybe it wasn't her at Copenhagen airport in the winter either. Perhaps he just imposes his memory of Grace on to other women who look like her. The stillness of the air becomes the intake of breath between them. It's her, all right.

Behind Grace, the sea flattens to a silk skin. Still. There's no movement, no time passing. Warm air like a sigh flows off the cliffs, on to the surface of the water. It settles glass calm, heavy, oily, sensuous. Not a wave or a ripple, but a lazy blue-green, flat like a bed, a whisper coming from the depths like wind through summer grass. She has sand on her fingers. Ryder notices this, and it is as if he has spoken it, for she runs the back of her hand down her skirt, shaking off the crumbs of beach, and tilts her head, squinting slightly to see him without shading her eyes. He realises that it is not so much that she doesn't recognise him but that she cannot see him properly in the low sunlight. His pulse races faster as the possibilities this opens up spark and ignite into another flame of excitement shooting through him.

A beep of a horn sounds behind him and Ryder almost jumps over the railing in surprise. He had not noticed the engine, the sidling yet sudden presence of Ed in his pick-up truck. He feels as if he is swimming up from the deep, breaking the surface and emerging somewhere brash and noisy. It surprises him to realise how intensely he had been moved in the previous moments. Or was it hours? Intoxicating. Surely what should be next in the programme for the day is more flirting, the magical disappearance of the children and a languorous hour or two of lovemaking with this woman who might be Grace. Nice fantasy, shame about the stark reality and the arrival of Ed. Ryder heaves a sigh.

'God, I'm sorry, I was miles away. Are you early?'

'Nope. Come on, mate.' Ed squints at Ryder, his head against the sun, low now and flooding pink across the still sea. 'I need to get back and tackle the rigging to get that sodding boat in the water before the owners arrive. We've got the tide for an hour or two now.'

Ed gets out of the pick-up and, feeling in the breast pocket of his shirt, pulls out a packet of cigarettes and lights one, breathing a cloud out over the cliff edge as he rests his elbows on the rail next to Ryder and looks down. Cool purple shadows are drawing a new surface across the sand, bringing depth to the red of Grace's skirt where it falls long in front as she bends to pull a garment over the head of the baby. Her hair falls across her face like another shadow; she doesn't look up again, but murmurs something to the baby and bends to kiss the top of her head. The encounter is over.

Ryder sighs again and turns to his friend. 'I'm all yours, Ed,' he says, rubbing his eyes, running his hand through his hair, kicking one foot against the tall white post with the life belt on it, and stretching tall, hands up in a spine-clicking arc, fingers interlocked and pulling the back of his head. His sketch pad is balanced on a post in front of him. He picks it up, sighing.

Ed raises an eyebrow. 'Where have you been? Away with the bleedin' fairies or what?' He scans the beach, his gaze moving past Grace and the children with not even a pause of curiosity. Ryder feels absurdly affronted. How can Ed not be intrigued by her? There must be something wrong with him. Ed digs his hands deep in his pockets and kicks a pebble into the dry grass beneath the railings. He purses his lips and half whistles, changes his mind and pulls his hands out of his pockets. Big hands, clasped now as he leans on the railings next to Ryder. A whiff of engine oil and a restless, slightly cross energy, emanate from Ed.

Even though the shingle rattling in the creeping water is louder now, and the slap of a wave on the groyne is like the crack of a whip as the air cools and the pressure drops, her voice rises over the cliff – not loud, but clear and gentle. 'Come on, you two, we need to go home before the tide comes in.'

Ryder grins at Ed and, wanting to engage him too, looks down again. 'Good view of Beauty on the beach from here,' he says, his euphoric interest in Grace spilling out of him in an attempt to involve Ed. Ed doesn't hear. Isn't interested. Perhaps she just isn't his type. Ryder was in Ed's workshop this morning, the radio was on, sawdust filled the air and, to the left of the door, was a carefully pinned and displayed wall of topless models. At the time, Ryder glanced at them without thought, but now he wonders why he has never torn a page from a tabloid and stuck it on the wall. Is it a desire to remain aloof or a thin-blooded lack of any desire at all? Do all men secretly want a pin-up and he is therefore a misfit? Or is it just something some people like and others don't? Simple. But hang on a minute, can anything where women are concerned be that simple?

He tries asking Ed now. 'Do you reckon every straight man has an inner yearning for a shag with a nameless model? Or is it just a fantasy that needs to stay fantasy?' Ed carries on leaning over the railings, staring at the sea. His eyebrows, Ryder notices, are doing just what evolution intended them for; they are full of sawdust and even though they are like small haystacks, they look as though they might collapse at any moment and the sawdust will fall into his eyes. He doesn't speak. Ryder opens his mouth to repeat himself, feeling foolish, but Ed has heard enough for it to be embarrassing so he can't just change the subject. But before he utters a word, Ed shifts around, tosses his keys from one hand to the other, and looks at Ryder with mock severity, 'For God's sake, Ryder, get your dick out of your arse and stop belly aching. You're not rarefied, you get laid like anyone else if you're lucky. Come on, let's go.'

Ryder laughs. 'Yeah, I guess you're right. I think my version has suspenders.'

Ed is on a different thought plane.

'There's something coming off the back of that wind,' he grumbles, looking to the horizon, and he reaches in through the window of his truck for binoculars. 'Yep, it's looking dirty over there.' He passes the binoculars to Ryder. Where sea and sky meet, so far away Ryder could swear he can see the curve of the earth, a black line is thickening. As if drawn by felt tip and then underscored, the darkness intensifies and Ryder sees it as a widening crevice pushing sea and sky further apart, though he knows that it is just rain seeping cubic tonnes of darkness and more and more water into the depths of the sea.

'How far away is it?'

Ed flicks his cigarette into the road behind him. 'Dunno. I don't think it'll hit us, though. But I wouldn't like to be out there tonight, the sea will be vicious. Come on, bring your colouring book and let's go.' He grins at Ryder and gets back into the truck. Ryder steals a last look down at the beach. There's no one there now. Like a shaken-out table-cloth, the wind cracks back into life, the sea hisses a response, and sound is all there is on the beach, apart from the ragged-edged hole dug by the children. She must be on the path, the zigzag concrete road made for tractors to get down the cliffs and haul out the crab boats from the shallows. A wind gust knocks over the small jug of sea lavender on the table where Ryder was sitting and the flowers fall into his empty cup and saucer.

Ed revs the engine. 'Look, mate, I'm gonna go; you can stay here if you like and I'll come by for you later, but I need the tide,' he says, his demeanour relaxed but determined. No more hanging around.

'OK, I'm in.' Chucking some change on top of the fluttering paper bill, Ryder grabs his notebook and the rolled charts he never quite got round to opening, and gets in to the pick-up. As Ed accelerates away, Ryder sees a billow of red skirt and wind-flayed hair in the wing mirror.

★ ★ ★

Jesus Christ, it's hot. Ryder's suit suddenly feels like someone else's bad joke. The road is frilly edged with cow parsley bobbing as it catches the breeze, tiny petals floating like confetti and the whole thing is festive and euphoric as if he is on the way to a wedding. This morning the countryside is alive with celebration, and being more accustomed to hanging out in the sea on rigs or in town on the boat, Ryder's senses are dazzled. Or assaulted, more like. The joys of the morning are not penetrating as yet. Waking up in Ed's house, on the sofa with a fuzzy head, and Ed's kids heaped in front of the TV on various giant foam blobs, Ryder was overwhelmed by the noise and action. He couldn't believe how lively they all were. And how callously oblivious to his presence. The television was unnecessarily loud, the cartoon creatures on it far too brightly green and cheerful, and Ed's children, all in pyjamas with tangled mops of hair, were rolling and somersaulting among the foam blobs like wind-up toys. There seemed to be about six of them, though Ryder was sure Ed only mentioned three. Or maybe four. The noise was intense.

Through the low window looking out on to the yard, Ryder could see Ed in his workshop, his cigarette billowing a cloud through the door. Verity, Ed's wife, was clanking buckets and chatting to Ed as she fed her horses, unbolting stables to reveal straw-lined spaces markedly more orderly than the house. Feeling like he had missed the bus, Ryder got off the sofa, trying to pretend to himself that he was neither stiff from sleeping scrunched up, nor in the wrong place, given that it was ten o'clock and he was meant to be on the other side of Norfolk. Of course he hadn't been given the sofa deliberately, Verity had shown him into the spare bedroom when he arrived, but when he and Ed finally creaked up the stairs last night, having seen the best part of a bottle of Scotch between them, Ed groaned on opening his bedroom door.

'Bloody kids,' he said, and tiptoed out to the landing where Ryder was leaning against a wall for extra support. Ed sighed, looking like his eight-year-old son for a moment. 'Natasha's in with Verity and I'm not going in her bloody bunk bed with Josie snoring away down below. I'm for the sofa, mate.'

Ryder was drunk, but not so drunk that he could let his host sleep downstairs while he tucked himself into the spare bedroom on the upper floor, with Ed's family in the rooms on either side of him. It wouldn't be appropriate. 'No, you're not,' he mumbled, blocking the way down the stairs with outstretched arms, swaying – deliberately, of course – to make absolutely certain Ed could not sneak through. 'I'm heading for the sofa; you get some kip in that spare room you fixed up for me.'

It would be a good idea to get out of the car and go for a walk or, even better, a swim in the sea this morning, but it's a long way round the coast to Winterton, and Ryder's adrenaline is pumping. He is anxious he might lose his nerve and bottle out of the christening and all it will bring up for him, if he doesn't set off to get it over with.

Immediately, he chastises himself; Christ, what a way to live, setting yourself up against even the gentlest occasion because you are so terrified of life. It's got to change. Driving out of Ed's yard, waved off by Ed with a small child sitting on his shoulders, Ryder experiences a pang of loss. Ed's life, full of kids and Verity and boats and too much work and not enough money, adds up to chaos, but good chaos. Not something Ryder has seen much of, but he likes it.

Passing the village where he saw Grace yesterday, Ryder takes his foot off the accelerator, seized with an irrational belief that she will open one of the doors of the flint-faced cottages and walk out into the sunshine. She doesn't, even though he is convinced that the yellow one with a pot of vibrant-orange flowers on the doorstep is hers. He indulges in a moment of self-torture, imagining her with her husband, laughing and chatting over breakfast with the children playing somewhere nearby.

Ryder's phone trills, breaking this fantasy before he has time to imbue the husband with all the qualities he himself does not possess, as well as jaw-dropping good looks and a big job. It's his mother.

'Ryder? Is that you?'

'I think so,' he automatically teases her. 'Is that you?'

'Yes, of course it is. Now will you be seeing the family before the christening? I mean Mac. And . . . and . . .' Her voice tails off helplessly. Ryder swallows, touched by her determined bravery.

'Mac and Lucy and the children? Sadly, I doubt it; I don't think I'll get there in time.'

His mother sighs, but pulls herself together. 'Well, it can't be helped,' she says brightly. 'We've sent some flowers, anyway; they come with helium teddy bears which we thought the little girls would like.'

'Good.' Ryder is out of the village where he is sure Grace lives now, and the road zigzags towards a cornfield sprinkled with poppies, and, at its farthest limit, a knife-edge ridge where the corn ends and suddenly becomes the swell of the sea, the whole horizon high in the view, as if the sea is rising to fill the sky.

His mother is still talking. 'Good? Do you think so? I hope so. And Ryder, will you take some photographs? I would dearly like to see Mac's daughters.'

'Oh Mum,' is all Ryder can say. He understands how much she would love to be here, and how impossible it is for her to come. And something soft in her voice tells him that she, like he, is thinking today how very lovely it would be to have some children to christen in their own family.

'Mum, Bonnie would have had great kids.'

'Yes.'

His mother was crying. Ryder felt it wouldn't take much for him to be crying as well. 'And I will, too, one day. I hope,' he says gently. He has never said this before, the notion of children has been even more taboo than the question of sex in his conversations with his parents. Not that they would mind the children talk, but Ryder has never wanted to face the unspoken monumental expectation of his mother's that she will become a grandmother. And he has left it and accepted it as one of the many unacknowledged areas where a splinter of pain from Bonnie's accident has lain festering for all those years. And in the end it was so bloody easy to say it's a joke. Ryder presses one palm against his brow; he is hot, despite the breeze from the sea. He wonders if it's the hangover talking, and if he has taken leave of his senses. But no, he is not bullshitting. He is quite sure that he will have children one day, and they will be great. And saying this to his mother is actually no big deal. Wow, and it's only taken all his life to learn this.

'Yes, you will,' she says, very gently.

Ryder pulls himself out of the reverie, rubs his hand over his eyes, and says cheerfully, 'OK, Ma, I'll take pictures for you, and I'll come and see you next weekend. I must get on now, or I'll be late for the whole thing.' The signal cuts out at the perfect moment and the car swoops over a rise in the coastline with a church on top. There's nothing else for miles, and in the distance ahead is the alien vision of the Bacton giant golfball, the early warning system.

12

Grace
Norfolk

Waking up on the morning of the christening, I lie in bed looking at the ceiling, remembering the rivers and faces I used to make out of the cracks when I was a child. Lucy and I used to spend hours in bed in the mornings waiting for Mum, and we used to invent whole worlds through the patterns on the ceiling. I had forgotten it in New York, but here in Norfolk in Lucy's spare bedroom, the ceiling is wall papered with tiny bunches of snowdrops scattered amongst pale green ribbons and I can imagine all the princesses and castles and exotic islands that we used to invent when we were small. Suddenly, as if conjured up by a genie, a small neon-green-clad princess with crown and sceptre appears by my pillow, breathing heavily.

'It's breakfast,' she says, and hands me a half-sized tin of baked beans.

'Great.' I am hugely relieved the tin is not open, and amazed by the insight I am getting into the eating habits of three year olds. Or maybe it's just Bella. Though it's not what she eats that's controversial, it's just the timings.

'I'll get up and we'll go down to Mummy, shall we?'

'Mummy,' says Bella dreamily, and climbs into the bed with me. She is so perfect I wonder if she can be a Stepford baby or a changeling from the *Day of the Triffids*. I still adore her after a whole day of being in charge of her and Cat. It's a miracle. I thought I would feel like a changeling myself in the company of small children for a whole day, but it was great. I love them and they love me. What could be better? The beach was a great success and I had them in bed before Mac and Lucy arrived with Mac's aunt Irene last night.

'Let's do something,' says Bella wriggling next to me, and I can feel a delicious tug of love in my heart. I pounce on her, and Bella squirms and giggles.

'I'm going to blow hot potatoes on your tummy.'

'Yes. NO. YES. NO. YES!!!!' roars Bella, wriggling more and more as I tickle her.

Eventually we notice Lucy in the doorway, the baby, Cat, in her arms. Lucy is wearing a coat over her nightdress.

'You must come and see, two lambs have been born and they're in the field between here and the church. It's Little Bo Peep for real.'

Following Bella out into the garden, I am overwhelmed by the full blossom and leaf experience of a May morning in the English countryside.

'This is amazing,' I murmur to Lucy. 'Nothing can be this perfect.'

Lucy smiles. 'Why not?' she says. Good question. We are by the wall bordering the field now; Bella has climbed on to an upturned bucket and is on tiptoe trying to see over. I pick her up. Two black lambs are following a very exhausted-looking sheep across the field.

'We've got to move them or they will get upset with all the people from the christening traipsing across.' As Lucy speaks, Mac and a man in a boiler suit appear at the far end of the field.

'How does he know how to do all this?' I wonder out loud, as Mac walks quietly up to the sheep and waits, watching the other man for a signal to pick up the lambs.

Lucy puts the baby down on the grass and leans over the wall next to me. 'He grew up here, and even though he went away for a long time, he knew he wanted to come back. But then he thought he couldn't bear to.'

'Why not? What's unbearable about here?'

Lucy laughs. 'Get you!' she teases, 'you're the one who ran away to America to escape this place, and now you're a convert.'

I grin, still interested. 'So,' I say, 'Mac – what changed him into someone who hated to be back here?'

Lucy moves closer to me, and we are side by side. She murmurs, 'I can't remember if I've told you this before, but when Mac was at university, his girlfriend died in a car accident on the way to see him. The first big love of his life. You know, he didn't even tell me about it until we had Bella. That's why her middle name is Bonnie. She's named after her.'

'Oh, poor Mac.' I look at him in the middle of the field, lifting one of the lambs and turning with it towards the gate. Suddenly I realise what I have said and how it might seem to Lucy. I reach out and squeeze her hand. 'Sorry, Luce,' I mumble, embarrassed and stuck now.

She smiles and shakes her head. 'No. I know what you mean. I feel it too. And there's no competing with a ghost. But there isn't any need to. It was long ago. And, you know, one of the things I am looking forward to today is meeting her brother. He's coming to the christening. Mac hasn't seen him for fifteen years. He's one of Bella's godparents.'

My eyes widen, I stare at my sister. A few freckles have appeared on her cheeks, and her hair has fallen out of the knot she tied it in; a tawny curl bounces on her shoulder and she looks a bit Grecian in her pale nightdress with her straight nose and soft pink mouth. She really is beautiful inside and out. I always knew she was, and it used to drive me mad, but now I feel huge acceptance. I know that not only could I never be like her, but I also don't even want to be any more. It is such a relief to finally realise my limitations and feel comfortable with them.

'Is he sexy, and is he single?' I ask, turning my face up to the sun, shutting my eyes.

Lucy laughs. 'I don't know about sexy, because I haven't met him, have I, stoopid,' she says. 'But he is single. Or, rather, Mac hasn't invited anyone with him, so he must be. Maybe he's gay.'

I feel like I'm having a full nature-style sensory massage with the cooing of pigeons and the gurgling laughter of Cat and the smell of grass and blossom and the warmth on my face. 'God, it will be strange for Mac,' I think out loud. 'Do you know what she looked like?'

'Mmm,' Lucy nods, 'I've seen a photo. She looks lovely, and she was so young it's devastating to look at it.' She breaks off to tumble Cat in the grass, blowing a raspberry on her dimpled arm. It's so sweet to see her so happy, and wrapped in her own family life. A yawn bursts out of me and I realise that at last the grey cocoon of jet lag has fallen away. Mac climbs the wall to join us and Bella runs to him, jumping to put her arms around his neck. He lifts her up and twirls her around him, laughing with her. My nose begins to run and I am gulping as if I am watching a soppy film. The notion of a happy family had never really occurred to me before as a desirable or attainable goal.

The bell tolling wakes me. I sit bolt upright, rubbing my face. I'm on the sofa, where I lay down after lunch promising myself I would be five minutes. Pins and needles in my arm and a shiver across my skin from being still tell me I have overslept. And I have certainly been noticed: two dolls, both wearing green tops and jeans, versions of what I am wearing, lie next to me. Apart from their clothes, they look like synchronised swimmers with their right hands thrown above their heads and their faces turned to one side, I suppose matching me while I slept. Creepy. Remembering that this is not voodoo but the work of a three-year-old child is a relief, but not something I have time to dwell on. I must get changed. The church bell sounds urgent, it's the summons for the christening. Racing upstairs is slow work, the landing is strewn with clothes as though a tornado has visited a Chinese laundry, and Lucy is standing in front of her wardrobe groaning pitifully.

'I can't stand it, I've only got one shoe. I've looked everywhere. Bella must have taken the other one for dressing up.'

'What's new, Cinderella?' I can't believe it, this is so familiar. Lucy and I fall effortlessly into the pattern we carved out for ourselves years ago when getting ready to go anywhere. Even with almost no clothes between us, like the weekends when we were sent to stay with our father, we still hurled every garment out of the small case we shared and spread them as far as we could in his flat. Standing here with Lucy half naked in front of her mirror, her expression catapults me back to that time and I realise I have forgotten about having fun. Lucy pouts. 'Oh it's all right for you with your fancy New York luggage.' We both look at my ancient, bashed-around zip-up bag. It has been in my studio for too much of its life and is paint daubed and marked with ink and tape. It looks like something a builder might use to take his overalls and tools around in. We burst out laughing.

'Mmm, yes, it's so fancy that I don't know how I could bear to bring it here,' I agree, delving through it. 'Hey, look! I've got some shoes here you can borrow.' I am half undressed too, by now, and pass the shoes while diving into a pink dress I bought especially. It came with a warning that crumpled was best, that was why I bought it. 'Oh my God, it's too tight.'

Lucy yanks at the dress. 'No, you haven't undone the zip, stoopid. Let me see. GOD, that's so unsuitable – I want it. Hand it over. It's gorgeous, I am the eldest.'

'But I look like a rhubarb fool.'

'No – plum tart, I reckon. Oh my God, Grace, that's so NAUGHTY.' Lucy is stroking the dress longingly, holding up a limp flowery one which she is about to put on, unable to let go of mine. She quickly ducks her head, saying about her skirt, 'Look at this, Grace – it came from Mum.'

She waves it bravely. I have unhooked the pink dress and am wriggling out of it. 'Here, Luce, you wear this one, I want to wear Mum's.' I am good at being determined, Lucy knows that, and the challenge in my eyes, as well as the fact that Mac is shouting in a stage whisper from downstairs, 'Quick, it's time, they're all arriving', stops Lucy protesting. Silently she takes the dress and pulls it over her head. I whistle under my breath. It's sexy, and just as Lucy said, most unsuitable. Thank God we've run out of time so she can't change. I wink at her.

'Very good . . . Luce by name and loose by nature.'

'Thank you, Grace. I haven't worn anything like this for years.' Her cheeks are flushed, her eyes bright, and she looks about eighteen. I hold up Mum's chiffon thing and slide it over my head. It is completely see-through. Mum certainly didn't wear this with us around.

'Oh shit.' I stare at the mirror in horror.

'Don't worry, it's only the light in the bathroom. She had it from when she was about twenty, I thought it was quite demure.'

'Lucy, you're a bloody liar! Maybe I should wear a cardigan, or will that just make it worse?'

'It will when you take it off, and it's going to be hot.' Lucy is putting lipstick on and being the older sister by setting an example of hurrying and having good deportment.

Defiantly, I reach into my bag again and drag out the borderline hat. Borderline ridiculous. I pull off the tissue from the layers dyed dark purple, almost black, at the crown, turning to crimson like a poppy. 'Look, shall I wear this?'

'Oh Grace, I love it! Yes, definitely, you must wear it. Those colours remind me of that poem you read at Mum's funeral, you know. "The pansy freaked with jet." You must wear it, it looks amazing. Honestly.'

Making faces at the mirror, I'm not sure. 'It's a bit vampy,' I suggest, 'and I don't want to give all Mac's aunts a bad impression. I want to be part of your family, not the black sheep.'

Lucy grabs my wrist. 'No time to change anything now, we've GOT to go, poor Mac is holding the whole thing together on his own.' And then, as we

254

clatter down the stairs, she turns to me, her face stricken. 'Do I really look like a tart in this dress?'

I raise my eyebrows back at her. 'Yes, it's great isn't it?'

The small front garden is full of people I don't know. I place myself close behind Lucy and Mac, fascinated to see them among their friends and family.

'This is Grace, Lucy's sister from New York.' Introducing and greeting, Mac and Lucy thread through the garden. 'We should be heading to the church now. I've just got to find all the godparents.' Mac marches off around the side of the house, Lucy moves on towards the lawn where the children are playing with Aunt Irene in charge.

'Hey, guys, meet Grace.' Lucy kisses a blonde woman and a man wearing a pale purple suit. I smile at them, and follow on in Lucy's wake. Briefly meeting Mac's family, I realise with a start that I am all there is left of Lucy's except for Aunt Sophie who cannot travel any more.

The garden is full of laughter and voices bubbling with enthusiasm. The apple tree by the gate has sprouted pink blossom, which almost seems to have happened since this morning. My shoe keeps slipping off my foot, when it's not sinking into the grass up to the top of the heel, so I crouch to tighten the strap. Everyone has started crossing the field towards the church, leaving silence a swathe behind them. A sudden chatter of birdsong pours out of the hedge beside me, and I try to look in without touching, guessing that I am close to a nest.

'Are you really interested in that hedge?'

The voice is familiar yet unknown. I squeal in surprise and clap my hand over my mouth.

'Oh God, you made me jump,' I mutter, my heart pounding, and everything contributing to self-consciousness in the peaceful summer garden. I have knocked over the flowers I was bringing in a small jug to put in the church porch. Crouching to pick them up, I push up the hat and find him beside me. He passes me a flopping sprig of lilac.

'Here,' he says.

It is him. Ryder. The man from Denmark. My immediate thought is not 'How weird'. It's, 'I knew you would come.' I am so surprised that all native wit and intelligence desert me.

All I can say is, 'Oh. It's you.' We look at one another for as long as it takes to blink, and I am so overwhelmed that I lapse into nervous superficial thoughts.

'Oh bugger, why did I wear this freaky hat and see-through dress? I look like a tea lady, and my underwear shows, and in a minute I'll have to stand up; how can I hide?'

Ryder picks up another gasping bloom from where it had fallen, and threads it into the jug between my hands and he doesn't look away from my face.

'So they're not your children,' he says. 'And I want you to tell me what you saw in that hedge just now.'

My knees are about to give way, I stand up, and try to stand only half facing him. Thinking about my knickers is making me blush, and I am distracted and confused.

'What? The girls? No, they're my sister's children.'
He is very close to me.

'I was looking for a nest in the hedge.'

He pulls a twig out of my hair and for a moment our eyes meet. I feel very shy, everyone has gone into the church, Lucy is beckoning from the door with the vicar, who looks like an angelic host in his long gown. I pull his sleeve, 'Come on, it's time to go in. It's my sister's children's christening, you know.'

He nods, and a smile is breaking in his eyes. 'I know, I'm a godfather,' he says. I stop and stare at him.

'Are you Mac's friend?'

'Yes. Does being a godfather make me related to my god-daughter's aunt?'

I have to cross my arms to make my dress more decent as we walk through the churchyard. 'Only distantly,' I tease him back.

We are almost at the door when he glances across and adds, 'I am so glad.'

'What? About the christening?'

'No, that they are not your children.'

'Yes, me too. Though of course they are lovely, but . . .' I suddenly realise that he is THAT friend of Mac's. The one with the sister, and as if I am having a divine experience, another understanding crystallises as we step into the church porch. Everyone else is inside and the vicar is saying something, his voice full of soothing cadences like a cooing pigeon in the shady summer space of the church. I put my hand on Ryder's sleeve to stop him and I whisper, 'What do

257

you mean? Why would the children be mine? What children are you talking about, anyway?'

'Yesterday I saw you on the beach,' he whispers. We are inside the doors now, he touches my back to guide me in and excitement races as clear as a bell.

'Oh God. Was that you?' All the fragments are rushing together and the picture suddenly makes beautiful sense. A lot of people are looking at us, and Lucy is making a 'hurry up' face.

In a moment I turn to him and I can't stop myself saying, 'I'm so pleased I've seen you again.'

13

Ryder
Norfolk

She smells of patchouli. A trace of it lingers like smoke next to him as he takes his place in a pew a few rows behind Grace where she has joined Mac and Lucy. Ryder smiles apologetically at the person next to him, and bows his head, relieved to have a spell of quiet contemplation thrust upon him for a while. Grace is Lucy's sister. Ryder finds he is experiencing a strong sense of completion.

All the way to Winterton, every moment until he saw Mac, he was haunted by thoughts of Bonnie, and how he could make it up to her memory that the children whose christening he was attending were not hers. It was irrational, but nothing to do with grief has ever been rational in Ryder's experience, and his sister was so clear in his heart that he could see her long dark hair, her laughing eyes and her dimpled smile.

Of course, Bonnie never asked him to make up for anything, but Ryder's need to do so sat like a lump in his throat.

He pulled up outside the gate of Chapel Farm Cottages and parked the car across the road. The house was low, built of knapped flint, most of the windows upstairs were open, and anyone leaning out of one would be able to reach a hand up and touch the rosy-tiled roof. No one was leaning out, but as Ryder shut the gate behind himself, a man, tall in a dark suit, appeared in the doorway and raised a hand in greeting. It was Mac, older, of course, but with the same silhouette, the same imprint on the world.

'Hey, Ryder,' he said, and walking over to Ryder he had a smile breaking, 'it's so good to see you.' Their arms wrapped around one another in a bear hug, and Ryder's heart was hammering so he could only just speak.

'I am here at last,' he said.

Mac nodded, gripping Ryder's hand. 'I'm so glad you could come, you know.'

'Me too,' said Ryder, 'though I've been worrying like hell that I won't make the grade with the vicar. Or with Bella. What's her take on the day?'

'Oh, she's excited – mostly, it has to be said, about the cake which she helped make, and which she has been licking secret dollops of whenever she can get near it.'

Mac and Ryder, hands in pockets, hovered together on the lawn in front of the house, talking about nothing, getting over the initial enormity of seeing one another. After a few minutes they moved inside. Ryder looked around, absorbing the happy chaos. He was beginning to recognise a few key elements – miniature shoes scattered about, dolls looking like victims of domestic violence, and a lot of low-level stacking and tidying.

Following Mac through the kitchen and into a hall with a flag-stoned floor which bowed in the middle with hundreds of years of wear, he felt his heart thudding again. It was a big deal coming all the way here, meeting Mac's wife and their children. But most of all, it was a big deal to see Mac again. All of it brought a layer of acceptance he hadn't realised he was looking for.

'I'm afraid we have no space downstairs that isn't carpeted with dolls,' apologised Mac. 'I've got used to it now, and I've noticed a tendency for the plastic nightmare to creep into some of my editorial work as well.' He grinned. 'But I'm hoping I'll grow out of it soon.' Mac stepped around a pink doll's pram which had been crashed into the bottom of the stairs and opened the door into a sunny room where a cat lay curled asleep on a crocheted blanket in front of the fireplace.

'You've got plenty here for inspiration though,' said Ryder, forgetting the rest of his thoughts as he noticed the two small girls perched on the arms of a big yellow sofa. How very odd. Not being a small-child expert, Ryder was inclined to doubt himself, but looking at these two, he would put hard cash on them being the ones from the beach yesterday. Same size, same hair. How many could there be like this in Norfolk?

Suddenly every whirling emotion he had experienced in the past few weeks collided within him and he had a sense that he might explode. Mac and the girl from Denmark? Surely not? But why not? No, it doesn't fit. Oh God. It can't.

Through the mist in his head he heard Mac explaining something to him, 'Lucy's upstairs changing, and I doubt she'll be ready before we are meant to be there, so I'll introduce you to my little ones.' Lucy. Ryder pulled himself back into sense. And in his head he reminded himself that she is called Lucy. He knew that perfectly well. Not Grace. Maybe they aren't the ones from the beach? After all, isn't one small adorable blond infant very much like another? Surely? He stared again at the little girls, and noticed they both had riding hats on. With party dresses and solemn expressions.

'What are they doing?'

'They're under starters order,' explained Mac. 'They've got the Derby coming up to compete with their christening.'

'Are they into gambling?'

'Oh yes,' said Mac, mock-serious as he pulled a betting slip from his pocket. 'They've each taken a punt today. Bella's on a long shot, Fuse Line, at fifteen to one, and Cat's gone for the second favourite, Dutch Landscape. I reckon she'll be in the money.'

Sparkling eyes stared up at Ryder and Mac. Ryder smiled and put down the bag he had been carrying. 'I like the look they've got,' he said, 'hats are great.'

Mac sat down on the sofa between his daughters and bounced them into his arms, where they fell in a giggling heap.

'Bella and Cat, here is Ryder, and he is my great old friend.'

Frankly, Ryder thought, the children looked as though they could take or leave him. He removed his sunglasses from on top of his head and tucked them in a pocket instead and proffered the bag hopefully.

'I've got some Barbie dolls for you.' He was embarrassed by how shy he felt, how humbled by the vibrant innocence and sweetness of these children. Both of them looked suspiciously at the bag. 'They used to belong to some little girls called Amy and Rachel,' he added, 'and they asked me to give them to you two.'

He had no idea where this had come from, and had forgotten that he knew the names of Anthea's children, but it seemed to be the right thing to say.

'Are they out of the box?' asked Bella.

'Oh,' Ryder cringed, 'yes, sorry.'

But she was smiling and clapping her hands. 'That's how we get them at the car boot sale; we like them out of the box,' she added. Grinning back, Ryder glanced across to Mac.

'They say all the right things,' he joked, 'they'll go far.' The girls jumped up from the sofa and delved into the bag.

'You got the password right,' replied Mac, 'and Barbie dolls are the best possible currency here – like dollars in Nepal.'

Ryder found himself floating away in his head again as the children unloaded a storm of tiny costumes and some naked dolls. Were they the same children? Could Grace really be Lucy? If he asked Mac if the girls went to the beach yesterday, what would it achieve? Would he seem like a weirdo and therefore not suitable as godfather? And what about Bonnie? In all the confusion of feelings he was experiencing, the one thing Ryder was sure of was that there were no amends to be made to Bonnie. His earlier anxieties on her behalf had dissolved and gone, but she needed to be mentioned.

As if he had spoken the thought, Mac got up from the sofa, opened the door into the garden, and stood looking out for a moment. Then he turned to Ryder with sadness in his clear grey eyes.

'It took me a long time, Kid. Really. Bonnie was wherever I was in her shocking absence every day for ten years. I felt like a part of me was missing. You know, the way amputees are supposed to feel? I really wondered if I would ever get over it, you know, and I'll be honest, it was like a curse sometimes.'

He half turned to look out of the door, swallowing. Ryder moved next to him and stepped outside to light a cigarette. 'I can imagine,' he said. 'I'm sorry, Mac.'

Mac took a cigarette too and both of them moved further into the garden, 'It's different now,' he said simply. 'It changed with Lucy. I will never forget Bonnie, but my heart mended when I met Lucy.'

Ryder meant it fully when he replied, 'I'm glad for you.'

Cars had pulled up, their doors clunking, their engines dying on the breeze. The church bell continued chiming along with snatches of laughter and conversation that had been gathering, and then someone saw Mac and broke away from their group to come over to greet him.

Chucking the cigarette away, Mac turned to Ryder. 'Come out and meet everyone. Mum and Dad are here, they'll be pleased to see you. I told them you were coming. I've got to get these girls out, too.' Bella has emerged from the house in swashbuckling mode, a Barbie pushed like a gun into the sash of her dress, twirling a toy ballgown on her fingers. 'That was a great present for them, thanks.' Mac picked up Cat who was squatting intently looking at a leaf outside the French windows. 'Here, come with me and we'll go and find everyone.'

Ryder, much to his surprise holding hands with Bella, who had reached up to him, tugging him, followed Mac through the gathered people. Then suddenly Mac walked away towards another open door into the house and out of it came a woman whom he put his arms around. She had her hair loosely up, and in the turn of her face as she leaned up to whisper in Mac's ear, there was something familiar that made Ryder's pulse race. A split second later it was as inevitable as it was astonishing that out of the door behind her stepped Grace. Sisters.

14

Grace
Norfolk

It takes my eyes a moment to adjust to the soft light in the church, where candles glow around the altar and the pink plaster on the walls bounces a rose tint into the aisle. Stepping into the space next to Lucy, I open the order of service. It is impossible to pay attention to the vicar as he delivers his sermon. How can it be that it is here and now that I have met him again? Is there significance attached, or is this just life revealing its shapes and patterns, flexing the push-me-pull-you of human connection? I don't feel really surprised to see him, it is as if he has always been in my life, and I cannot dismiss this notion even though it makes no sense. But neither does his being here, at the furthest point east on the very edge of Norfolk with the sea moving steadily towards us and the land crumbling into it. And we are here for this tiny homely family christening. Ryder has appeared in my dreams once in a while, and in my thoughts a little more often through the last five years, but I never had a sense of truly wanting to see him again until yesterday. And yesterday I dismissed it as crazy. So last night, when I was telling Lucy, I made a joke out of the whole episode and I said, 'When a guy flicks a fag over the cliff at you and reminds you of a lost moment five years ago, it's a sign you need to get out more.'

Lucy laughed too, but she squeezed my hand and said, 'True. But it also means you must be over Jerome. You will find someone new now.' And it was a relief to find no lurch of the heart or contraction of feeling when Jerome's name is mentioned. The bruise has healed. The sun beams in, engulfing the soft candlelight and suffusing the church with joy. The vicar reaches the denouement of his sermon, and I wish I had been listening, as he draws himself to a conclusion.

'There is wonder all the time in the world, it is our choice to see it or not. I know of no better expression of this than William Blake's "Auguries of Innocence":

> 'To see a world in a grain of sand,
> And a heaven in a wild flower,
> Hold infinity in the palm of your hand,
> And eternity in an hour.'

Every small detail is lit with significance today. But then, maybe it always is, and usually we are too busy to notice. Cat, the baby, is in Lucy's arms next to me. She reaches out her hand, turning it in the shaft of sunlight, absorbed in her own world while all of us gathered here are absorbed in her and Bella's celebration. We stand up, rustling an introduction, as the organ pedals rattle and the tune to 'All Things Bright and Beautiful' pours into the church. Lucy and Mac are edging out of the pew to go to the font at the back, and beside them Bella skips in the aisle. She trundles towards the vicar, and then, in a block of sunshine, she stops and slowly twirls around, a tiny Degas in her shuttlecock skirt.

It's a bit like waking up in a room full of people to look around at the other guests. There are not many people, perhaps twenty or so, and among them old friends of Lucy's whom I recognise and find myself half greeting with a semi-smile and invisible internal code to which I imagine they are responding similarly. There are a couple of aunt-like figures who must be related to Mac, as Aunt Sophie, our only proper relation, is too frail to come.

Mac's family are exotic-looking, I remember Lucy telling me they were Italian, and Mac's dad ran a fleet of ice-cream vans on the beach at Great Yarmouth and Gorleston and was waiting for Mac to tire of photography and take them over. His parents are opposite me, and they remind me of the parents in a pack of Happy Families cards. Marina Perrone has a sculpted wave of auburn hair and gold jewellery enhancing a gleaming suntan the texture and colour of butterscotch ice cream, and Mac senior has wings of silver hair ending in glistening sideburns and thick black eyebrows. In the gathering of Lucy and Mac's

268

friends they look more surreal than the small boy in a
Spider-Man suit and red Wellington boots who is
flexing his spider skills by attempting to climb up the
bell rope behind the font. His mother Felicity is a
friend of Lucy's from university, last seen by me wearing hot pants and high boots to her graduation
ceremony. Of course, they were hidden by her gown,
but the pinkness of her face as she strode on to the
stage to receive her certificate was a glaring reminder.
Her mermaid-like long red hair is a crisp bob now
and her shoes are sensible and low. I am sobered by
the changes wrought by age and domesticity and at
the same time attracted to her serenity. She has been
tying a small pink hat on to the large head of a baby
who is identical to the tall man holding it, and she
finishes this before gathering up Spider-Man. Her
quiet patience is a quality I have seen in Lucy since
Bella was born. I thought it was just exhaustion, but
now I see it is actually love and I am chastened and
pinpricked with curiosity. There is a collective theme
running through the appearance and stance of all
Lucy and Mac's friends, subtle in as much as it is
revealed in outward details – many of the women
wearing coloured shoes, or the fact that none of the
men is wearing a tie and even the ones with suits have
rumpled linen shirts or T-shirts under them and no
one's hair or, indeed clothes, have a military cut. But
it is more, Ryder both fits in and stands out. The vicar
has separated the godparents and parents from the
rest of the flock with practised skill and is busy extract-
ing promises from them.

'Do you turn to Christ?' the vicar asks.

'*I turn to Christ,*' everyone responds.

'Do you repent of your sins?'

'*I repent of my sins.*'

'Do you renounce evil?'

'*I renounce evil.*'

All of us are around the font now, and Bella is on tiptoe, trying to peep over the edge. Lucy and Mac look like one entity standing close together, Cat in Mac's arms, solemn and attentive. Ryder catches my eye as the vicar moves towards the godparents, and in the glance we exchange I feel a thrill of possibility and I bite my lip hard and look away to stop myself smiling.

'Do not be ashamed to confess the faith of Christ crucified,' says the vicar, sounding somehow reproving, and all of us mumble the response like naughty children giving an excuse. 'Fight valiantly under the banner of Christ against sin, the world and the devil and continue his faithful soldiers and servants to the end of your lives.'

When I dare to look back at Ryder, he winks at me and looks down at the order of service in his hands, the corner of his mouth a smile. I feel incredibly naughty to be flirting in the middle of a christening, and it's such fun too. The vicar moves on to bless the water of baptism, and I keep my eyes fixed on the children. Cat is wriggling away from the water as if it is deathly poison, climbing up her father's arms like a marmoset. Bella is like the apprentice to the vicar and picks up the silver dish he uses for pouring and passes it to him as if she is a mindreader, just as he is reaching for it.

He doesn't falter, but smiles at her, and pours a trickle on to her head, intoning as he does: 'Bella Bonnie, I baptise you in the name of the Father, and of the Son and of the Holy Spirit.' With his thumb he makes the sign of the cross on her forehead and Ryder and her other godparents chorus 'Amen.'

It is Cat's turn. Bella's godparents move away from the font back to their places in the crowd of us grouped nearby, and suddenly Ryder is standing next to me. I feel absurdly proud of him, and confused. Nothing today has made sense since I looked up from kneeling in the garden and saw him. Thoughts and feelings rush and form in my mind in fast succession, but none of them add up to anything except a dopey, stunned happiness that has no foundation. Now the vicar has lit two candles.

He gives one to Ryder, for Bella, saying, 'Receive this Light.' He gives the other one to Cat's godmother and, waving his arms to encompass the two children, who are both automatically pouting ready to blow, he says, 'This is to show that you have passed from darkness into light.' He gets the final words out as Bella gives in to her own desire to blow, but although the flame shivers, it does not go out. Maybe it's just me, but the pause that follows is electric, I must have been to a christening before, but I have never taken any notice of the words of the service, or the symbolism. There is nothing that does not feel significant. I wipe my eyes on my sleeve, not wanting to detract any attention from the babies.

'Here, it's clean.' Ryder has pulled a bright yellow spotted handkerchief from his pocket and passes it to me. Somehow I am holding it before he lets go. We both tug at once and the look between us smokes. I am ridiculously overexcited. The service speeds towards its conclusion. The blessings are over, and the vicar and Mac and Lucy lead the way out of the church into the breezy sunlit churchyard where nature is creating a celebratory welcome committee with giant saucer-sized elderflowers nodding and bowing against bright green leaves, and the cow parsley beneath them is like a bank of lace. Ryder is by my side. I remember walking into the gallery in Copenhagen with him, wondering then if he would touch me, a leap of desire like the lick of a flame sparkling. He left on his boat in the dark, and I was so caught up in the suspended tension of the moment that I completely failed to notice the sliver of loss like a tiny blade of ice in my heart, unacknowledged but nonetheless there for all those years. And now it is melting. I thought I would never see him again. For months after the evening in Copenhagen I wondered if he would somehow get in touch. If I had known his number or how to find him, I might have tried, but the different time zones, the fact he hadn't given me that information, and the secret conviction I could hardly let myself hear, that he could find me through the gallery if he wanted to, all stopped me doing anything. I wanted a man who would come and find me, I didn't want to have to go looking for him. I guess that's why I went for Jerome. He came and found me. Or tripped over me, more like, as I was floundering through the disorder of my life as a foreign resident in New York. After that I think I shut down my heart and I really gave up. And now the horizon is limitless again, and it has not been like that for a long time for me.

15

Ryder
Norfolk

Ryder's mind flips and weaves, cresting on a wave of excitement – she is here, he has found her, and everything will be wonderful now. He looks up at the vaulted roof, and the shadowy carved angels standing like figureheads on a ship's prow at intervals along the ceiling, and his thoughts take an abrupt nosedive. How come, after all these years, I have re-met Mac, and I am taking part in his daughters' christening, and all I can do is lust after a woman?

But there is Grace, with a beam of sunlight bouncing on to her shoulder, like a girl in a highschool musical. When she moves her hair falls across her back, and everything, just everything is on the up. Ryder forces himself to read the words on the service sheet, to think thoughts of tedium and distraction to get himself back under control. It's excruciatingly embarrassing being a man sometimes. Right. Now. Watch. Join in. No perving. Mac leans towards Lucy and she passes the baby into his arms, their eyes meet and in the shape of their bodies and the way they fit together but are separate beings, there is such love and such mutuality. Lucy's hand rests against Mac's chest for a moment and then they move out into the aisle with Cat in Mac's arms and Bella stomping along in front.

In the aisle, Bella shuts her eyes and slowly turns, her arms above her head, in a dance she has learned at ballet lessons, unless a pirouette is implicit in all small girls. Actually, it probably is. What a girl. Bella, his god-daughter, is sublime. Ryder had no idea of the new levels of the word adorable that were untapped until he met his god-daughter. Mac and Lucy have gathered her up now, along with the baby, and they are walking to the font. In a minute he will be, too. Grace follows them and he feels a pinprick of light, the possibility of happiness, as she passes him and her patchouli scent wafts into his soul. The other godparents move out of their pews, and with a start Ryder follows them, glancing at people he doesn't know, mildly curious and wondering what exactly his bond with them is now. Or is about to be. He finds himself standing across from Grace, and he wishes he was next to her for two reasons, first for the magnetic attraction he feels to her and secondly because now he can see her he can look nowhere else. Her dress is low at the front, and beneath it her breath rises and falls. She has sexy underwear on, and the light falls like lace across her, revealing much more than she is

probably aware of. Oh God, it's profane to be thinking like this in church, especially when you are there
to take part in something as wonderful as a baptism.

Stealing a glance at Grace, Ryder finds himself
shed a layer of self-protection in order to get closer to
her in his thoughts. All this and she isn't even looking
at him. Then she does, and back into his head comes
the verse the vicar read earlier:

> 'To see a world in a grain of sand,
> And Heaven in a wild flower . . .'

And Ryder suddenly knows as he looks at Grace and
she looks back at him, that this is what he has been
yearning for. He winks at her and pulls himself
together to concentrate on the service.

'God is the creator of all things . . .'

Grace

Is this what it feels like? Is happiness this close all
the time? This morning I read in the newspaper
that there is no time that a New Yorker is further
than eight metres from a rat. It used to be fourteen
metres. Is happiness like a New York rat? Coming
closer and closer? Was it there all the time like the
moon is, even when we cannot see it? And if it is,
why did no one say so? Life can be full of love
and light or fear and darkness. All of it is lurking
ready to pounce on us at any moment. So all the

happiness we will ever experience is ready and waiting. We will not miss out.

'Will you come for a walk with me?' I jump almost out of my skin. Ryder's voice in my ear is unexpected and though he whispers, it sounds like a stage whisper and I am sure that Mac's Aunt Irene sitting under the lime tree nearby has heard him and can read my mind and sense the leaping excitement. Is it just circumstance that is making this meeting into a big deal? I don't know, after all, people meet people and even fall in love with them every day. But this version of it is new to me.

'Well?' I still haven't answered Ryder. He lies down on the grass next to me and closes his eyes. I have to move or I will touch him.

'Irene, would you like another drink?' I bounce up as though I have been scalded. And over my shoulder in a hurry as I am walking towards the table and the drinks, so it seems throwaway, I say airily to Ryder, 'Oh yes, I'd love a walk. Let me just bring Irene a drink.' I purposely don't look at him. Actually, I can't.

Irene shakes her head. 'Please don't,' she says, 'I really don't want any more.'

'Great. Ready when you are.' Ryder is grinning, I can hear the smile in his voice. I still can't risk looking at him. Irene turns her piercing gaze on him; she has yellow eyes like a tiger and very unreal black-and-white-striped hair like Mac's dad but more extreme. She's Italian, but she could almost be an elderly Chinese warlord's concubine.

'And whom might you be?' she asks. 'Are you one of Mac's boxing friends?'

'Boxing?' Ryder shakes his head. 'Err, yes. I mean no. That's not how I know Mac but I did box with him a bit. It was long ago. God, it was great, I should get back to it. Does Mac still do it?'

Irene nods. Her topaz eyes are warm and lively. 'Yes, though he does more coaching now. He takes a class once or twice a week. I sometimes watch the training.'

I try to imagine anyone enjoying the salt-and-metal taste of blood in their mouth, the heat of swelling on their lip, the sense of outrage and pumping adrenaline all piling into every blow you take, and though I recoil, I am fascinated and excited too. Thinking of Ryder boxing turns me on. He is looking sheepish, but before I can ask him more, Lucy is there, holding out a small plate, smiling.

'Now, Irene,' she says, 'will you let me give you some cake? I've got to take Grace and Ryder away, but look, here comes Mac instead.'

She shoves me in the small of my back, muttering, 'You go, quick! It'll be fine.' Lucy seems to know what is happening better than I do. Walking out of the garden I am burning with the conviction that everyone is staring at me. I might as well be naked, breathing is impossible, so is looking round to see if Ryder is with me. I am gloomily expecting that he isn't, but I can't turn back. Out of the gate and on the road I sigh, pause and dare to glance behind me.

'Oh.'

'Oh what?' Ryder is walking towards me. My heart

leaps, I am not sure if it is fear or excitement, and suddenly I blurt out, 'Thank God you're here.'

His eyes are very clear, his gaze straight at me.

'Where would you like to go?' He is opening the passenger door of a car for me. I almost get in, then step back and away.

'Aren't we going for a walk?'

'Yes.'

'Well, why are we getting into the car?'

He shrugs and shuts the door again, reaching out his hand to me. 'Automatic reflex of a town dweller, I guess. Come on, let's walk to that church instead.' He nods towards the sea and a round-towered church on the cliff. 'Am I a proper town dweller?' he says, almost to himself.

'Where do you live?'

'On a boat.'

'I don't remember that about you before, where is the boat?'

'It's in Little Venice, you should come and see it some time.'

'I'd like that, thank you.' We leave the road and climb up through a gap in the hedge until we are crossing heathland, the mossy grass springy and silent beneath our feet, gorse wafting a scent of coconut sun-oil I had forgotten about. It's the smell of the Hawaiian Tropic stuff we used in my teens. I can't even make a joke about it because my senses are on overload and speaking is becoming increasingly difficult. Ryder's physical presence, his shoulder next to mine, his arm bumping me occasionally as we walk, the scent of him, renders me stupid with desire.

Luckily he hasn't noticed and is looking out to sea.

'Look, they are trying to build a kind of dam in the sea; it's supposed to stop the tide, but all I can think when I am told about it is that King Canute couldn't do it, and neither can we.'

'Why do they ignore something like that?'

'Oh, it's not a scientific fact and there's no money in listening to folk stories.'

'But it's not a folk story. King Canute is history, isn't he?'

We reach a wall running around the churchyard where we pause, side by side. Ryder leans over and picks a buttercup growing just within the wall. He hands it me and I notice the scar running down from his thumb into his sleeve raised and white like a fine cord.

'That's the thing. You said it, sweetheart, he is history.'

Without knowing what I am doing I catch his hand and run my fingertip down the scar.

'Can you feel this?' I ask, and he looks at my mouth when he answers, 'Yes.'

'But scars are meant to have no feeling.'

'I know, but this one does.'

The wind flies suddenly into my hair and I try to push it off my face. Ryder stops the movement of my hand with his. Clumsy with charged excitement, I stand on his foot. It's a good ice breaker, we laugh and begin to walk up the path in the churchyard.

'Another church?' Ryder leans in the doorway, the sea is behind him, white horses riding the churning indigo waves. Anxious to clean up my mind I muddle up entering a spiritual place with having chaste thoughts, and eagerly push open the door into the church.

'Let's look round, this one is so pretty, I came here ages ago. It's got pink walls.'

Ryder

'Good.' Ryder follows her in, wondering if he will be smitten down by a thunder bolt if he puts his hand up Grace's skirt in here. She walks into the middle of the church then moves towards a small table beyond the pews to read the printed leaflet about the church. He is behind her, pretending to look over her shoulder at what she is reading, but in fact he is breathing in the scent of her and looking at her skin.

'So it was built when the Saxons were still here, and there is an ossified boy in a tomb somewhere over there.' Grace looks up, biting her lip, turning her head. And he is there, so near her their breath mingles as their eyes meet, and both of them are saying yes.

Ryder bends his face and kisses her, for a moment just his mouth on hers, then more, and his hands are finding her too, one on her waist, the other around the back of her head, then his hands pull her against him and she is supple and her body melts to his and the heat between them burns, and he pushes her against the wall and she gasps. The rough sensation of plaster against soft skin is exciting. Grace tilts her head up and Ryder's mouth runs over her collarbone, his hand warm against her skin but making her shiver.

Grace pulls away, breathing hard, her pupils black and big with desire.

'This is a church!' she gasps, but she doesn't look as though she wants him to stop. Ryder's hand is on her thigh, under her skirt. He kisses the corner of her mouth.

'You can't kiss in church! I mean we can't – you can't kiss me here.'

'Why not? They do when they're getting married.'

Grace laughs, her arms are around him, her body is soft yet taut, like the string on a violin, a breath of surrender floods from her and in the moment she is somehow infinitely closer to him without physically moving. 'Yes, but not like this.'

Ryder brushes her hair off her forehead, and looks at her.

'No,' he agrees, 'not like this.'

'Let's go outside.'

In the churchyard the soft air feels blissful, a breeze wafts fragrance through it, and all of it adds to the surreal reality. Grace sits down on a bank beneath the hedge, Ryder comes and lies beside her, throwing his arm over his face against the hazy heat of the sun. Grace turns over on to her side, and props her arm on the ground, her head on her arm. He breathes in her excitement and it mingles with his own, and he wonders how he can possibly be falling in love with this woman whom he hardly knows. It feels like love, but what does he know? Anyway, whatever it is, he likes it, and he's not trying to escape from it.

'What are we doing?' Grace is fidgeting next to him.

Ryder opens one eye, props himself up for a moment, then lies flat and shuts it again. 'Lying in the sun in a graveyard.'

'I can't believe I finally got to meet you again after all.'

One eyebrow goes up. 'Can't you? I can't believe the opposite. How can we have missed meeting one another for the past five years?' He is so close she can feel his ribs rising as she breathes. 'I left you my number but you never called.'

She looks straight at him, 'I never got your number,' she says. He looks surprised and comes closer, rolling over, pulling her under him.

'That explains it,' he says, 'and we've got a lot of catching up to do. I need to know you.' Grace looks at him looking at her and her mouth is red. The connection between them is warm and potent, like a silken bath, but then Grace frowns, sits up and clutches her arms around her knees.

'I think it's all going to go wrong. The sky will fall on our heads, you know the sort of thing.'

'Do you think so?' says Ryder. His hands are stroking her back, his eyes have flecks like crystals in the iris, and Grace is reflected in the black of the eye in the middle. He can see himself reflected back in her eyes, warped and in double on the curve of her corneas.

'Don't forget there could be a tidal wave as well. There is something called the Coriolis force which determines the direction the wind moves in.'

He is stroking her arm now, tracing down to her wrist, linking his finger and thumb around it. She lies back down. 'In the northern hemisphere, the Coriolis force causes deflection to the right, so I guess a tidal wave could come here from the Atlantic. It would probably lose most of its momentum coming into the Channel, but you never know. Actually, a tidal wave doesn't really happen in shallow water like this, so probably you're right, it will be the sky falling on our heads.'

Ryder realises that he sounds as if he is making it up. 'Sorry, you don't really need to hear me boring on, I need to get out more.'

Grace's eyes are closed, she smiles and murmurs, 'No, it's nice, I like it. It makes me feel safe – something to do with you knowing all that stuff even though none of it is in our hands.' Speaking of hands, Ryder can't keep his off her. Of the five senses, his sense of touch is eclipsing all the others by miles at this moment, and his fingers are magnets to which every nerve ending in his body is drawn as he traces around her belly button. All his focus is on the hot electric energy which begins where they are touching one another, and darts deep inside him. Grace is clearly oblivious lying with her eyes closed beside him. He drops his hand down beside her, reaches for hers and is still. Grace's eyes open and both of them stare at the clouds, wisps of pale smoke in the sun-bleached sky. Surely love is meant to be all the clichés? Agony and ecstasy, despair and liquid joy. Not eating, not sleeping and obsessing wildly on a cliff top? Just now, though, holding hands, lying still and quiet, doesn't feel like any of that. It just feels real. Can love be real? Ryder has never allowed a thought of love into his head or his heart at this stage with anyone. They have only just met, it's not likely that they will meet again because why would she want to? So what is the point of any thought of love? This is surely desire, naked, straightforward lust. Nothing more. But also, nothing less. It seems for ever since Ryder last made love with anyone, let alone someone he wanted as much as he wants Grace.

To distract himself he dredges up some more local information, wondering as he opens his mouth how he thinks he is going to get away with being so boring, but comforting himself with the thought that at least it's less desperate than jumping on her in the churchyard.

'And the cliffs will be eaten away so there will be less of here. In fact, here will move over there.' Ryder gestures vaguely to the west.

Grace grins. 'Oh. Are you still talking?' Her face is close to his, her breath against his collarbone, she smells of warmth and flowers and possibility in the sea air, but with a kick of musk that jolts inward and flashes sex like a beacon in his mind.

He opens one eye. 'Are you still listening?'

She blushes, meets his eye then glances away. Ryder strokes the hair off her forehead and his voice runs over her. 'Anything can happen, and we will have no warning. It's like love, appearing out of nowhere and slicing right through everything that went before.' He turns over, he is nearer, he can't help it. She slides back from him; disappointment leaps like a jumping fish inside him.

'Oh my God,' says Grace under her breath, and suddenly she is close again. Ryder is still. Grace puts her hands on his chest, the base of her palm on his sternum not far from his beating heart. 'I can feel your heart,' she whispers.

It is impossible not to respond to her. Ryder tries, but when her hand is on his chest and she is just above him, he strokes her hair and rolls her over so she is flat on the grass and he is kissing her, his body so near hers that he is aware she is trembling, and he pulls her towards him and it is irresistible.

This is so much more of a result than Ryder was anticipating. Well, of course he wasn't anticipating any sort of a result, so this is great. But it's more than great, this is the beginning. Isn't it? Grace is lying on top of him now, the weight of her making him aware of the earth beneath the grass underneath him. He needs to pee and he has a hard on. But practical matters aside, he is elated and excited and fearful. Be careful what you wish for, he thinks wryly, rolling her over and off him and standing up.

A familiar voice inside him is suggesting it's time to get out before it gets messy. It's too intense with this girl. He wants to interrupt the flow because it is so delicious, and he cannot believe it will last. He cannot bear it to end. He stands up. She is lying on the grass, Ryder is standing facing away, wondering where he can go to pee. The hedge is straggly with a few gaps. He pushes through one of them as a cloud moves over the sun.

Grace has her arms around her knees when he returns to her.

'It's cold,' she says.

'I'll keep you warm, and the sun will be out again in a moment.' He lies down next to her and pulls her on top of him.

She laughs and wriggles. 'Am I too heavy? I must be squashing you.'

He shakes his head. Actually, he feels a panic of exposure – she is so close, he can hide nothing. There is a moment when he fights this internally, then he breathes out, grinning because of the weight of her on top of him dropping with his deep breath, and says, 'This may sound odd, Grace, but I mean it. I have thought about you so much since we met in Denmark. I want to be with you, to get to know you.'

Ryder has never wanted to say this to anyone before. Not wanting to say it has never stopped him, though. He has, of course, said versions of it and so much more. How many times has the average guy said, 'I love you' without meaning it? Or meant it when he says it for that moment, post-sex, caught up in a tangle of sheets and hot skin and desires. There is a spell which weaves impenetrably around the desire to please and be pleased which can never be sated. Now, though, Ryder hears himself and it is as if he is on the other side of a glass window. The tenderness within him, behind the language, is new, he feels as if he is stepping out into thin air. No rope, no platform, no protection, just a drop to the depths of his feelings, previously unplumbed. Not a place he wants to go. His thoughts move from unplumbed depths of feelings, to the bottom of the ocean. The mountains beneath the sea that form a jagged edge around the coastline of America. The canyon, twenty miles wide and unfathomable that lies beyond those mountains. The unknown is always more exciting than the known, and the sea bed in that canyon is unknown. His feelings for Grace are unknown. Jesus Christ, he's back on the subject he thought he was escaping from. But under the sea, at its deepest point, it is unknown to anyone on earth. It is a mystery, a reality no one has experienced. It is the best thing and the worst thing about it.

Grace

We stroll back towards the village and the house and I don't know how long we have been out, but the light has changed to a rich evening gold and around us trees hum with the whir of swallows' wings swooping past after a fly and the bittersweet tune of a blackbird, liquid and intense. I am panicking. What do you say when a man you want actually wants you too? Is it allowed to be easy? A dream coming true is hard to handle, and I am caught up with desire – desire for love as much as desire for sex. My past experience screams 'No!' at me. 'No, don't trust it, you cannot have what you want.' But I don't have to believe that any more. We get back to the garden, and all the guests have departed, and empty chairs sit around in congenial groups, a pair of shoes lolling under one, a semi-clad Barbie doll beneath another. I am strung out and nervous, and I feel trapped. Mac comes out of the house and says, 'Who's here for supper?'

'I think I've got to go,' I answer before I have thought anything through, it is just a reflex of self-protection. But as protection it is useless.

'Oh.'

Ryder and Mac look at me amazed. Ryder's expression is concerned. I backtrack as fast as I can. 'I mean, yes, but I think I've got to go,' I mumble. What am I talking about? Of course I haven't got to go. Ryder begins stacking chairs, pacing about. He coughs and I can tell he is trying to sound casual.

'Well, if you leave it until tomorrow, I can take you.'

'Er, I'm not sure. I'm . . .' I am midway through refusing when Mac puts his arm around me and draws me towards the kitchen.

'That sounds perfect,' he says. And I am grateful. He is right. I can't believe I was about to throw all this afternoon with Ryder away because I feel scared. Ryder stops pacing and comes and sits at the table. Mac passes him a chopping board and some muddy vegetables.

'OK, we're cooking for Lucy and Grace tonight. What's it to be?' says Mac. Ryder has a look of panic on his face as he confronts an aubergine.

'Er . . . Not sure. Grace, I bet you can cook. What works for an aubergine?' He is smiling, looking at me. He holds out his hand, he squeezes mine, and with a rush of surprise I realise he is not angry, and he is not trying to duck out from anything. I smile a grateful apology and squeeze his hand back and, raising an eyebrow at the aubergine, I say, 'Well, we can do a lot with it, shall I help?'

'Definitely. I can do breakfast, and steak, but living vegetables are different.'

Mac pours wine into glasses and takes two to the door. 'I'm going to give Luce a hand with bath time,' he says.

'That's fine, we can do this,' I tell him. Gratefully, Ryder moves along and passes me half his vegetables.

'I'm all yours,' he says, 'show me what to do.'

Mac has left a pan hissing with frying garlic and onion. 'Stir it and add this.'

I pass him the sliced aubergine. His hand rests on my waist as I slide the slices into the pan and stay close to him. He looks sad.

'Is it difficult for you seeing Mac with Lucy?' I wonder as soon as I have said it if it is intrusive, but he rubs his forehead and meets my gaze.

'No, it's not that. Not at all, it's lovely seeing them together, they are a bloody good advertisement for couples. I'm tired, though, and I didn't like the thought that you might go.'

'I'm glad I didn't.'

He leans over and kisses the hollow of my neck.

'Yeah, so will the others be. Dinner is going to be a lot nicer with your input than if it was left to me. What shall we do with the beans?'

I slice them with a huge smile because I feel so happy in the kitchen with him. I think I could feel happy anywhere with him.

'Tell me your favourite sport?'

'Boxing,' he says promptly. 'Oh, and pool of course. Yours?'

I giggle. 'No one usually cares about girls and sport. I like yoga, if it's a sport to do, or cricket, if I am in England in the summer.'

He puts down his knife and twirls me into his arms, kissing me in a ham dramatic way.

'Perfect girl. You like cricket,' he says, then begins chopping again.

In mock alarm I nudge him. 'What's all that about?'

'You'll see as you get to know me that you have touched something very dear to my heart,' he says solemnly then winks and passes me my glass.

'A bath-time toast to Mac and Lucy for bringing us here to cook,' he says, and we raise our glasses towards the ceiling, above which a herd of small elephants seems to be charging back and forth squealing with laughter.

'To Mac and Lucy,' I agree.

The next day Ryder drives me to London. To his boat. It is sad leaving Mac and Lucy, and I am nervous as I hug my sister goodbye. She holds me tightly and whispers, 'Just have a nice time, Grace, that's all you need to do.'

Ryder opens the car door for me and passes me an earring as I get in. 'You left it in the bathroom,' he says.

'Thank you.' I am very touched that he noticed. We drive away from Winterton with Ryder beeping the horn and the windows open to wave. Ryder drives calmly, and without a map.

'How do you know where we're going?' I ask after a while, when we have turned at yet another tiny crossroads with no signposts.

'Oh, I don't know, really. I came this way yesterday a bit, and I know which direction London is in, roughly.' He breaks off to pass me a bottle of water. 'Here, sorry it's not cold. Yeah, anyway, don't worry, we're not lost yet.'

On the motorway, he drives fast, but I feel safe. He reaches over and puts a hand on my thigh. I am watching his profile, enjoying his ability to focus. A lazy sexy saxophone plays on the car music system and I drift into sleep. When I wake up, we are almost there.

'I can't believe I was asleep all that time.' I shiver, rubbing my eyes. We are at traffic lights somewhere on the edge of London. He touches my cheek.

'You're lovely, Grace,' he says. I look sideways at him grinning, dazed and still sleepy.

He winks at me, laughter escapes between us and I stretch and yawn. 'Mmm, this is so nice.'

He looks pleased. 'I agree. And now we're nearly there.'

Before we get out of the car, he turns to me. 'Grace, if you can stay on with me for a bit, I could take you out, or keep you in. Whatever.'

My heart pounds with excitement. I was dreading leaving and now I don't have to just yet. On a deep breath I try to speak and give up and just nod my head.

He kisses me hard and murmurs, 'I think you need to go back to bed, jet lag is getting the better of you.'

'Sounds perfect,' I follow him away from the traffic. Ryder's boat is tucked down by a bridge on the canal in a part of London I have never been to before. It is like another world, stepping down off the pavement and on to the towpath where the boats lie waiting, like trains in a station. The geraniums on the boat next to Ryder's catch my eye as we cross the small bridge and enter. He opens the door and the space inside is bigger than I expected. A sofa covered in a Mexican rug and a table made from a slab of walnut fill the main room. Ryder takes my bag through another door and puts it on the bed. I have another rush of panic at the thought of staying here with him, and then I remember he must be nervous too, and I flop on to the sofa and make myself be calm.

'Why do you live on a boat?'

'Because it can be anywhere, and I didn't really want to live in London so this seemed a good way to pretend I'm not.'

'It's lovely.' Although the space is small there are photographs and pictures and odd objects everywhere. A yellow boxer's punch bag hangs in a corner above a teetering pile of books. Squinting at them I realise they are all the same, or, rather, different editions of *Wisden Cricketers' Almanack*. In another corner a pale blue bicycle frame hangs on the wall, its tyres spooled over the handle bars, and on the floor by the sofa are two skin-covered drums.

Ryder sits next to me, then he puts his arm around me and whispers in my ear, 'Shall I make you a cup of tea, or shall I take all your clothes off and make love to you?'

'Both,' I whisper back, pulling him closer. We draw the curtains around the little port holes and stay in bed. It's Sunday, and there isn't any reason not to. In fact, we need to do it.

Ryder is lying on top of me, brushing my hair from my face. 'We have five years to catch up on, Grace,' he says, 'so please stay here with me for a while.'

I love the way he is able to say what I need to hear, I love his steadiness and his passion and his gentleness. When I try to tell him he puts his finger on my lips. 'We found each other, everything else can come later.' I thought I would be nervous, but every moment I am with him deepens my sense that I have always known him and there is nothing to fear. Later, we walk west along the canal as the sun sets, and the water is so still that the houses and warehouse buildings are reflected as if in a mirror. A plane curves through the sky and Ryder puts his arm round me.

'I'll come and see you in New York soon, but I'm hoping I can persuade you to come back here.'

'To live?'

'Yes.'

I feel as though he has lifted the blanket I have been hiding under all my life and he is seeing me as I am, and he still wants me. It is uncomfortable, like taking off your sunglasses to look at a beautiful day. And of course I want him too.

'I think I will, but it might take a while.'

'We've got a while,' he says. We turn off the canal and walk back through the evening. Summer is breaking through in London and outside pubs and bars people are gathered on the street. Everything has a dreamlike quality, but the happiness is less ephemeral, and it is still there when I wake up in the morning and look at Ryder asleep beside me. We spend three days together, doing the sort of things I have always wanted to do with any boyfriend and never have. We go to the zoo. It's a hot day and we walk back along the canal past the hyenas at the edge of Regents Park.

'They are incredibly cheerful-looking for hyenas,' Ryder comments, taking my arm and walking around me so he is on the canal side of me as we saunter along the narrow towpath.

'Well, what should they look like?'

'I dunno. I just imagined them to be gloomy. Like vultures.'

'Stoopid!' I poke him in the ribs. 'They're famous for laughing, of course they're cheerful.' We explode giggling and loll on a bench while a red-lacquered boat glides past full of tourists. The next evening we drive down to the river to walk along it in the dark. Ryder holds my hand and we lean over the Millennium Bridge and he talks about his family.

'I'd like to take you to see Mum and Dad. They will love you.'

'Will they?' I don't mean it to sound as disbelieving as it comes out.

Ryder hugs me, and I can hear his smile. I don't have to look at him to feel it warming me.

'I mean, they will love the fact that I have met you,' he says. 'They took so long to live again after Bonnie died, and now they finally want to.'

'Tell me about Bonnie.'

'Well, it's not easy, sweetheart.' He pauses, trying to assemble all the love and memories to tell me something. 'It's hard to explain someone I love to someone I love without sounding over the top.'

'I don't mind if you're over the top, darling.' The Thames rushes beneath us, spangled with light reflections like stars, and, on both sides of the dark banks, glitter and sparkle sprays out like jets of water from the buildings. The air is warm, and all sound carries through the night; rushing cars, the occasional wail of a siren and the murmur of voices from people passing us. We walk on from the centre of the bridge towards the South Bank. Ryder puts his arm around my shoulders and we walk side by side.

'She was any guy's dream sister. She was such a good friend of mine, too. I told her everything, and it was mutual. She had lots of friends and though she was only nineteen when she died, she really filled her life up.'

'You must miss her every day.' I cannot think what it would be like not to have Lucy in my life, and sad compassion for Ryder smarts behind my eyes.

'I don't know. I think I do, but it's the way life is,' he says.

'I understand a little.' I squeeze myself closer to him. 'Our dad died a while ago and then our mum, so I understand loss. But maybe not the kind of love you're describing.'

We are at the Tate, and it is late-night opening. I lead him in. 'I want to show you my favourite paintings.'

'Wow, I can't believe it's open at night and you know about it even though you live in New York, and I don't.'

The Rothko Room is empty. My heart pounds as if it will burst. Ryder is silent.

'Have you been here before?' I whisper.

He shakes his head. 'These are amazing.'

'They were painted for the Four Seasons hotel in New York, but he felt they were too gloomy so he gave them to the Tate.'

I lie down on the big leather banquette. Ryder sits next to me. 'They are intense,' he says finally.

On Tuesday night, anxious because I leave tomorrow, I begin to panic at the thought of saying goodbye, making plans to meet soon, missing him, trying to make dates to meet. And what has felt like the most natural existence, hand in hand with Ryder, doing everything with him, is suddenly remorselessly finite. And a continuation seems impossible, there is so much distance between us in our lives.

I take a deep breath and speak into the silence that has been growing around us.

'I want to be with you more than anything in the world, and I love you, but I don't think I can do it right now.'

Ryder is lying next to me, almost asleep. He sits up, staring at me.

'What are you talking about? I love you. We are together now. You're just going home for a while, that's why you're nervous.'

I can't look at him, I hide my head. 'No, I don't mean that. I mean I'm too scared. I don't think I'm ready to be with you. It's not you, I love you, it's just me.' It feels as if a cliff has crumbled away inside me leaving nothing. I just need to get back to New York to think straight.

At the airport Ryder kisses me and I cling to him. I am numb in my body, but tears keep falling from my eyes. I don't know what has happened, I can see happiness so near, but it is as if it's through glass. Maybe I am testing him, I don't know. Maybe I am testing myself. Ryder takes me to the security section. He cannot come through any further. He hugs me again, and I never want to let go of him.

'It will be all right, you know,' he says.

I watch him walk away, and he turns to look at me three times, and I stand there like a stupid statue until he vanishes among the crowds. I cannot believe what I have done. Except that it is what I always do. In the departure lounge I find a seat and call Lucy. She is horrified.

'But I thought you were staying with Ryder in London. I thought you weren't going back for a bit. Oh Grace, why?' She sounded so disappointed you would think it was her life I was sabotaging.

'I can't. I need to go back. I need to work.' I can't explain to her that I just need more time. But I try.

The loudspeaker starts calling my flight. I launch in, my fingers in the other ear so I can hear my sister. 'Oh Luce, I don't know. Maybe I need a bit more time.'

'No, you don't. You need to get a life and stop hiding behind your work.' I have never heard my sister shoot back at me with such a steely tone to her voice. 'You will never not be afraid. We all are. You just have to take the risk, Grace. It won't kill you.'

'But when I panic I feel it will kill me.'

'Well, go ahead and ruin your life then.' Lucy is furious. I garner my spirits to argue, to answer back, to insist I am right, but the fight has all gone out of me. My eyes flood with tears again, I can't see the numbers on the gates.

'I know, I think I already have,' I say, 'but I don't know how not to.'

'Did something happen that worried you? You seemed to be really into one another when you left here.' Lucy's anger has abated, one of the children is in the background, then both of them.

'Oh nothing. We were having a really nice time, but I couldn't deal with it, so I said I was going.'

'You couldn't deal with having a nice time? Well,

who do you think you are anyway?' Lucy breaks off to talk to the children, then comes back.

'What did Ryder say?'

'He said if it was meant to be, we would find one another again. He's only just gone, he came to the airport with me. It was awful.'

'Oh Grace.' Lucy sighs. 'He's right, you know. If it is meant to be, it will sort itself out. Love finds a way.'

I begin to cry quietly again. Not quietly enough, though.

'Grace?'

'Yes?'

'You should get on your plane, go home, pack up your life and then call Ryder and get him to come and get you. Please don't end it like this, you will regret it for ever. You are such a stubborn ass sometimes.'

'Bye, Luce.' I turn off my phone for the flight.

16

Grace
August

Back in New York I am lovelorn. I am a real bore to myself and my friends. The only good thing is I am working a lot, manically painting my frustration and gloom on to canvas. Ryder called me as soon as I got back.

'I will come and find you, Grace, but you have to want to be found,' he said.

Now, two or three months have passed and we still speak quite often, but with no plans to meet. At home I function like a robot. Breakfast is something I do standing at the fridge. Eating would make what I am doing sound like a sensory experience, which it is not. I seem to have left my tastebuds in Europe, and food tastes of nothing, it is just a series of feeling different wet or dry substances in my mouth. As I force down some yoghurt and blueberries, I think I have got stuck in terror. Most of me just misses Ryder and wants to go back to London and marry him and have babies for which I am sure I am ready, or just as ready as anyone ever is. But some stubborn and crazed part of me is clinging to fear and I don't know how to stop it. Lonely, frightened or whatever, I am grateful when Stephan and Ike ask me out to supper. Stephan works in the gallery on the Upper East Side where my next show is happening, and he needs photographs of the work.

'Only if you feel like it, honey,' he trills, when I call him to arrange where to meet. 'Let's go for dinner downtown. Ike is working late and he'll join us.'

Stephan and I have drunk two Mojito cocktails each by the time Ike arrives and we are heavily into a conversation about my work which has become a kind of therapy session. The restaurant is noisy, the tables close to one another, but as everyone is talking loudly and Cuban music tumbles through the spaces between the conversations, it offers perfect sanctuary to blurt out my sadness.

'So, I left and came back here, and I speak to him occasionally on the phone, I spoke to him today, in fact, but not with a plan to meet. Not with a plan for anything. I can't do it, I'm too scared.'

Stephan is aghast. 'Darling, you have to go and find him. Where is he?'

I laugh. 'Oh, he is unreachable. He's on a gas platform somewhere in the sea near Denmark.'

'Well, get on a plane and get over there. Haven't you seen the movies? That's what you do. That's what you have to do for love.'

'That's ridiculous.'

Stephan finally takes off his sunglasses and looks me in the eyes.

'No, it's ridiculous to walk away,' he says.

I try eating a bit of bread to see whether I can taste anything. It's not bad, there's a hint of rosemary and the crumbling bite of salt. I feel as though I am defrosting from the tip of my tongue.

'Keep talking. I think you might be able to convince me.' I actually feel, for the first time, that I have got through whatever it was I needed to experience by coming back to New York. And I think it was just a bit of time alone. To see I could do it and live. OK, I may have overdone the experiment, and eating has been a disaster, but here I am, I still have a few friends and a sliver of my sense of humour, I didn't go mad, and I am still very much alive. And I love Ryder. I pray it's not too late.

'You know what—' I say to Stephan.

Suddenly Ike is at the table, like a visitation from another world, tanned and crisp and finished in his suit. He reminds me of Jerome. Stephan and I gape at him as he slides into the chair next to me and leans across to take Stephan's hand for a moment.

'Hey, Grace.' He kisses me and his smile is warm and expansive though he presses his fingertips into his eyes before leaning over to take a glass of water from in front of Stephan.

'I'm sorry I'm late, we had a gas platform blow out on a company I deal with just as it's about to be bought by one of the big guys, and it sent panic through the clients like a Mexican wave.' He opens the menu, reads for a moment then looks up, glancing between Stephan and me, his eyebrows raised in a question.

'What's up? You two have gone very quiet.'

'A gas platform?'

'Yes, it's off the coast of Denmark, it's causing chaos among some of the clients.'

I grab my bag and lunge out of my seat.

'I've got to go. I'm going now.' Making little sense, I kiss Stephan, wave to Ike, and rush out of the door. Every vestige of mist in my head and the internal fear in my heart has gone. Out on the street the late summer evening hits me with a blast of heat like an oven. The light is yellow and everything shudders in dust and warmth. I take a deep breath of hot air and make my way towards the subway. Then I change my mind and hail a taxi. There is an urgent clamour in my head. I need to find Ryder and I have to go now. My heart begins to hammer when I think again of the explosion. But it can't be him. I pray it can't be him.

Ryder
August

'I'm going to supper tonight with Stephan – you know, my friend from the gallery. I'll have to go straight from the studio. I'm going to go now or I'll never even get to work today.' Grace's voice has the small pause of long distance, and Ryder feels a desolate ache because she sounds so far away.

'OK, sweetheart. I'm stuck on this boat for a while, but it's nice to talk to you. Thanks for ringing. Bye.' The phone clicks and the line hums in New York before he can say anything else. The silence when she has gone is empty. He wonders what she is wearing, what her apartment is like, whether they will ever meet again. When she left after those few days in London, he felt as though he had been beaten up. It was not over, it was only the beginning, and yet she left. What is she doing now? Whom will she be doing it with? Suddenly in his mind's eye she is there, walking out of the door, down the road in the silky summer morning. She will not be alone, she will see a friend at the studio, she will chat to the guy in the delicatessen where she buys her coffee. It's so easy to imagine it all as wonderful, rich and various from where Ryder is, namely in the deathly quiet cabin of an efficiently air-conditioned supply ship on the way to the rig.

Ryder is alone. Apart from the crew, who don't speak any English and to whom he is seemingly invisible. They are a team from Shanghai, and operate their shifts and duties with a homogenous rhythm and group body clock that Ryder notices without being either affected by, or included in, it. Being alone like this has taken some doing, and Ryder has made a spectacular effort this time. Surpassed himself, in fact. He is miles from anywhere, and that isn't just north, south, east and west, but even from the bottom of the sea as well. He is on a boat taking cargo to the gas platform off the coast of Denmark. Funny to be near Copenhagen again and to speak to Grace from near where they first met.

He recalls his moonlit boat ride into the harbour, drawn like a moth to the extraordinary liquid light of Grace's work on the wall of the gallery. Is it significant that he is near Copenhagen again, or not? Frankly, Ryder feels he has no judgement any more. This is ridiculously isolating. Bringing new meaning to the middle of nowhere. It's late morning in New York. Grace is probably at her studio by now. Photographing her work. She may have got a friend to help her. Probably a male photographer. And photographers, Ryder broods, dragging himself on a swivelling chair towards a computer screen, are all after one thing. For Christ's sake. Maybe he should just stop obsessing and get himself to New York? But what if she doesn't want him? Ryder flicks the screen to standby. The other cargo ship is about to dock with the rig, so his vessel still has hours to wait. He steps up and out of the cabin on to the deck, adjusting his mind fast as the sound of the engines and the sea roars in his ears. He cannot get Grace out of his thoughts. How did he let this one in to his soul, where he thought he had built a citadel?

On deck, the curving horizon swells like a blue knife edge, cutting through the dense and restless sea, all flattened by sky. It is impossible to take on the scale of where he is, and unbearable to contrast it to land, home and heart. A familiar claustrophobia wells in his chest, a feeling he has gone to such lengths to escape that he finds himself here, alone, crazy with longing to be somewhere else, and that, too, is familiar. That is what has driven him. What would it be like to lose that feeling?

Ryder closes his eyes and breathes. Everything that has been wound taut pings into free fall. And it is like an elevator losing its machinery in a lift shaft, so fast is the plummet inside him, as he tries to imagine not wanting to be somewhere else. For a start, he would not be here in the middle of nowhere. Oh no. Hang on a minute, there he goes doing it again. Just for a minute, just for now, he wants to try what it feels like to be where he wants to be. So that means here and now in the middle of the sea. Far from the land in every direction, on the surface of the ocean, halfway between earth and sky, floating at the centre of his own world. And just for a moment, he glimpses the sun coming out in his heart and the full and happy sense of the warmth it brings, makes his heart sing with the exhilaration, the expansion, the joy of being where he wants to be.

It's amazing; for a flickering moment he understands what a privilege it is to be alive on earth, or rather on the sea. It is a privilege he has earned through all the choices he has made to bring him to this point.

He remembers where he was a year ago. Then he was watching an iceberg move down from the shores of Labrador and Newfoundland, trying to plot where it would get to before it melted in the Gulf Stream. He was unutterably miserable. No one whom he cared about knew where he was, and no one needed to. The loneliness of that feeling inhabits him again, and brings a clanking sadness.

We are the hollow men . . .
At the hour when we are
Trembling with tenderness
Lips that would kiss
Form prayers to broken stone . . .

He read Eliot's 'Hollow Men' at Bonnie's funeral. It was his favourite poem, but it meant something different after that.

A different line, from a different poem, floats into his mind now, a softness, a sense of destiny and change flooded his feelings.

Suddenly Ryder knows what to do. In the end it's simple. He will go and see Grace. He will ask her to marry him, and he will wait for her in New York until she can tell him one way or the other. It's the only thing to do.

Turning back to the cabin and the telephone, Ryder notices the gas platform has come into sight on the horizon ahead of them. A giant unsymmetrical construction, yellow and black like a giant toy from his Meccano set when he was small, it squats like a spider in the churning sea. Ryder's boat is still some distance away, so what he is seeing is more what he is expecting to see than what he can actually make out. He is moving closer, and with each minute that passes he can see more clearly what he is approaching. Nothing about it looks safe. And as if this thought is a self-fulfilling prophecy, Ryder is struck still with horror where he stands as a vast ball of fire leaps from the heart of the rig, up into the sky, spinning and mushrooming bigger, then hurtles back on to the metal structure. As it falls down again, black clouds belch from it like spores, spreading, ballooning out and back, bigger and bigger, and the red-hot heart of it throws long spears of burning flames into the foaming black-stained sea and through every level of the platform. Debris and machinery fall and vanish in puffs of smoke, and the fire rages and pulses with life. Until today Ryder could not have been sure he believed in God, but now he finds himself praying.

Grace and Ryder
Copenhagen

'Hello, Ryder?'

'Grace, where are you?'

'I'm here, at the airport. Just coming through. Where are you?'

'I'm here too. I'm just past the customs bit, waiting for you. Oh hang on. I can see you, turn round.'

She turns round and their eyes meet.

'I can see you walking towards me,' she says, but before she has finished speaking Ryder is pulling her into his arms.